VEILED

BY

DESIRE

CANDACE ROBINSON

For Alexa,
May all your desires come true!

One

Tavarra
Seven Years Ago

As Tavarra tried to leave the gravitational pull of the powerful ocean waves, each one crashed and pounded against her strong body. She swished through the murky sea, her tail flicking at the rough current as the liquid attempted to haul her back into its clutches.

Tonight was a chance for her to escape the haunting depths she so desperately dreamed of leaving behind. Tavarra pushed her head out of the sea's liquid claws, finally finding herself near the sandy shore. She took a deep breath through her mouth, no longer needing the gills etched on each side of her neck.

Holding steady, she stared through the last rays of the waning day, searching for him. But the young man wasn't anywhere in her line of sight yet. Keeping on top of the liquid swells, her gaze fixed on the caramel-colored sand. As her arms repeatedly cut through the vigorous surge, a hint of desperation filled her—she couldn't get swallowed back up. At last, her body struck the grainy granules, swept in blackness.

She sighed in relief.

With no time to spare, Tavarra dragged her exhausted body by her forearms across the sand. Each tiny grain rubbed against the delicate skin between her fingers and nails. She came to a halt and rolled herself to a sitting position, letting the edge of a cool wave caress the end of her tangerine tail. Bony plates fused together with a fleshy covering lined the tail's body, and the tip came to a curled point.

A heavy breath forced its way out and tugged harshly at her lungs. "Goodbye," she whispered, half to herself and half to the ocean cage that, for seventeen years, had never been a true home. "Please let this happen." Tavarra's heart pounded rapidly, and had it beaten any harder, her sternum would have cracked.

Bringing her sandy hands to her waist, she glided them down her moistened tawny skin until they met the vivid exoskeleton. The silver of the twin moons shone down in answer, as if telling her it would work. *It must work.*

Tavarra had recently heard a tale of when the twin moons would rise, there would be a way for her sea dweller kind to truly walk the land of Laith. She desired it with everything in her. If this worked, she would never return to the watery home—her underwater grave.

Slowly, she slid her thumb beneath the soft plates of her tail. To her surprise, the tail pushed away from her skin, as if it were never a part of her at all. She thought there would be pain, but there wasn't, only a filmy residue left behind.

Tavarra's lips pulled up on each side, and she let out a rumbling, giddy laugh to the moons, to the ocean, and to herself. Tugging the tail a little more, she shimmied out from the exoskeleton and found smooth bare legs underneath—as she had hoped. The story had been right. If only she knew sooner that legs rested beneath the tail—then she could have been doing this every time the moons were at their fullest. A continuation of delighted laughter echoed from her as it bounced off the waves and into the darkened forest.

She kicked these new-found creations, releasing the legs in their entirety from the confined appendage. To her it felt natural, more than surreal.

"Tavarra?"

The deep male voice caused her to whirl around and fall to the sand, catching her upper body with her forearms.

Darkness surrounded them as the night grew to its peak, but he would always be visible to her eyes—whether he was carrying a lantern or not. Brice—one of the main reasons she wanted to stay. Satiny black curls fell against the pale skin of his shoulders. His features became clearer as he approached— that soft, pouty mouth she had kissed time upon time, and the delicate nose which came to a sharp point. A blue tunic accented his broad shoulders, and with each shift of his body, the muscles flexed beneath it as he drew closer. She could never return now—not when he was there, real, breathing, waiting for her.

"Yes. It's me, Brice." Tavarra pulled her new legs to her chest. As his boots scuffed through the sand, she didn't tear her gaze away from him. The ocean sounded with musical whispers, its way of luring her back. Instead, she focused on the crushing of his shuffling steps.

Brice knelt directly beside Tavarra, shining his lantern toward her tail on the sand before he examined her new limbs. His mouth agape, his green eyes opened even wider. "I don't understand," he stuttered and stared at her face with both longing and confusion written across his own.

Lifting her hand, she ran it down his cheek, and the rough stubble scratched her palm. "I told you I had to show you something." Tavarra smiled. She had wanted to tell him earlier that morning but decided that a surprise later would be better.

She had loved Brice since the day she first laid eyes on him. There had been sea dweller females and males she'd been cozy with, but no one ever held her interest—until Brice. Each morning, she had swum to the same shore to let her body lay in the sand while the waves continuously beat against her tail. One sunrise, when she thought she'd been alone—he had stumbled upon her. For the past year, they had shared kisses, secret touches, and endless dreams together. It wasn't just all kisses, though—he had told her stories, and she had confided in him all her fears and hopes.

Brice studied Tavarra's stiff legs for a moment, then returned his focus to her face. "Is this temporary?"

From the story a water sprite had told her, it was only meant for one day. But she would make it permanent, regardless of what the tale said. The story could be wrong. A fish could never be with a bird, just as she could not live another day with only meeting Brice for stolen moments.

They had wasted enough time. Tavarra pulled Brice's forehead to hers and stared into those bright green eyes that gazed at her, glinting with something forbidden and exciting. He ran his hands through the wet tangerine hair that brushed her hips, and she molded her lips to his.

Brice slid his palms up her naked body, enfolding a hand around her breast. He tugged his tunic over his head and pulled her into his lap. It was not the first time she had felt his sizzling touch on her naked skin, as they had pressed their upper bodies together time and time again. But this… This was infinitely better, and not just because she could feel the part of him that *wanted* to be against the new piece of her.

She tore her mouth away from his, long enough to make him as bare as she was. Without any pause, she let herself press down on him, and a moan of pleasure escaped them both. They had waited and waited, and there could be discussions tomorrow, but tonight she wanted him in the ways she never could have had him before.

In the morning, Tavarra awoke to an empty blue tunic and her tail, both lying beside her. Brice had whispered he would return that evening, but she hadn't understood why she couldn't come with him. She slipped on the tunic to cover herself and waited for his return.

The day bled into night as the dark pink sky faded to blackened whispers. Tavarra was hungry, tired, and desperate to find Brice.

He still did not come.

"Sister?" a familiar female voice called from behind her.

Nezarra.

What is she doing here?

"Go home!" Tavarra snapped. She loved her sister more than anything. Perhaps not anything, since, to her, staying ashore was more important.

"No." Her sister appeared determined, a hard frown on her face.

Tavarra's jaw fell open when she fastened her gaze on her sister, *walking* to her and carrying a tail. Nezarra's emerald hair fell to her waist, and her skin practically radiated. Above them, the night sky had flecks of blue-diamond sheen highlighted by the moons. Her sister was moving on two legs, same as Tavarra now could.

Nezarra wore a pair of brown trousers and a white tunic, her feet just as bare as Tavarra's. Her sister must have been keeping secrets back in the hidden depths of the sea.

"You've done this before, haven't you?" Tavarra seethed, realizing that her sister had always known something she hadn't.

"Yes, but only because I can handle it," Nezarra said softly. "I can come here and return back to our home without yearning to stay and destroying myself."

"Destroying myself?" Tavarra's body heated with rage. She didn't understand why Nezarra had never told her about this.

Her sister knew how much she had wanted to live off the shore.

Sighing, Nezarra swept her emerald hair over her shoulder. "There's a curse if you stay out of the water too long."

"I can't go back. I have Brice." Tavarra hit the sand—maybe her sister was lying.

Nezarra ceased moving, her eyes shifting to the side. "No, sister, you *don't*." Her gaze locked on Tavarra, a hint of sadness in her dark eyes. "I know what you told me about him, and that's why I've been coming to the land, learning about Brice. He isn't yours. There are others." She paused and took a deep breath. "He has a wife … and a baby at home."

Everything inside of Tavarra stiffened, and the blood flowing through her veins halted. "You're lying. You're only envious." With each word that passed her lips, Tavarra's heartbeat thundered in her chest, choking her, stifling her. It couldn't be… *He wouldn't have!* But Nezarra's conviction seeped through her relaxed body language, even as she stepped closer to her sister.

"No, sister, I love you." She gently lifted Tavarra's chin, meeting her gaze. "Now let's go home."

"Then prove it to me." Tavarra ripped her chin from Nezarra's hand and took a step back. "Show me Brice's wife." She believed her sister wouldn't because it was all a lie, a deceitful untruth Nezarra had concocted in hopes of sending Tavarra home to wither away in unhappiness.

"Are you sure?"

Tavarra slowly nodded.

"Then follow me." Her tone was somber.

After picking up her tail, in case it wound up missing, Tavarra followed her sister away from the beach and the murmurs of the ocean. They trampled through the darkened forest to the new sound of fluttering wings and animals' chirping. Brice's tunic brushed against Tavarra's thigh, and a harsh pain needled her feet from stepping on sharp rocks and twigs.

Dark shadows moved within the forest. Her nighttime vision was better than most, so she could see where she was going.

Nezarra latched onto Tavarra's shoulder as they silently trudged through the trees the remainder of the way. Tavarra did not remove her sister's hand because a nervousness had started growing in her, despite her conviction of Brice's innocence.

Eventually, the trees parted, and they came to a village filled with small wooden shelters.

"This is where Brice lives?" Tavarra asked, watching smoke pump out of several tiny chimneys.

"It is." Nezarra avoided looking at her sister. Stepping forward, Nezarra pulled Tavarra in the direction of a logged shelter with a window lit by a golden flame.

Once at the glass, Tavarra hesitated to peer inside. *What if my sister is right? What if she isn't lying? Brice said he loved me when we were together last night. Love is ... love conquers everything.*

Shaking away her senseless thoughts, she pressed her forehead to the cool glass and peered through. Inside was a rectangular room with a lit fireplace, flames licking up its walls, creating smoke that rose out of the chimney.

Two people sat cuddled in front of the fireplace—one, a woman with chestnut hair pulled into a bun, the other, a man, with his arms draped around her. It was Brice.

Tavarra's body deflated, collapsing in on itself. Her eyes angled to a small wooden cradle beside the two lovers, where a small infant cloaked in a cream-colored nightgown quietly slept.

Nezarra reached out to comfort Tavarra, but she ripped her arm out of her sister's grasp, leaving Nezarra standing there as Tavarra stumbled into the secure blanket of the forest. She held back the tears and let the bitterness eat away at any sadness, willing it dormant and hidden away. *Humans are liars, and I should have known.*

The rustle of Nezarra's steps echoed behind her, and she quickly caught up. Tavarra could tell her sister was used to running on those legs. "I didn't want to show you *that*. I wanted you to forget about him and move on."

Tavarra spun around and tapped at her sister's chest. "If you had told me this to begin with, I wouldn't have let my heart become so enamored with him. This is all your fault!"

Nezarra sighed in defeat. "I know."

Tavarra's shoulders slumped. "It isn't your fault. It's his. He should have told me." She pointed at her own chest. "I shouldn't have fed into his lies."

But he was good at telling them.

"Are you ready to go home now?"

The truth was, she wasn't. She wanted to stay there where she felt unchained. But maybe she could go home for a little while and return again as Nezarra had. "We can come back together? Another time?"

"Of course." Her sister smiled.

"Can we stay one more night?" Tavarra wanted to feel the sand between her toes once more while taking in the fresh air before she had to breathe in water.

"I don't know." Nezarra hesitated. "What about the curse? It is believed that you can't be out of the water for too long."

"I've only been out of the ocean for a day, not a year. And what does this curse say anyway?"

"The curse states for more than one day." Nezarra rubbed her bicep, biting her lip. "I don't know more than that."

"Well, I'll get back in before it reaches two days—it will still be one day." The water sprite hadn't mentioned anything to her about a curse, only that she had to come back after a day. Nezarra could be right, but she could also be wrong.

Nezarra paused for a few moments and then softly said, "All right."

After they reached the shoreline, Tavarra sat down in the

sand, sliding her tail off her shoulder and resting it beside her.

"You will be all right, sister." Nezarra set down her tail and wrapped an arm around Tavarra's shoulder, drawing her closer.

She wouldn't cry that night—or any other night—for Brice. "I have you and now know that you're the most important person in my life. I'm sorry I did not realize it before." *But the sea is not your home*, a voice whispered at the back of her mind. She ignored it.

Nezarra smiled, letting a single tear streak down her cheek. "You're not the only one who has ever been in love. I have had my heart broken, too…"

Tavarra reached out and wiped her sister's tear away. "Tell me the story?"

"How about tomorrow night, when we're back home?"

As much as Tavarra wanted to hear this story, she could tell it was still too raw for her sister. Setting aside everything she had felt from the night before, Tavarra interlaced her fingers with Nezarra's, same as they did when they were little. The sisters laid back on the sand and stared up at the twin moons, talking in soft whispers before finally drifting to sleep.

The night that started out as beautiful dreams of walking across all of Laith turned into nightmares about Brice. A knife stabbing her in the heart caused Tavarra to rip open her eyelids, reaching for her chest. She was still whole, away now from a torturous dreamworld she never wished to visit again. Tavarra was in Laith, with her sister. And even if she wasn't ready, she was going home.

With a yawn, she lifted her hand to brush the emerald hair away from Nezarra's forehead to wake her. Tavarra's sister's eyes were open wide, staring endlessly at the cloudless blood sky. Her hand stilled and she blinked several times, waiting for her sister to do the same. She shut her eyes tightly for a moment before reopening them, knowing once she did, her sister would be fine.

But Nezarra was still lifeless, without the smallest amount of life present.

Her gaze floated down to her sister's chest, and Tavarra released a high-pitch scream that could shatter all of Laith. Red liquid saturated Nezarra's entire body. Her sister's tunic was ripped to shreds, stomach torn open, organs scattered and half eaten, displayed for all to see. There was blood *everywhere.*

Frantically, Tavarra stood and backed away with shaky limbs, darting her gaze side to side, searching for any sign of help or danger. There was nothing. Her heart pounded and pounded uncontrollably. Then she peered down at her hands and let out another terrified scream that hurt her own ears.

Claws. Tavarra's fingernails were now sharpened claws soaked in dried blood and bits of brown skin. Nezarra's skin. Tavarra looked down at herself, and to her horror, patches of tangerine fur lined the back of her legs, the side of her arms, and down the center of her shoulder blades to the middle of her spine. The shirt she wore—Brice's shirt—was now ripped and torn.

She swept her tongue against her teeth and tasted it—blood against newly sharpened teeth. It was her. *She* had done it. She had killed her sister. There was one way back home, and she reached for it, only to find that her tail was now a pile of tangerine ashes.

"This is the curse, isn't it? It does exist," Tavarra whispered. To roam forever on the land as a beast and never return to the sea—locked inside her new cage. She screamed and screamed, causing birds' wings to flap and reverberate through the trees as they flew to get away from the shrieks— from her.

Two

Rhona
Ten Years Ago

$\mathcal{E}$ach and every day, nine-year-old Rhona woke before the others in her small village. She knew she'd have to come back after a few hours of the suns' morning light had passed. There would have to be time left for swordplay.

Although Rhona liked her sword and daggers, she loved to dance more than anything: dancing in the rain, dancing under the heat of the suns, and dancing under the luminescent silver light of the moons. It was a forbidden game she liked to play alone—one that her leader, Belen, didn't allow. Belen was someone she wished she didn't fear.

Today, Rhona wanted an adventure of her own. She planned to secretly venture out farther than allowed, and a broad smile crossed her angelic face at the thought. Rhona's mama always said she looked like an angel with her tight blonde curls and bright blue eyes, but there were no angels in Laith. Only fairies. Maybe there had been hundreds of years ago, back when the humans were on Earth, but she didn't know those answers. They were only stories passed down over the years.

With quick feet, she darted around each cone-shaped tent—some were bright in colors, while others had no paint at all, only the barest of bones. Thankfully, Belen lived secluded in the back of the village, so she didn't have to scurry past his home. A hand clamped down on her shoulder just as she passed the very last cone-shaped tent. Her small body jumped at the touch.

Rats, I've been caught, she thought.

As Rhona slowly turned around, she plastered on an expression to make her appear as if she'd only been lost. "Oh, thank goodness, you found me. I didn't know where I was going." She came face to face with her best friend Perin. He was a year older than her and already more than a head taller. "It's only you." Rhona let out a heavy sigh of relief. Her mama would've been angry if she knew where Rhona planned to truly go.

"You're not lost, Rhona, you haven't made it out of the village. Yet. Where are you going?" Perin asked, frowning. He was always frowning. She wondered if he had any other facial expressions. Even when they were having fun together, he was always frowning. But he was her best friend anyway, and she'd decided a long time ago that she quite liked his frown.

"I'm going to go pick wildflowers in the north field for Mama," she lied, knowing Perin hated picking flowers. He'd rather be practicing with his wooden sword, preparing for the real one he'd soon be receiving. He spent most of his time tinkering with objects, building things that never came out quite the way he wanted them to. And she'd nod her head and pretend it was the greatest thing in the world so he wouldn't get upset. Because there would always be that look of frustration on his face when he didn't get something right.

"Mmm. I suppose I'll see you at sword practice then." He didn't move right away, hesitating and eyeing her with suspicion. Even though he was only a year older than her, he sometimes acted more grown up than the adults did.

Smiling, she gave his back a small shove. He sucked in a deep breath and hurried to place his hand on the spot she'd touched. She rushed forward, her gaze scanning him. "Did I hurt you?"

"No, I fell yesterday." He pulled away from her before she could roll up his shirt. "I'll see you later." She watched his back until he turned and vanished behind a tent. After he disappeared, Rhona counted to sixty to make sure he stayed gone. Without a sound, even the tiniest of breaths, she adjusted the daggers at her hip and yanked up the white hood of her cloak to cover her wild blonde curls, then darted in the direction of the river.

The pink sky looked more scarlet, signaling it might rain later that day. As she ran past tall pine trees, she leaped over their brassy-hued needles shed across the ground. The wind blew against her hood, but she held it tightly around her face.

After running for a while, the foliage changed, opening to pear trees sprinkled in with others that she couldn't name. Stopping only for a moment, she reached up and plucked a light-green fruit. Her ear perked up when she heard the sound of rushing water.

The river.

Something else floated through the air. Something that sounded almost majestic, magical—a melody.

Closing her eyes, Rhona pulled back the hood and let the music sink further into her ears. She wanted to get nearer. Clutching the pear, she crept as quietly as she could to get a closer look.

Gingerly, she pushed a large leaf that was bigger than her head out of the way. The new view gave her access to the sparkling river, flowing at a rapid speed, carrying leaves and other objects to their destination. Then her eyes fell to something seated at the edge where liquid met earth. No, not something—*someone*. A boy.

The young boy faced away from her, his obsidian hair cut

short, and he wore an acorn-colored tunic with matching breeches. His feet were bare and … *filthy*. Black dirt covered them. Rhona crinkled her nose while peering around a wide tree. Thick vines wrapped around its belly, making it easy to hold onto and spy.

Her heart thudded in her chest when music drifted closer and closer. Every inch of her ached to dance to it. She couldn't see what he was holding, but whatever kind of flute he blew into, the instrument made the most miraculous sound.

Rhona decided to be brave, because if she got into trouble for being out here, so would he. When she edged forward, he was so consumed by his instrument that he still didn't turn around. She pressed a firm hand onto the boy's shoulder. "Hello."

The boy whirled around so quickly—his olive skin changed to various shades of greens and darker browns to blend in with the surroundings, until she couldn't see him.

"Troll," she whispered and shakily stepped backward, tripping over a small rock. Her body tumbled to the ground and she dropped the pear.

As she scurried to her feet, she frantically thought of skin, muscle, and bones melting, then liquid moving. On command, her body disintegrated into a puddle of water, swishing between the dirt and grass. *Well hidden*, she thought.

The boy stared down at her, his skin slowly turning back to olive. "I'm not a troll. I'm human, like you." His tone was harsh. "Have you ever *seen* a troll before? If you were going to use a proper term for blending in, you might as well have called me a chameleon."

Too frightened to move, Rhona kept quiet. He wouldn't have been able to hear her thoughts anyway, only if she spoke.

When humans came to Laith hundreds of years ago, it was said they had gained abilities to adjust to their new world as soon as they crossed over from a dying Earth. Some were said to have had strength, fire, wings, but no one she'd heard of had hers. As time passed, and those humans had new children of their own, the abilities had started to die out. It was as if the world of Laith knew the humans no longer needed abilities as they learned more about the land.

"I can still see you," the boy pointed out as if he was a know-it-all. "The suns are making the liquid specks shine."

She still didn't move.

"If this is hide and seek, then I've already found you." He knelt to one knee and craned his neck above her. "So, your turn."

Maybe he wasn't so bad. Or maybe he was. She could now see he wasn't a troll, but he was from another village. Belen always said outside villagers were to be dreaded. There was only one good outsider, and that had been Rhona's papa, murdered by his own villagers. She'd never gotten to meet him since he'd died before she was born.

Lengthening her liquid puddle, she wasn't afraid any longer. Her daggers were still at her hip if she needed to take down this boy. He shifted forward and a tingle spread through her.

"Take a step away then!" she shouted. "You're on my leg!"

"Oh! Sorry!" The boy hopped back and almost fell.

Rhona thought of being stitched back together and liquid becoming skin. In a matter of seconds she rose from the ground, and the clear water took shape. She was back to herself.

"You're not from around here." The boy narrowed his eyes.

"Neither are you."

"I come here every day."

"That doesn't mean you *live* here." She didn't know what village he was from, nor did she care to find out either. He was already starting to annoy her.

Rhona's eyes fell to the instrument in his hand that appeared to be multiple flutes twined together.

"It's a pan flute." He smiled, holding it up, beaming with

pride. "Wanna try it?"

For a moment she thought about reaching for the instrument, until she remembered his mouth had been near it. She curled her lip in disgust. "No."

"You just blow in it." With a deep inhale, he pushed out a few breaths into the open holes—a lovely sound poured out. "See?"

Before she could nod, he held it out to her, his golden-brown eyes meeting hers. She stared at the pan flute then back at the boy. Maybe he wasn't so bad, even though his feet were filthier up close. Yet other villagers could have hidden tricks.

Without a word, she reached forward and yanked the flute away. She took deep breaths and blew into the open piece a bit too hard, warm spittle sprinkling out from her lips.

"Gross! Not like that." The boy grabbed the pan flute from her grasp as she tried one more time. A withering blow came from her lips, and Rhona jerked her head back, cheeks red when she noticed the flute was no longer in her grasp.

The boy wiped the tip of the flutes with his tunic. "Why did you call me a troll?"

"I don't know. Don't trolls morph?" She'd never seen one, but when his skin had changed to different colors before he vanished—he had seemed like he could be one.

"So wouldn't that make *you* a troll, too?"

"No…" She folded her arms across her chest. "But you are from another village. My papa was the only good outsider to ever walk the land."

The boy let out a high-pitched chuckle and turned around, playing his flute again.

All the blood within her began to boil, her anger blistering. Rhona snatched the instrument from his hand and took off. Staring up at a broad, sky-scraping tree, she climbed as quickly as she could up the trunk, then craned her neck down at the little brat.

"Hey, give that back." Two hands were propped on the

boy's hips as he gazed up at her. His voice wasn't angry, as if it was all only a game to him.

"Why don't you make me?" Rhona pulled the pan flute closer to her chest.

"I can come up there, too! You're not the only person in the world who can climb a tree!"

"Then do it!" she taunted.

And he did, but she was ready. Right when he got to the branch she was perched on, she leaped off. She would have been fine if it wasn't for the sharp branch that struck her leg on the landing. When she looked down, warm blood bloomed profusely to the surface of her leg, and tears were already falling down her cheeks. A small moan and a grunt came from her as she tried to hold the sounds back. She was used to pain.

The boy jumped down next to her with a loud thump, his dirty hands already lifting her leg and examining it intently. "I can run home and get some thread to mend it."

Rhona pushed his hands from her leg. "No, it will heal." As if at her command, the wound closed, but crimson still coated her skin.

"Fancy trick you got there." He smiled, and it grew wider with amazement.

"Yeah." But there were a lot of times where it wasn't fancy, because of Belen. She shook those images away.

"Come here." Grabbing her by the wrist, the boy dragged her to the river and tugged off her boot. He rolled up her trousers a little past the knee and held her leg near the water. Dipping his hand into the river, he splashed the cool drops against her skin and rinsed the blood away. She watched in surprise. For such a young boy, he seemed rather focused. Maybe he had younger siblings at home.

"Good as new," he said and stood.

"You aren't so bad, I guess—unless you're hiding the trickery."

"That's for you to find out, isn't it?" The boy arched a brow and she rolled down her pant leg.

The pan flute was still clutched in her hand, and Rhona thought she should give it back since he had performed a good deed. Even though she could have done it herself. "Here."

The boy, who was still nameless, shook his head. "No, you keep it. I have more at home."

Was he really offering her a gift? She stared down at the flute in wonder, excited to have one of her own. "By the way, what's your name?" she asked.

"Quilan." He paused. "But you can call me Quil. And you are?"

"Rhona, and you can call me Rhona." She found herself smiling.

"Or maybe Rho?"

"Maybe." No one had ever called her anything besides Rhona before.

"I was actually going to search for a four-leaf clover after I finished playing the flute. Wanna come?" Up ahead, he pointed at a wide field covered in bright green clover patches.

She stared up at the suns and still had a little time before needing to return home. "Okay, but I have to leave soon."

Rhona ended up staying longer than she probably should have. In the end, they had no luck in finding a four-leaf clover. But there were copious amounts of ones with three leaves and even a couple of fives.

"How about we do this again tomorrow?" she asked, surprising herself.

"Same time?"

"Yeah." Rhona nodded and pressed a hand to her pack. "Have you ever heard the story *Peter Pan*?"

"No."

"I'll bring it tomorrow!" With a quick wave, she ran through the forest all the way back home.

As she came upon the ornate-painted tents, the clanking of swords filled the air. Class had already begun.

She found Perin seated on a wooden bench, watching two girls swing their swords. His eyes met hers, accompanied by a frown on his face.

"You're a little late," he said, his gaze shifting to his father, Belen, who stood with his back turned toward them. Belen had the same shade of brown hair as Perin, only his father wore his in a long, low ponytail while Perin kept his short.

Before she could move her lips, Belen turned around, his blue eyes locking on hers. "Where have you been?" he demanded, striding toward her and Perin. His features were always sharp and fierce. Sometimes he would pretend to treat her kindly by giving her sweets, but other times he wasn't so caring. She tried to keep her body from trembling with fear as he approached.

"Rhona was picking wildflowers in the field for me," Perin answered.

Belen's head whipped toward his son. "Did I ask you?"

"No, sir." Perin held his stare.

Belen looked back at Rhona. "Don't be late again. Afterward, you need to come by my office."

"We're doing something after," Perin chimed in.

Belen's gaze became icy as he leveled Perin's gaze. "You'll come, too, then." He turned around from his son and walked back to the two older girls who were challenging one another.

Perin stared down at her hands with his lips pressed into a thin line. "Yeah, so where are the flowers?"

Rhona peered at her empty hands and had to quickly come up with another lie. The only new thing she had from the forest was the pan flute, and she couldn't show him that.

"I ended up leaving a large bundle by the tree for anyone to take to someone as a present."

"But I thought you wanted them for your mother?" Suspicion laced his tone.

"She has plenty. Maybe I should have really brought them for you instead." She smiled.

He didn't smile back as he handed her a wooden sword. "Nah, let's get to the field." Rhona had never beaten him at swords, not once.

As she looked at Perin's profile, she knew he didn't believe her. He had known all along she lied to him, but he had defended her to his father anyway. She would have done the same.

Three

Tavarra
Present Day

Seven years of this. Tavarra closed her eyes and gripped the chains around the tree that bound her wrists together. She howled with urgency, screamed, and bared her fangs. As she stared up at the twin moons in the darkening sky, she knew her fate was coming. A fire spread throughout her entire body with a wicked touch, and she shook violently.

"The chains will hold this time," her friend Eza said, landing on Tavarra's shoulder. If Tavarra killed the pesky bat, there would be nothing, no one, and she had grown to love Eza after all these years.

"Get out of here, Eza! Now!" Tavarra screamed.

"I'll be right here," the bat murmured and flew up into the tree above. Eza looked incredibly similar to a fairy except for the thin blackened wings, fangs, and sharper-pointed ears. She was a little taller than the size of Tavarra's hand from wrist to the tip of the claw on her middle finger.

Tavarra was trying to fight the change. She would win this time. As she breathed in the scents of Laith, Tavarra knew it was a lie, and indeed, she knew she'd failed when her skin began to stretch. She could feel her face taking on a new shape, and that was when the terror came because the night would be unknown to her. That was what haunted her the most. Tavarra held back the tears, unwilling to break, unwilling to bend and show weakness.

All that remained in her soul, heart, and existence, was hunger. She yearned and thirsted for blood, meat, and bones.

Dark orange fur sprouted and wrapped around her legs, arms, and torso. The shirt and pants she wore tightened and ripped as muscles elongated. Her teeth became longer, sharper. The snout protruded, and she could smell *everything*.

She became the true beast then, with no speck of her true self left—only the monster. She jerked forward, and something confined her, holding her back. Shaking the chains fiercely, she needed to get free, wanting to be free. Her insides were starving, hungry, and thirsty for blood of any kind. She *would* be fulfilled. A smell permeated the air, of flowery meadows—a small creature—she needed to find it!

The heart in her chest beat with destruction, and the rage within her shook the entire world. The iron at her wrists held on tight. With her sharp claws forward, she scraped at everything she could.

"You're doing great!" a voice called from above.

Tavarra whipped her head back and through the dark, she could see a small wisp of a thing—a winged creature she would eat as soon as the iron broke at her wrists. That was the flowery scent she smelled—she licked her lips, preparing herself for the morsel.

Gathering her strength, Tavarra howled with fury, roared with the pain of needing to kill the little disease. She would rip its head off and then hunt through the forest to find more.

As she shook the tree harder and faster, one of the links stretched. With one quick and hard thrust, the chains broke.

Tavarra's shoulders relaxed and her snarl became more like a smile. There were sounds within the forest that she couldn't identify, but her focus was on the little creature above. Baring her teeth, Tavarra studied the black wings that almost blended in with the night.

The thing had the indecency to speak. "We'll have to find stronger chains tomorrow." It sighed. "Again."

Without hesitation, Tavarra tried to scale the trunk but fell. Her hands and feet were too clumsy to do it. That only made her angrier. The creature flew, and Tavarra lunged for the winged nuisance. She leaped forward for the creature, but it flew higher. Her fist was left empty as she landed on the ground, shaking the dirt with a heavy vibration.

The creature took off into the distance and Tavarra was left alone. Other sounds filled the air, sounds that called to her, sounds she wanted to taste. The sweet nectar of flesh and bones she would lick clean. Slowly and deadly pulling herself on to her haunches, she knelt forward to one knee and sniffed the air. *Meat.*

Tilting her head over her shoulder, she listened closely, protective of her prey. In the distance, a low murmuring being transferred from one creature to another could be heard. Not willing to wait any longer, she shot forward in an eastern direction that would lead her straight to what she ached for.

As she ran in a hunched position, her clawed, fur-covered hands striking the ground with each leap, she could see various winged creatures in the sky above, dancing and enfolding themselves together. Things she wanted to rip apart, but they were too high and too bothersome. So she would go for the ones who could not get away.

She pounced up a darkened hill, the night wind striking her fur until she crested the top. The grass threaded between her clawed toes and fingertips, and she took a whiff of the air, smelling them. They weren't too far off.

Her body snaked down the slope of the hill, crawling past several trees.

A shushing sound traveled right up ahead. "Quiet, I think I

hear the beast."

So they want to kill me, she thought as she crept closer.

"We should have waited until daylight," another voice whispered, adjusting something over his shoulder.

"No one's ever seen it during the day," the creature that spoke earlier replied.

"Let's just kill something else, and we'll say it's the beast and still get a reward."

Tavarra slinked her way forward, staying as low to the ground as she could. Even the bugs hidden in the grass and dirt seemed to be afraid of her as they tried to flee. She crushed their tiny bodies below her when she moved forward.

The two creatures stood in front of her, facing away. *An easy target.* She watched her future prey, her taste buds coming to life. One was covered in wrinkles, while the other creature looked younger, but not a babe. Old blood tasted just as sweet.

As the older one glanced over his shoulder, his eyes finally met hers, and Tavarra lunged forward and tore his throat to bloody pieces before he could scream. Only a gasp escaped him.

The other one held up an arrow and released it, hitting her furry bicep. It didn't slow her down, barely even caused a sting. She growled and jolted forward, leaping through the air and pushing the creature down. He tried to roll to his side, but she tackled him and held his body down by his shoulders.

His frantic gaze locked on to hers, knowing it was his time to die. She held up a hand, the moons illuminating her claws, and dove it straight at his chest. Her claws broke through the barrier, tearing apart his rib cage, until she fisted the organ hidden inside. The oddly-shaped thing beat against her hand, then ceased as she brought it to her mouth. The taste and suppleness of the beautiful heart that chose whether one lived or died were now hers, almost fulfilling her.

What she did next was what the beast did best—she

finished them off.

The darkness behind Tavarra's eyelids transformed into a hazy orange. She fluttered them open to the bright morning light from the two suns. Sighing to herself and lifting her hands, she could see she was no longer strapped to the tree. One chain hung limply from her right wrist, while the other was free.

"Sorry, Tav, we need to find stronger iron." Eza fluttered her wings above Tavarra's head, blocking the sky from her eyes.

"What did I do this time?" By the fresh appearance of the dried blood streaking her hands, it didn't look good. Even after seven years of this, when she woke to blood on herself, she thought about Nezarra.

The only favorable thing about the forsaken curse was that she never remembered what she had done. That was Eza's job—to always reveal exactly what had happened, whether Tavarra wanted to know or not.

"You killed two human men." The bat shrugged. "They were out to kill you anyway, so they kind of got what was coming to them."

Her insides tightened at the thought of ripping apart and eating human flesh. Tavarra rolled to her stomach and pushed herself to her knees, then brushed her tangerine hair from her face. The shirt and pants she wore were split to pieces.

"I just got these, too." She usually only removed her boots at night because those were harder to scavenge.

"I've told you to just sleep naked. Easier that way." Eza cocked her head. "But fear not, my monster friend, there's a village up ahead that's filled with new clothes and chains for the taking."

"Did … did they have a family?" Tavarra didn't know who

she had killed, but in her head there was an image of a family sitting at an eating table together with small children running around.

"Probably." Eza was ever the one to tell things as they were. "But they should have stayed home, and then they would have been fine."

The monster side of her had rarely ravaged villages before—there was plenty of nightlife in the forests to feed her hunger and thirst. She stared at her hands again, seeing her sister's face, that expressionless stare. Tavarra often wondered what Nezarra had thought when her own sister, who hadn't listened to her about the curse, attacked her. Nezarra had probably died hating her.

"Why are you looking as if you are dying?" Eza asked. "You didn't know them."

"I was just … thinking about my sister." There were some days when she didn't think about it as much, but the memory always lingered.

"Tav…" Eza flicked her dark braids over her shoulders and flew up in front of Tavarra's face. The bat's gray eyes fixed on hers.

"I know," Tavarra started. "I can't undo the past, but wouldn't it be easier if I wasn't here anymore? So many nights it's like this." She had thought about dying, had thought about ending her life at times, but she still chose to fight in the end.

"Not every night."

"No, but a lot of them." It wasn't all the nights, but even those where she didn't change, she still left herself tied or chained to a tree. A punishment or atonement for the things she had done.

"Without you, there's no me." Eza reached a hand forward and swiped her fingers across Tavarra's forehead.

"You were you before I met you." Tavarra hunched her shoulders forward and drew her knees into her chest, wrapping her arms around them.

"No. I was on the brink of death. If you hadn't been there, I'd have withered and died."

"Funny, you looked pretty happy and well-fed to me."

"All right. All right." Eza waved at the air. "I'd be alive if you weren't here, but what a miserable existence it would be."

Tavarra stood from the ground and looked around. The two bodies—that she had known were torn apart somewhere— were nowhere in sight, and that part helped her breathe steadily.

Despite being a little hungry, she wandered in the direction of the lake to clean off. Later she and Eza would need to raid a village for more things. She hoped tonight wouldn't be another excursion of murder. Sometimes the change was days apart, sometimes it happened the very next day.

When the only death she found the next morning was a small, murdered animal, it didn't bother her as much. She did that during the day for meat anyway. But she hadn't torn apart an animal the night before, it had been humans. She pushed away the images that were forming.

As the sparkling lake lay before them, Tavarra angled her head up at Eza. "Do you think the Stone of Desire really does exist? It's been years and we've never found it."

One time on the beach, when Tavarra had still been a sea dweller, Brice had told her that the humans had passed through a gateway—known as the Stone of Desire—years and years earlier in order to get to Laith. With everything in her, she had desperately tried to find it for her sister—since it could be an answerer of desires. But it had been too late for Nezarra, anyway.

"We'll find it. Whether we stumble upon the Stone ourselves or find some poor soul who will lead us to it, we'll get there." Eza's tone was certain. Tavarra's thoughts were not.

"What if we find the Stone, but it turns out it was only a tale and I stay a monster forever?"

"Then we'll make the chains stronger and continue to fight it together. I may be small, but I'm here."

"I know you are," Tavarra whispered.

"Hey, if the Stone of Desire can't help you, maybe it can make me become larger so I can contain the beast better."

"Do you want to be bigger?" Tavarra lifted a brow and watched Eza float through the air back and forth.

"Nah, I like being a little sneak." Eza laughed, then turned serious. "Also, we've been here too long—more hunters will come after last night."

Tavarra contemplated where to go to next, and this time, it was a place she thought she would never visit again. "I want to go back and see the ocean."

Eza didn't ask why, only nodded.

Tavarra tossed her scarlet-stained clothes to the side and let herself drift to the middle of the lake. She cleansed the blood from her face and arms, struggling to not think about her sister. Not a day went by where Nezarra wasn't on her mind, and not a day would ever go by where she wouldn't feel guilty.

Four

Rhona
Present Day

Clink, clink, clink. The sound of Rhona's sword striking Perin's grew louder as she tried harder to take his ass down. Eight times … eight times he had caught her off guard and she'd fallen at his feet, practically prepared to kiss his boot.

She could beat everyone else, but never Perin. This was the one skill she wanted to best him in. Her mother, Thea, sat on one of the benches, watching, her long blonde hair falling over her shoulder. Noticing her daughter's concerned gaze, Thea shrugged in a delicate manner—as if to imply Rhona shouldn't worry if she lost again.

"You can do it, Rhona. But I'm not going to make it easy for you," Perin said in a serious tone.

"You're a real bastard sometimes." Laughing, she lunged at him. He was quick, boots angling to the side as he brought up his sword to block hers.

Belen held up a hand. "Continue. I'll meet with you two later. I have a meeting with Thea." Rhona's gaze drifted to her mother, who set down a cup of tea at her side next to Jasmine. The doe-eyed girl stared lustfully at Perin's muscles.

Rhona narrowed her eyes at Belen's back as he walked toward Thea. Perin caught her devilish stare and shook his head for her to stop. She didn't.

"I'll see you in a little while," her mother called before leaving with Belen's hand loosely holding onto her elbow.

It was now only the two of them left outside—everyone else had gone off to do other things—except for Jasmine, who hadn't taken her eyes off Perin. His sleeves were rolled up, shirt drenched, and his forearms slicked with sweat—the whole scene had Rhona rolling her eyes. She lifted her sword. "Just go with Jasmine at the next fire."

When the moons were at their fullest, the villagers would celebrate with a bonfire where they would toss something into the flames in hopes of a wish. The wishes weren't real, but the idea of dreaming about something had its appeal, especially after she lost everything. But for the past two years, Rhona hadn't gone because there was nothing to wish for. *Even though there is,* a voice spoke in her head.

"There is," she whispered.

"What is?" Perin arched a brow.

She shook her head. "Nothing, just go."

"And no, I don't want to go with Jasmine." He swung his sword, striking hers and making her hand vibrate. "I'd rather be alone."

"But you talk to me."

"That's because you need me."

"Nah, I think you need me maybe a little more." She thrust her sword and tried to kick his feet out from underneath him, but it didn't work. It was as if he knew every move she'd make before she did it.

Rhona looked over her shoulder to tell Jasmine she needed to try harder with Perin, but the girl had already left. She turned her head back to Perin, who had an apologetic expression on his face as he shot forward. With a stumble, she tripped over her own feet, falling on her ass. "You could have waited.”

“You could have tried to not set me up with Jasmine, too.”

Even though he was now twenty, she’d never seen Perin with a man or a woman. Not that there was anything wrong with that, but something, or someone, needed to take his frown away—the same that was on his face right now.

“You do know I used to have an ability that could dehydrate you, in turn making me win.” One she desperately wanted back.

“Then that would have been cheating, now wouldn’t it?” Perin reached a hand toward her to help her up. Giving him a hard stare, she placed her hand into his. Even after all these years of growing up together, he was still a true friend.

As she brushed the dirt from her pants, Perin glanced over his shoulder. “I need to show you something.”

Rhona peered in the direction of his gaze but didn’t see anything that held her interest. There were only rows of weeping willow trees and the cone-shaped tents. “Does my friend have a dirty little secret he’d like to share?”

“Just come on.” Pivoting on his heels, he waved her forward. “We need to be fast.”

Fast? Rhona’s frown mirrored Perin’s. “All right.” Something seemed different about him, his jaw clenched tighter than usual and his shoulders tense.

As they passed several tan tents covered in different paintings of flying birds, she perked her ear up. No sounds— as if everyone was still asleep. There wasn’t anyone outside their homes, no one working or playing.

“Where is—”

Perin grabbed her arm and pulled her in the other direction until they stopped in front of one of the enormous willow trees. He pushed the large brush aside so she could step through.

When he let go of the leafy green limb, he turned to face her with a desperate look on his face. Rhona grew panicked.

He isn’t going to kiss me, is he?

"Perin, I ... I don't like you like that." She held up both hands to make that clear—he was like a sibling.

"*What?*" Scowling, he took a step backward.

Her hands relaxed at her sides as she took a deep breath. "Kissing you would be like kissing a brother. And my heart..." She didn't finish that sentence, couldn't finish it. Luckily, he finished it for her.

"You don't have to worry about that." His scowl only deepened. "*Ever.* All right?"

"Too grotesque?" Maybe she would never have feelings for him like that, but the way he said it—as if she was a hideous monster—kind of pissed her off.

"Stop being ignorant." He brought his hands to her arms and held them firmly. "Now listen."

Her entire body stiffened, and she moved back out of his hold. Out of nowhere, something struck Rhona inside her head like a rock. Her heart sped up, and she found it hard to breathe. Another sharp pain pulsed at her temples, and the words she was going to speak became less and less clear. Each throb became sharper, more torturous, until she let out a scream that was a half-gasp. Her knees buckled and she drooped downward.

"Shit. He's here." Perin shot forward and wrapped his arms around her, preventing her from slamming to the ground. "It'll be all right. I'll explain everything later." He brushed a golden lock of hair away from her face. Rhona curled into his chest, but the pain wouldn't lessen. Then everything around her became a bright glow of white—she couldn't see anything. Only once before had everything around her gone white— when her ability vanished—with Belen. She still felt Perin's arms holding her while she clung to him. The pain only increased as the white glow became brighter and brighter until she couldn't think of anything anymore.

Rhona woke up even earlier that particular morning, unable to keep her giddiness to herself. She pushed the Peter

Pan *book into her leather pack and ran through the forest to meet Quil. This time, she'd have to make sure she came back to the village on time. Belen had made her work harder with her ability after sword fighting lessons, and she still mentally felt the sting from the cut he left her with.*

She had wanted to tell Perin about Quil, but she just couldn't. It would be her little secret.

As she ran under the tall leafy trees with sapphire blooming flowers, they seemed to speak, begging her to turn around and go back home. However, she didn't listen and avoided her imaginary whispers.

Once she entered the edge of the forest, she stopped in the exact spot where she'd found Quil the day before. He wasn't there. Her excitement disintegrated. Sighing, her tiny shoulders slumped, until her gaze fell on a shadow in the meadow, digging through the clovers. The inside of her chest filled back up with delight.

"Find one yet?" she called, taking a step closer.

With a wide smile, he looked up at her. "Not yet! But one day!" He stood, letting a clump of clovers fall to the grass as he strolled toward her. His clothing hung loosely over his lanky body, and she realized they were the same height when he stopped in front of her. She hadn't paid attention to that yesterday.

"Look, I brought it." Rhona hunched down, unbuckled the strap of her pack, and pulled out the withering book.

It was old and probably didn't have much life left in it. She still hoped to be able to pass it down one day.

"Sit?" he asked, already finding a spot near the tree she had jumped out of yesterday. A fat amber-colored beetle crawled above his head, but he didn't seem to mind. So she wouldn't either.

Rhona sat beside him, and Quil scooted closer until they were knee to knee. He pulled something from beside the tree and handed it to her. "I made you something yesterday."

Only Perin or her mother had ever made her things before, but this was the best one she'd ever been given. It was a crown with twigs woven together and dazzling pink and blue leaves intertwined. Radiant green clovers were inserted as well. "It's beautiful."

"Sorry, there isn't a four-leaf clover in there." His cheeks pinkened as if he was embarrassed that he could only find ones with three leaves.

"I like it the way it is, but maybe one day." Grinning, she set it upon her head—a perfect fit. "So does everyone in your village ... change colors?"

"Does everyone in your village melt into water?" he countered, his voice teasing.

"You should know that answer."

"How can I if I don't live there? And in that case, then you should know mine."

"So, just you?" Rhona guessed, since she was the only person in her village who was able to turn into water.

"Just me." Quil shrugged.

"We're both one of a kind then."

He nodded and studied the object in her hands. She pulled the book out of a sheer material that supposedly had only been found on Earth. Then she cracked open the cover to the first page.

Quil's hand caught hers before she could turn to where the story started. "Did you write that?"

She looked down at the words that had most likely faded over the years, but short ones she had read over and over.

To Luca,
Together, we'll survive anything.
Love,
Wes

"Your name isn't there. Who are they?" Quil asked, pulling

the book so it was between them.

"No. Luca and Wes were my great-great-great grandparents somewhere down the line. Luca's the one who saved our ancestors and brought us here," she said with pride. "His mother, Bray, was a bat, so in a way, I'm descended from one. Haven't you heard about him?"

His eyes widened. "Yeah, but I didn't know that was 'the' Luca."

Rhona supposed a lot of people had been named Luca over the years. There were several in her village. "I'm sure he was some sort of royalty for a while, but it's obviously faded over the years." She wasn't anywhere near royalty—not even close.

"Go ahead and read to me." He edged closer to where his shoulder was right next to hers.

Rolling her eyes, Rhona then read him the story of a boy who could fly, a girl who learned to take chances, and a fairy who was a good friend. When she finished the book, Quil looked awestruck.

"I brought your flute back if you want to play?" She reached for her pack, but he had already pulled one out.

"Nah, told you I had more." He paused to look at her. "But you can play with me."

"No, I'd rather dance this time while you play."

As he produced musical notes against the tree, Rhona stood up and danced the way she could never at home, spinning in dizzying circles and laughing with the wind. She told Quil to dance, too, but his cheeks pinkened as he shook his head, yet didn't miss a beat on his flute.

"Fine, Quil." She smiled because it was the first time she'd used his name.

And he grinned against the flute.

After Quil finished a few tunes, Rhona hurried back home and made it with plenty of time to spare. She slid onto the wooden bench to get ready for sword practice with the other girls and boys.

When Perin arrived with Belen, her friend sat down beside her. "I see you came back with something this time."

She touched her head and felt the crown, remembering how she'd lied the day before about picking flowers. "Yes."

"I like it." He brushed his finger against a leaf.

Belen grabbed two wooden swords and dropped them at their feet. "What is that on your head?" he demanded.

"I made it this morning," Rhona lied, not meeting his angry eyes.

"Quit wasting time on things." He ripped it from her head and smashed it under his boot, before walking away.

Tears welled in her eyes, but she held them back.

"I'll fix it for you, Rhona," Perin whispered, picking up the broken crown and setting it on the bench.

She nodded and tried to smile but knew in her heart that this would be the last time she would bring anything home again.

☾

"Quil?" Rhona asked as her eyelids flew open. The last time she'd seen him was two years ago when she was seventeen. It was her fault she hadn't gone back—she hadn't known the gap between them seeing each other would be so long. When her eyes peered around the room, she jerked forward, only to be pulled back. No one was around inside Belen's home. Her wrists were bound to a wooden chair, and her ankles strapped to the legs.

Rhona's head still tingled from earlier, but it wasn't in pain. *How did I get from the willow tree to here?*

Numerous daggers decorated the wall above his desk. "Hello?" she called. "Perin?" Nothing.

The thought of skin, muscle, and bones melting followed by liquid moving came to her. But it hadn't worked in two years and didn't now either.

The door to the room swung open, startling her as Belen slithered inside. His dark hair fell in curled waves right between his shoulder blades in his low ponytail.

"You're awake." His voice was low and raspy, baring a menacing tone. "I've been waiting a while."

"Untie me this instant. My mother isn't going to be happy," Rhona seethed, trying to pull her hands from the rope, but it only burned at her wrists, creating red marks. Red marks that wouldn't heal the way they used to.

"I'm going to untie you in a moment, but first"—he held up a finger in front of his lips—"I'm going to tell you a story. If you don't do as I say, your mother will be dead. I have her somewhere … private."

The blood drained from Rhona's face. Her mother? He always made threats about her mother or Perin.

"Okay," she whispered, if only to entertain him while she thought of what to do.

"You see this?" Belen produced an object from his pocket, the color of ivory. He flipped it around so she could see it clearly—a triangle at each end, parallel sides, *a prism*. "It's done wonders over the years."

She didn't know why he was telling her this, or what he wanted exactly.

"I need *you* to help me find the other one."

Prisms? She had heard the tales of two prisms hidden in Laith—together they could create wonders, together they could end everything. "How did you get this?"

"Before you were born, I was able to locate it. Let's just say, it's prevented you from using your ability against me." He tossed it up in the air, easily catching it. "It also helped me take them away."

"You bastard!" she shouted, shaking the chair.

Belen leaned forward, so close to her ear that she could feel his hot breath—it sickened her. "Your *father* never died because of other villagers."

"You killed my father?" she whispered. As much as it should have surprised her, it didn't.

"I'm…" He paused with a smile. "Well, we'll save that for another time."

"It was you who knocked me out, wasn't it? How?"

Twirling the prism between his fingertips, he held it up again. "As I said, this little beauty can do magical things. For instance: hide your mother, take away your ability, let me put the entire village to sleep while I absorb their lives—anything, really."

"If you've had this for so long, then why are you just now tying me to a chair?"

"It's been a plan since the beginning, my dear. Now. My son is going to help me locate the other one."

Rhona's body stilled.

"Perin?" he called.

Her friend walked into the room, not meeting her eyes. Belen held up the prism, and Perin slumped to the floor, gripping his chest.

"You see how I can make him do things?" Belen asked.

"Stop!" she screamed.

"Now as I said, you and Perin are going to travel through the Crimson Forest to retrieve the other prism for me. I can then take a journey to the Stone of Desire. The last time I went, I only had one prism and it didn't quite work out."

Rhona had heard about the Stone of Desire numerous times from village tales told to her by her mother. It was how Luca, and humanity, crossed over from Earth to Laith. Her mother had mentioned its location before when telling the story, but she'd always been more interested in her ancestors than finding the Stone who didn't answer to humans anymore. She couldn't remember the location now that she thought about it.

Leaning closer, the prism vanished from his fingertips as Belen stared at her. She leaned forward to bite at his face, but a loud screeching sound forced her to stop. It wasn't coming from the outside—it was coming from inside her head. She wanted to push her hands to her temples, but they were strapped down. The sound finally dissipated.

"If you disobey again, I can make it much worse. This will be different than a cut to the flesh, or perhaps a beloved kitten dying." Belen glanced at Perin who was on his knees, breathing heavily but didn't appear to be in too much pain when her friend's eyes met hers. He finally stood, his hand clenching his chest.

"Why can't you go yourself?" she spat.

"I'd rather have my children help me. I can't risk something happening to myself or the ivory prism, now, can I?"

"I'm not your child."

Belen shrugged. "I'm going to untie you, and you're going to go with Perin."

Rhona tried to quiet the fire she knew showed in her gaze, and unclenched her teeth. It wouldn't do for Belen to see past her façade, to her true intentions. She'd play along—for now. "I'll go."

As soon as Belen freed her, she shot forward—her body was flung back to the ground. Rhona's lower back throbbed with a harsh ache.

"Didn't I say I was protected?" Belen smirked. "Anyone who comes too close gets thrown back. Now, grab your things." She didn't want to look at Perin at that moment, so she didn't as she exited the house. He stayed close on her heels, not saying a word.

Up ahead, Jasmine was on the ground outside a tent. Rhona rushed to her side to wake her. She tugged the girl by the shoulder, and Rhona gasped, falling to her backside. Jasmine looked shriveled, as if she'd aged sixty years. Her eyes were closed and sunken, skin yellow, with wrinkles all over her face, yet Jasmine's chest rose and fell as if she was only sleeping.

"We need to hurry," Perin said. "There's nothing we can do for her."

Rhona tried to wake her, but nothing worked. And Belen had her mother... What if he was doing the same to her? She got up and hurried toward her tent without looking back at Perin. She couldn't bring herself to think about him luring her to that willow tree, or what he was doing with his father.

Inside, Rhona expected to find her mother, but she was *gone*. Hands shaking, Rhona grabbed the hidden pan flute and the *Peter Pan* book from beneath her bed and shoved them into her pack, along with a few other necessities.

She swallowed the lump in her throat that had gathered there. Everything felt like a nightmare—it didn't seem real, nothing at that moment did. Rhona should have guessed that other villagers hadn't been responsible for her father's death, but how could she have known?

Placing the daggers at her waist, and the sword at her hip, she opened the curtain that led back outside. There stood Perin, already packed. She shoved his chest and took off running. Belen might think she would bring the second prism to him, but he was wrong. She planned to use it herself—to defeat him.

Five

Tavarra

Tavarra watched the little drogwai dig through the hardened dirt, hunting for something to eat. She sat perched on a thick tree limb and tried to avoid the smallest of movements. She and Eza had been traveling for a few days now, and they were both in need of food.

Well, I'm hungry, too, you little furry ball, she thought, licking her bottom lip in anticipation. She hadn't had anything to eat all morning, or last night for that matter. The monster had decided to stay hidden.

A sweet scent filled the air as the gust of wind blew harder, causing the tree branches and leaves to make a loud rustling noise. Tavarra didn't move a single muscle. The drogwai, smart as he was, lifted up his oversized head, extending his overlarge pointy ears up to the sky. Black and white fur coated its body, and from the many she had eaten, she knew it was soft to the touch.

The drogwai sniffed the air slowly, then gave two quick sniffles. Tavarra continued to stay still and blended in quite decently with the tree, except for the brightness of her hair. Perhaps the little thing thought her orange hair was flowers. The rest of her body was covered in brown clothing.

Thankfully, Eza had gone on her own hunt for food—she would have been too loud.

The creature's ears lowered back to the sides of his oval head, and he resumed his hunt in the dirt for insects or worms.

Stroking the inside of her cheek with her tongue, Tavarra shifted forward, jaw opened, and teeth ready. From her left, an arrow flew with quick precision in the air, striking the drogwai through the skull. Tavarra froze and grasped the limb tighter. The creature slumped to the grass without even the tiniest of squeaks—dead to the world.

Tavarra jerked her head up and narrowed her eyes. Whoever had shot her food would now have to answer to her. The scuffing sound of heavy boots trampled across the ground, crunching leaves and breaking twigs in their wake. Not one, but two sets of feet thumped against the earth, one quieter and smaller than the other.

As soon as a man with short dark hair and a little girl wearing an oversized dress entered her territory, Tavarra leaped from the branch. She ran forward and wrapped her hand around the larger human's neck, slamming him hard against the trunk of the tree.

The man tried to groan, but it sounded more like a gurgle. His familiar green eyes met hers, and she released him as if his skin had burned her. Even though Tavarra had stayed away from him, she had always dreamed of this moment. But she had hoped to avoid him on her journey back to the sea.

Her hand clamped back around his throat, squeezing harder.

"Let my papa go," a weak voice behind Tavarra whimpered. Perhaps she would have felt sorry for the child if she had never met Brice. But she *had* known him, and he was the seed of it all. As much as she didn't want it to, fury lingered, rising to the surface in that moment.

"If your little spawn comes any closer, I'll rip her to shreds." Tavarra sneered, her claws digging in at his throat.

She had never purposely killed anyone, but she would do it to Brice and his pathetic weasel of a child. It may not make things better for her, but she would be happy doing it. A life for a life—redemption for Nezarra.

Brice's eyes widened and he grunted out to his daughter, "Go home!"

Being the little weakling she was, the fragile girl ran, leaving Brice and Tavarra to themselves. The last time they were alone together had been in very different circumstances. She gripped his throat tighter and slammed him roughly against the tree again, his head flinging back into the bark.

"Tavarra?" he finally whispered. The same expression was on his face now that there had been every time she had met him in the past. One that she had thought was adoration, but it had never been that at all. It was only him wanting to have entertainment outside of his wife.

"So… You remember my name?" Her fingers loosened only a fraction.

"What happened to you?" Brice's face looked the same, only a little older, but his hair was cut shorter. His eyes didn't leave her sharpened teeth that she had fully bared just for him. If he was disturbed by only a few pointed teeth, then he would be even more so on the nights she became an untamable beast.

"This is because of you," she spoke in a low and deadly whisper. "You *lied* to me. You told me you loved me." The words of the past played through her head over and over: him saying sweet nothings while resting by the ocean, while eating with her, stroking her face, kissing her. At least the beast she became, from what she knew, didn't have to remember those things.

"I did—*do*—love you," he said with sincerity. "I came every morning to the shore for months and months, searching for you."

"All to go back to your wife and … child at night?" Her claws tightened around his throat, a sliver of crimson sliding down from where her thumb dug in. She inched closer to the throbbing purple vein, as if it was begging for mercy. The pulse beat against her thumb. It would take only a moment to end his life.

"I'm sorry," he said in a choked whisper.

Tavarra released Brice and pushed away from him, disgusted. "Sorry?" she screamed. "You're *sorry?* So fucking sorry! My sister is dead because of you." Her cold eyes met his, wishing for the impossible—a second chance to do things right. Through clenched teeth, she said, "I wish I'd never met you."

Brice only stared at her, his lips parted.

"Yeah, yeah, I've learned quite a few new words these past seven years, not being under the sea and all."

"I was going to leave her … for you." Another damn lie. Would he have left his wife for all the other females he had secret rendezvous with, too?

In answer, she slapped her hand against his cheek—her claws left hairline cuts behind. Reaching for his face, Brice took in a heavy breath. Tavarra was prepared to finish him off when an annoying set of wings flapped beside her ear. Then two small legs settled onto her shoulder.

"Not now." Tavarra gritted her teeth, not turning her head.

"The child didn't leave," Eza said. "She's watching from the other tree." Tavarra wished she could smack away the bat who should have still been gone.

"Go away." Tavarra brushed the bat from her shoulder, but Eza stayed near her, creating a buzzing sound with her wings.

Thinking he had an opportunity, Brice tried to dart to the side, but Tavarra prevented him from escaping by pushing him in the chest with all her strength back to the tree. "Not so fast."

"You will hate yourself, Tav," Eza said, attempting to be Tavarra's good conscience.

Tavarra already hated herself, so she thought, *why would killing Brice even matter?* For stupid reasons, she shifted her head and met the frightened eyes of the little brown-headed child. Her body poked halfway around the tree, silently watching.

Perhaps it was a better punishment for his family to be ripped apart by his actions, and him living with it.

With a frustrated groan, Tavarra released him. "Go. Now your child knows what kind of deceiving human you really are. Nothing you say will ever make her forget what I said today—what you said. She knows now what you've done. What you are most likely still doing."

"I really am sorry," he murmured, before turning and skulking away. That day, long ago, flashed before her, a young girl waiting for her love on the beach, and him never showing up. He wasn't sorry, only a pathetic excuse for a human.

After his steps faded into the distance, Tavarra relaxed her shoulders and took a deep breath in and out. Finally, she reclined her head to look up at Eza, who was seated on one of the lower branches. Her two inky braids swung forward, and her gray eyes stayed directed on Tavarra. Eza ran two small hands down the front of her violet dress.

"I loathe you," Tavarra breathed, trying to keep the sadness away.

"No, I don't think you do, Tav," Eza replied with a smirk, crouching as she peered down.

"It would have made me feel better. He's why I'm a monster, why I can't go back to the ocean." She knew with all of her heart that it was her fault for not returning right away with Nezarra, but she wouldn't have been at the beach in the first place if it wasn't for Brice.

"But then you wouldn't have met me." Eza propped her hands on her chin and flapped her wings.

"But then I wouldn't have killed my sister…"

"But I'm also like a sister."

"An annoying one who won't go away." Tavarra turned around and Eza flew down, landing on her shoulder.

"Did you find any other bats while you were out here? Preferably of the male-kind, only because I need to increase the bat population once again."

Is she serious? "Are you teasing?"

"Yes and no." Eza shrugged, keeping a straight face.

Since Tavarra had been on land, she had not encountered or seen any other bats. It was a rare species, and Eza had become a one of a kind pest that wouldn't go away, but she was *her* pest nonetheless.

"Did you find anything while you were gone?"

"An apple tree." Eza hopped off Tavarra's shoulder and hovered in front of her face.

"Look what I have for our next meal." Tavarra bent down and plucked up the dead drogwai from the grass and brought it to her chest. If Brice had reached for it on his way out, she would have chopped off his arm and not have cared. He could have still gone back home to his *precious* family with a missing limb. Thinking about Brice was getting her fired up again and she wanted to go after him to rip his arm off.

Even after seven years, she could remember that night on the beach, her younger self so happy, so in love. Not in love, *infatuated.* A seventeen-year-old sea dweller who knew absolutely nothing, and had her head buried under water for so long that she didn't know what the above world was really like. Eza was the one who had helped her learn so much—how to hunt, how to survive, how to trust someone again.

"As long as you cook it this time!" Eza sang and drifted back to Tavarra's shoulder.

"Sometimes that takes too long, but if you show me where the apple tree is located, then I'll cook it just for you." Tavarra tried to smile, but it came out more as a snarl because she couldn't get her thoughts away from Brice.

After she had tried to return to the water without her tail, after she had gone back and tried to piece her sister back together and had carried her to search for the Stone of Desire—

a myth she had never found—she ran and ran until she curled up beside a tree where she found Eza.

Tavarra sensed that her strength had increased. Stronger than she had ever been, even as she carried her sister's lifeless body. She didn't know which direction she was going in anymore. Gently, she lay Nezarra down on the ground beside a tree and chose to fold into herself on the dirt.

There was no one—she had no one. Brice. Nezarra. Her parents were both dead. Everyone else was deep in the sea, and she didn't care about any of them—only Nezarra.

Hot tears that felt as if they were on fire slid down her face as she sobbed into her open clawed hands.

"You don't look to be one of the jovkins," a meek voice said from above.

Quickly, Tavarra sat in a straight position and jerked her head to gaze up at a small winged creature. "Go away, fairy!"

"Um, the correct term would be bat."

Tavarra had never seen a bat before, but all she wanted was to be left alone with her sister.

The nosey bat stood and walked across the branch. "Why are you carrying around a dead body?"

The creature had no sensitivity whatsoever. In fact, she flew down, moving her dark wings back and forth as she hovered over Nezarra.

Tavarra swiped her hand across the air. "I said go away."

"Nah, I quite like you already." The bat shrugged. "It's been weeks since I've talked to anyone."

A loud and heavy sob came from Tavarra. "I killed my sister."

There was barely even a pause before the tiny stranger spoke, not seeming the least bit frightened. "Oh, we all do things without thinking. You look to be regretting it now."

"It wasn't on purpose!"

"I've also had people I love killed. My parents were murdered—by a jovkin. Now, that was a creature with no

regret." The bat angled closer. "Then I was raised by a human family, and they were killed, too ... by volachs. Those stone creatures aren't regretful, either." The volachs were a large giant of a creature. Bodies made of stone, always angry. Most of the time they kept to themselves, though.

The way the little creature spoke was strange, as if having two families die had been an everyday occurrence. "You don't look to be too heartbroken about that."

"I am ... but I hold it in here." Flying in the air, the bat drew a small shape over her chest that may have been a heart.

Tavarra looked at her lifeless sister. "You wouldn't happen to know where the Stone of Desire is, would you?"

"Can't say I've heard of it, only know about a couple of prisms. Those won't bring your sister back to life, though." The bat flew off, and Tavarra wished the creature had stayed. It would have made her feel less alone, even though she didn't know the bat.

A loud thump sounded beside Tavarra, and she looked down near her hand where a luscious red apple now sat. She had eaten those with Brice before—she scooted the fruit away, as if the memory would leap from it.

"You looked hungry." The bat said, flying back down in front of her. "Do you want me to help you bury the body?"

Tavarra narrowed her gaze at the bat. "No." With one look at her expressionless sister, she knew that even if she had found the Stone of Desire, her sister was gone—truly gone. She didn't want to return her sister to the sea—she wanted her on land where she knew she was somehow with her. Not meeting the eye of the small creature, Tavarra sliced at the ground with her new-found strength and dug a hole until it was deep enough to place her sister inside.

In silence, the bat watched, not making any movements, which Tavarra appreciated. However, when she covered up the hole, the little creature came forward to help push the dirt with her small hands until they were finished.

"Where to now, friend?" the bat asked.

Friend? Tavarra had no friends now and didn't want any, either. "I don't even know your name."

"I'm Eza."

"How old are you?" Tavarra couldn't tell because the bat was already so small.

"Fourteen." Not too much younger than Tavarra then. "And your name?"

She let several moments pass before deciding to continue. "Tavarra."

"Hi, Tav. Not the best circumstances, but we'll get through this together. We're family now."

Tavarra thought that if a monstrous beast had found Eza in the tree, she would not have called it family. Then she remembered that she now was something similar.

"But I am a beast."

"How are you a beast? You have sharp teeth, claws, and hair in some strange places, but you look very human to me."

Tavarra reached up to feel her throat—the gills hadn't come back. Without responding, she walked for a long while until she came across a small lake. Eza had followed her. Tavarra took off Brice's blood-stained shirt—only a reminder now of the most painful night of her life. There were rips up and down the back, as if she had grown overnight and torn it.

Peering down at her claws, she shook her head and splashed water on her face. Dried blood that wasn't hers came away. Then she washed the scarlet as best she could from the shirt, while scrubbing her skin clean to the point it was rubbed raw.

"There's another apple tree on the other side of the lake," Eza called.

"I'm not hungry."

After she finished and slid on the wet clothing, Tavarra curled up beside the lake and fell asleep. Something disturbed her out of her slumber. Flicking open her eyes, she gazed up at the twin moons in the sky, shining above her. Her body trembled, and she felt pieces of her tearing, growing, and hair sprouting. A howl of pain ran up her throat and out her mouth.

"Tav?" a voice shouted.

She was so hungry. Then it all faded to black.

In the morning, Tavarra looked down at her shirt. There was more blood and more rips on it than before. But the day before she had washed the shirt as clean as she could get it. Unless she was bleeding. Then she remembered the pain, the aching intensity of it.

"You're not the one bleeding." Eza cocked her head and pointed in the direction up ahead. "But you did save any possible living bats from potential harm."

Crinkling her forehead, she stared out at the scattered body parts of two horned creatures. They had been ripped apart and eaten. "Jovkins?"

"Jovkins," Eza confirmed, rubbing a hand across her chin. "Remember when I said you looked mostly human?"

Tavarra nodded.

"Well ... not last night."

Six

Rhona

Rhona needed her ability. When she was younger, she'd pretended it wasn't there—Belen had made her hate it at times. But when her entire being transformed into water, that part she loved—every single piece of her turning into liquid. As Rhona ran away from Perin, she now wished she'd spied on Belen. Or killed him—but she had always been frightened of him, and it wasn't going away now that she knew the truth of his treacherous spirit.

She tugged the hood of her cloak over her head, the edge falling at her waist. Holding the straps of her pack close, Rhona took off in a hard sprint north toward the Crimson Forest. She knew Perin was probably not far off.

After distancing herself well enough from the village, a hand clasped her shoulder. She turned around to find narrowed blue eyes staring at her.

"Leave me alone!" she shouted. Her heart sped up because Perin was her best friend, but he was also Belen's son. Something didn't feel right, especially after he had led her to that willow tree. And now people in her village were turning into corpses, her mother possibly being one. She shivered as she remembered the decrepit skin of Jasmine's face.

Her gaze fell to the pack on his back, the cloak across his shoulders, and the sword at his hip.

"Listen, we have a new mission," he said in a flat tone and started walking ahead of her.

"You planned this. You knew about that demonic prism!" she cried, catching up.

"Yes." It was all he said without looking at her, not meeting her eyes—*again*. "But I got you out. Now, we have to retrieve the dark prism from the Crimson Forest. Together we will use it against Belen."

She gave his arm a hard shove. "I got myself out, idiot!"

He kept on walking.

She had never not trusted him with anything. Or maybe she had because she'd never told him about Quil.

"Why didn't you tell me about the ivory prism, Perin? Especially after you knew my ability had been taken away!" Snatching his arm, she tried to twist him around to face her. He was much bigger than her, though, so his feet stayed planted in the dirt.

"Because he threatened to kill you," he said softly.

"But you could have still told me! We could have figured out some way to get it back from him or *something*."

"I couldn't risk your life." Sucking in a breath, Perin moved forward again.

Rhona caught up with him. "But you *were* risking mine. I was just strapped to that chair, and now we're risking my mother's!"

He let out a long sigh. "I knew what I was doing. *You* are important to me."

"I'm scared now. Apparently, I can't even touch your damn father. I don't understand!" She tapped a finger against his chest. "I don't even know what he wants to do with this stupid dark prism!" She knew Belen was going to try to do something wicked with it, along with the ivory one, if he was able to take them to the Stone of Desire.

"You know how I feel about my father." His gaze locked on hers. "*Nothing* is what I feel."

Rhona struggled with words, confused beyond understanding. "Why didn't you ever try to kill him then?"

"You saw what happens when you try, and I wouldn't have attempted anyway because that would have affected you."

Rhona stared at him, wondering how in the hell he could be both her best friend and this complete stranger at the same time. "There's no reason for me to trust you." Then she thought about Belen using the prism on Perin. Him falling to his knees back inside Belen's home. That was the first time she had ever seen Belen hurt Perin. If anything, his father ignored him most of the time, as if he was nothing.

He frowned as they parted bushes and moved down the grassy trail. "About the willow tree… I didn't know he was going to do it right then. I was trying to tell you…"

"Look," she interrupted, choosing to give Perin the benefit of the doubt. "My mother's missing, so we need to go. *Now.*" She wrapped her hand around his bicep and tugged him forward.

Her heart pounded as they ran past willow trees and grass greener than emeralds. After a while, they slowed to a steadier pace.

"You know things will only get darker the farther north we go, right?" Perin said.

"Somehow you survived being your father's son," she shot back.

"Yes, and it's been lovely. How about we go back for some afternoon tea?" He frowned, his sarcasm awful.

Rhona's whole body stilled. "Perin, has Belen ever hurt you before? Or was that the only time back at the house?"

"You've asked me this before, and you know the answer. I have no special ability. My life consists of my father threatening to harm you if I don't do as he says. It always has. And in case that isn't clear enough, the threats have been again and again and again." His eyes stayed trained on hers, and her body relaxed, even though hearing that made her angry. She couldn't handle it if Perin had been treated the way she'd been by Belen's hand.

"You shouldn't have listened to those threats."

"Come on." He walked ahead once more.

They wandered deeper into a thicket until they reached the edge and came across hills of greens mixed with pinks, violets, yellows, blues, and oranges. The hilly landscape resembled rainbows, and Rhona watched in delight. She had never explored all of Laith. Always the obedient child—besides the times she'd spent at the river with Quil, so maybe she had never been a good child after all.

"Do you remember these hills?" Perin asked.

"No, I wasn't awake on that journey because of Belen, remember?" Rhona shut down the bitter thoughts that were already surfacing as she studied the radiant colors, letting the vibrancy swirl around her.

"I know… I could *kill* him," Perin seethed before gathering his composure. "Come on. We'll have to find somewhere to sleep for the night. I'm not sure how many days it will take to get there."

"I think the Crimson Forest is supposed to be on the other side of the sea." Despite her words, Rhona wasn't really sure.

"You have a boat, then?" He quirked a brow, but received only a glare from her in return.

"We've got arms."

"Mmm. Have fun swimming and then drowning because you're too tired to finish."

She smacked his arm.

"But no, crossing the sea isn't the way." He almost smiled, and she swatted his arm again.

They stayed silent as they hiked up to the top of a large grassy knoll where everything was quiet. Taking a rest, Rhona sat down and pressed her hand against the swaying grass. It felt softer than feathers as the blades laced between her fingers.

Staring down at the bottom of the hill, Rhona was almost tempted to roll down it—but she wasn't a child anymore.

Movement to the side drew her attention. Perin pulled out slices of dried meat and an apple. He split the rations between them. She drank a little from her canteen but wanted to save some in case they didn't find a water source.

After the colorful hills, nothing else stood out besides trees with leaves of magenta. "Do you see it? Up ahead?" Perin asked.

Lifting her head, Rhona saw a pale-white rabbit nibbling at a piece of green foliage. Her stomach rumbled at the sight, and she didn't want to have to eat dried meat again. They needed to be saving as many provisions as they could for what promised to be a long journey ahead.

With quiet precision, Rhona slowly withdrew her dagger from inside her belt. She squinted her eyes for a moment, to focus, before letting the dagger fly.

The sickening thud of the weapon hitting its mark echoed in the forest. She smiled with a bit of pride.

"Perfect aim." Perin sounded impressed as he moved to pick up their dinner.

Above them, the suns' light was beginning to die. Rhona and Perin found a spot beside a few hefty boulders to cook the meat and sleep for the night.

Perin gathered leaves and twigs to start the fire while Rhona skinned the fur from the rabbit. He took the skinned animal from her and pushed its body onto a larger limb, then held it over the crackling fire. The intoxicating scent filled the air. Rhona inhaled deeply, and her hunger had gotten to the point where she could have eaten it before being roasted.

"Can I tell you something, Rhona?" Perin asked as he pulled the meat from the fire and let the air cool it down.

Rhona stared at the meat, prepared to whisk it away and

shove the entire thing in her mouth. "You can tell me anything."

"There once was a girl who loved to dance, but one day she stopped. Why is that?"

Rhona knew he was talking about her, but she played along. "Because when they moved, there was nothing to dance for anymore." What she really meant was there was *no one* to dance for.

"Maybe one day."

"Maybe." When she leaned back, something sharp scratched her hand. She brought it up to the fire to inspect it. Blood. The wound didn't close—she should be used to that by now. Maybe she'd secretly hoped the farther they went away from Belen, that her ability would come back. But she should have known better.

"What's wrong?" Perin asked, peeling off a rabbit leg for her.

"Nothing, just a scratch."

He bit his lip and must've read the expression on her face. "I suppose we'll both be mortal on this journey, then."

"I suppose." She dove into the meat and it filled her stomach, but she still wished there had been more rabbits to eat. One split among two people was nowhere near enough— but it would have to be.

Perin had already fallen asleep by the sounds of his even breathing. Before lying down, she tossed a few more limbs into the fire to keep the flames going for a little while longer. The only noises she could hear were the clicks of bugs and the beating of fragile wings. She would try not to think of her mother or Belen during the journey. She needed to gather all the inner strength she could to find that prism.

With a yawn, she placed her pack behind her head and closed her eyes. One thing that prevented her from sleeping was knowing how close they were to their old home. It meant they were closer to her friend—and at night, she always thought of him before falling asleep.

"I have something to show you." Rhona grinned, looking over her shoulder at Quil.

He was trying to peer around her, craning his neck as far as it would go to see what she was doing with her hand.

Over the past three years since Rhona had met him, Quil had grown, too. He wasn't as scrawny as he had been, but he was still on the thin side. One of the teeth near his front tooth stuck out a bit too far to make his smile perfect, but it was perfect to her.

She tilted her body to the side so he could see her hand hovering over the bright-yellow daisy.

"A daisy? Is that the surprise?" he huffed.

Closing her eyes, she thought of draining water. When she opened her eyelids, Quil was now hunched down in front of her with his jaw hanging open. She peered down at the flower to see that the life was now gone. It was brown and droopy and looked a bit melancholic.

"You killed it!" he shouted, eyes not blinking.

"No ... I, uh, well, yeah, it's dead now. But only because I had to show you." She stared down at the flower. "Sorry ... Daisy Sunshine."

"You named the flower Daisy Sunshine? After it's already dead?" he asked, incredulous.

"Oh, get off your high horse, Quil, you yank up clovers every day, killing way more than I ever have." If anyone was a plant killer, it was definitely Quil.

"We're going to pretend you didn't just compare a colorful daisy to a weed."

"A weed you want to find desperately!"

He bent his head closer to the dead flower as if to take a long whiff. "So, when did you learn this new trick?"

Pursing her lips together, she avoided his gaze. "Today..."

"You little liar." He grinned one of the biggest smiles she'd ever seen.

"Little?" She straightened to a standing position. "You're the same size as me."

"When?" he asked, lengthening his spine beside her. It didn't make him grow any taller.

Rhona took a moment to answer, so she could remember when she'd first found out. There'd been a flower she'd chosen that was already on its way to dying. She thought she could save it, but it only shriveled farther. Her mother had been with her that day and had comforted her when she ran to her crying after the ordeal was over.

"All right. All right. I learned it when I was five."

"And you didn't tell me? For three years?" His voice went up several octaves. "You sneak!"

"I'm not a sneak! I just never thought to show you." That was true. It wasn't as if she went around killing flowers and trees all day. After Belen had made her try things, she didn't want to do it. But he had stopped making her.

"Whatever. What else can you do?" In awe, he gestured to the sister flower beside the now dead one.

"Well, I can heal, turn to water, dehydrate things, and..."

"And..." he echoed, pointing with an annoyingly quick motion at the living flower.

"I need two flowers."

He waved his hand at the brother flower next to the sister one.

"Fine," Rhona drawled, "but be forewarned that I can do this to you if you ever make me mad."

"I make you mad all the time, yet here I am!" He gave one of her curls two tugs.

With an annoyed grunt, she closed her eyes and focused on the sister flower, thinking about water turning to ice.

When she opened her eyes, Quil was already touching the flower. "It's cold!"

"I made the water inside turn to ice."

His face looked completely mystified, all wide-eyed and

mouth hanging open again.

Next, Rhona directed her attention on the brother flower, concentrating on water boiling. After she opened her eyes, the flower tilted in a wilting position and Quil reached for it. She snatched his hand away. "Don't touch it! It'll burn you."

"So that's it, then?" He leaned back. "No other things?"

Furrowing her brow, she thought for a moment. "Well, there's one thing I always wanted to try, but I never have."

"Well…" Quil's body angled closer, even though she could kill him in a second if she really wanted to. But hurting people wasn't in her nature.

"You have to trust me."

"You know I do." There wasn't a single pause in his words. She trusted him, too.

She held up her hands between the two of them, waiting for Quil to press his against hers. When he did, she closed her eyes, intertwining their fingers. Skin, muscle, and bones melting, followed by liquid moving.

Together their skin turned to a translucent blue, and they swished to the ground. As soon as they hit the grass, Rhona thought of water reshaping, and they rose back to their original position, fingers still interlaced.

"What if I had been left as a puddle and only you came back?" Quil didn't sound frightened, even though the answer could have been. She wouldn't have let his hands go.

"You took the risk."

He smiled and stared at her for a moment, their fingers still woven together. "So, I wanted to ask you something."

"Yeah?"

"Have you ever been kissed by someone before?"

At twelve, she'd never even liked anyone. "No. Have you?"

"Yes … plenty of times," he rushed the words out and stared at the ground.

"No, you haven't! Who's the liar now?"

"Okay, I haven't." Something about his expression made

her feel sad, and she didn't want him feeling that way.

Taking a deep breath, she leaned forward and gave him a quick kiss on the mouth, because he was her friend. "Now you have."

"We both have."

"Now all the girls in your village will be fighting over you." She peered down at his bare feet, covered in dirt. "If you clean your feet first."

Laughing, he let go of her hand. "Before you go, do you want to dance?"

"You know the answer to that." She'd always want to dance out here to the sound of his pan flute.

Quil picked up the instrument from the top of his pack and played a new melody that made her body want to dance, her soul to fly, and her heart to beat with the rhythm. Rhona wished she could stay here, live beside the river, and dance to his music all day, every day. But that could never happen.

Seven

Tavarra

Tavarra stood where it all began: the sea. The waves were once her life. She hated living in the sea, but she never hated looking from the outside in. Now, the push and pull of the water only felt like death because she hadn't been herself in a long time.

Even though she could have come the day before, she hadn't. Perhaps because she had run into Brice. So, Tavarra had ventured back out a little farther for the night. She hoped the new chains she and Eza had scavenged from a village would remain strong. Last night they had held her, and as always, she remembered none of it.

That morning before coming to the sea, she'd unlatched the chains, feeling a small amount of measured hope. It had come from somewhere inside her after being buried for years. With that tiny emotion, she had made way for the beach that she hadn't been to for so long.

"Last night you were wilder than ever since you couldn't break loose," Eza said.

Tavarra believed it. She rubbed at her wrists, still sore from where they had drawn blood. Her jaw hurt from where her teeth must have been clenched so tightly that she wondered how any were left in her mouth. Sometimes, Tavarra wanted to know what the beast looked like. When she stared down at her reflection in the water, she wanted to see the monster for only a second. Instead, it was always her, and with her fangs, she still appeared deadly, but that was more because it was hard to find a smile when Eza wasn't around.

Tavarra stared out at the horizon and inched closer to where the forest dirt became sand.

Letting out a sigh as her heart started to quicken, she turned around and asked Eza, "Do you mind if I go alone?"

The bat pressed her hand to Tavarra's forehead with a delicate touch. "Since this is going to be a day of mourning, I'll go do that for a bit, too."

She already knew Eza would only be sitting in the branch of a tree and watching over Tavarra to make sure she didn't fall apart. However, Tavarra nodded and walked through the sand.

The grainy texture shifted as she took uneasy steps to get to where she wanted to be: at the center. She moved forward with small paces, almost afraid to let the water touch her feet. As if meeting a lover, the water met the sand, giving it a brief kiss before rolling back. A sense of braveness washed over Tavarra, and she pressed her feet into the wet part of the sand, letting the waves swish back and forth against her toes.

Closing her eyes, she thought about her life down below. Tavarra's parents had been older when she and her sister were conceived. When she was twelve and Nezarra fourteen, their father had passed, then two years later their mother followed—it was expected. She still missed them, and they were kind enough to their two daughters, but they had never been close.

Tavarra knelt into the sand, sliding forward on her knees into the water. Even after everything, she still didn't want to go back, not really. The depths of the sea would always be a cage for her, regardless if she was this *thing* or not. Her heart never sang for the ocean—she didn't know what it sang for anymore. It was only there to keep her life going.

"I'm sorry, sister," Tavarra murmured, stroking and picking up beads of wet sand. She let the pieces rain back down as she rubbed her fingers together. "I know I selfishly didn't bury your body in the ocean. But I'd like to think your soul came back to it, to take care of all the wayward dwellers like me who felt they needed something more." *Who still feels this way.*

She thought about her recluse life, the people she never wanted to get close to—only those dalliances that came and went.

Despite being close with her sister, they'd never spent all their waking hours together. Yet even after days of being apart, when they would reunite, it was as if they had never been away from each other. She had always loved her. Even if they had ended up being separated with Tavarra on the land and Nezarra in the ocean, she still would have come to the sea to visit her.

Picking up a small shell from the sand, she treaded her way farther and farther into the liquid, until it was brushing hundreds of tiny fingers at her waist. She didn't want to go deeper than that—it felt as if the water would chain her in place if she did.

With the shell resting in the middle of her palm, she pressed it to her lips and whispered a message inside. "Nezarra. Wherever you are, you're a much better dweller than I ever was. I love you." Taking a deep breath, she threw the shell as hard as she could and listened for the plunking sound as it struck the water. Somewhere out there, it would sink and drift to a new beginning, not knowing where it was going. No different from her, but at least the shell was home. Tavarra never truly had one of those. She had always drifted from place to place, and she still did.

The good thing was the beach no longer reminded her of Brice, only her sister. After shutting off her thoughts for a few moments, she finally walked back to the tree where Eza was.

"I know you're still there. You don't blend in with those bright leaves."

"Drats, I thought my camouflage and position were good this time." Eza stepped from behind a yellow leaf.

"You sure you don't want to mourn?" Tavarra could go somewhere else for a little while to let her friend have time to think.

"As you know, I wasn't around my real parents long enough." She sighed. "But can I show you something? It's about a day and a half from here."

"We have plenty of time, Eza." Maybe they could find someone along the way who knew where the Stone of Desire was located.

"It sure seems like it, doesn't it? Seven years later and here we are." Eza smiled and hopped from the branch, flapping her wings.

"What will happen if you ever encounter another bat? Will you go off to your new-found tribe?" It was meant to be Tavarra's attempt at a jest, but instead, her heart plummeted when she thought about Eza leaving.

In the air, Eza stretched her spine straight and put her fists on her hips, making herself as tall as she could. "I would say, 'hello, bat, let's mate to expand our kind and then you can help me protect Tav or go away after you implant your seed.'"

"Can't expand your kind if it's a female, though," Tavarra pointed out.

"That's true, but we can still mate."

"Might have to settle for a fairy." Fairies might be like little demons, but they would most likely be fine mating with a bat.

Eza's face slowly disintegrated into a grimace. "He would probably suck my blood dry or our little creation might do it while in the womb. I can't risk that!"

It had been seven years since Tavarra had those type of intimacies, and she didn't think she ever would again. But maybe Eza could find a small family one day and be happy.

"How about you lead the way and take me to this place you want to show me." Tavarra was more than a little curious.

"Sure, but first can you pull out a piece of fruit? I'm starving." Eza flew around Tavarra's head, rubbing her belly as her wings created their small buzzing sound.

"But you just ate." Tavarra laughed, removing her leather pack. "For such a small thing, you eat more than me."

"That's because you eat a lot at night time." Eza zoomed closer to the pack.

Tavarra's eyes widened, but her stomach didn't sink as it would have years ago.

"Too soon for those kinds of jokes?"

"As long as I never eat a baby, I'll be okay." She paused and stopped opening the bag. "Wait, have I eaten a child?"

"Not a human child…"

Tavarra clamped her jaw shut, motioning for Eza to stop talking. From the pack, she grabbed an apple resting on top of her chains and spare clothing. Closing her bag, she placed it on her back and led the way while holding out the apple for Eza to take bites.

The forest was quiet. Out here, the trees reached incredible heights, their leaves a golden yellow. Tavarra realized that Eza was leading her the same direction in which Nezarra had taken her before. Her stomach did sink this time when she thought about the small village.

"I don't want to go this way." Tavarra scowled.

"Don't worry, we're not stopping here. You can run if you want." Eza sped up and Tavarra followed her. When the wooden shelters all slid into view, they looked different. Perhaps because the first and only time she had seen them had been at night with her sister.

Noises echoed all throughout the village—children laughing, someone hammering, humans shuffling around. The smell of meat cooking filled the air, and she had to leave. This was home to them—a home she wished she had.

"Let's keep going," Tavarra said. Ignoring the shelters, she marched on, careful not to stare in the direction of the homes for fear she might do something she would regret. The male species from this particular village could wither and die if they were all like Brice, which she thought they probably were.

Past the village, their journey didn't take quite a day and a half. They slept for the night without Tavarra changing and didn't linger long when they ate. Tavarra caught a large feathered bird, eating most of it. As they continued up a steep hill covered in vegetation, Tavarra held another apple in her palm for Eza. Every few moments, the bat would take a small bite.

After going down the hill, there wasn't much forest up ahead. A luscious green valley with mismatched hills and a waterfall leading to a river slid into view.

At the river, Tavarra leaped over the narrow flowing body of water and then hopped over a decaying log before hurrying up the small hill. Toward the top, under the suns' beams, there was another village.

But this one wasn't like Brice's village—all neat and tidy. Instead, small wooden shelters were spread away from each other. Some looked to be falling apart but the others seemed to be nice and sturdy. Up ahead, people tended their gardens and children played.

Eza paused midair and slowly turned around. "It's not the same anymore."

"How's it different?" It looked like a village to her, except for some shelters on the verge of collapsing.

"When I left, *everything* was in ruins. This is where my parents lived—my human ones. I wasn't really theirs, but it always felt like I was." With wide eyes, Eza took off without another word.

"Come back, Eza!" Tavarra shouted and chased after her. Her feet struck mud, but she didn't stop to wipe the splashes from her trousers.

Eza was deaf to her cries, heading toward a man tending a garden. At Tavarra's shout, he turned around, and that made her slow down. She didn't want to talk to anyone—she didn't really want to see anyone, either. And she wouldn't let these humans, who she didn't know if she could trust or not, capture her friend.

The man tending his garden was burly, surrounded by pink and white flowers. Eza had already stopped in the air in front of the man, appearing to be speaking to him. Placing a small shovel on the ground, he turned his head and scratched a dirt-covered fingernail across his ebony cheek.

He opened his palm, as if luring Eza into it. *Of course, she would do it.* The bat dropped down to his open hand, and Tavarra hurried because she didn't trust him one bit.

She snatched Eza out of his hand. "Touch her again, and I'll rip you to shreds."

The man dropped a tiny rake, beads of perspiration sliding down his forehead and neck. A gray mustache hovered over his upper lip, matching the color of his hair. He kept quiet, body nervously shaking as he stared at the fangs she was baring.

"Tav, drop me this second!" Eza shouted, wiggling in Tavarra's grasp. "This is Mr. Sivley."

Opening her hand, she released Eza.

"Sorry about that, Mr. Sivley." Eza adjusted her dress. "This is my friend, Tav."

The man stared at Tavarra, his hands twitching. "Good day, Miss."

She attempted to smile, but it probably looked more like a sneer. *Not all humans are deceitful, I should remember that.*

Eza shifted in between them. "I was asking Mr. Sivley about the village. When I left, the volachs had destroyed everything, killing so many. Most people had scattered."

"A lot of us did leave," Mr. Sivley said, clearing his voice, "but only for a bit. This is our home. If rebuilding is all we had to do, then that's not too bad."

"Have the volachs come back since?" Eza asked.

"No, but we're better prepared this time."

Tavarra didn't think he could swat a bug away, especially with how nervous he had gotten over meeting her.

"I believe it," Eza said. "You were always so kind to me and my family."

Mr. Sivley tilted his chin in the direction toward the back of his shelter. "Your home is still around if you want to have a look. No one's fixed it up yet."

"I will, but first, can I ask you a question?"

"Any kind you want." Mr. Sivley bent down to collect his shovel and rake.

"Have you heard of the Stone of Desire?" In all of Tavarra's nervousness, she hadn't thought to ask the man about that.

He sucked in a deep breath of air. "It's supposedly what helped save humanity. When the savior, Luca, placed his hand against the Stone of Desire, it allowed access for a lot of people to cross over from a dying Earth."

"Do you know how we can find it?"

"I couldn't say, never seen it. Wouldn't even know what one might look like. Maybe try the Crimson Forest?" The hope that Tavarra had started to develop slowly faded. "But!" He held up a finger. "I can ask around while you go take a look at your old house if you wish?"

"Yes, please." Eza pressed her hands together. "My friend is desperate to find it."

Jaw clenched, Tavarra stared at the bat, wishing she could kick her up the hill right then.

"I'll see what I can do." With a tilt of his head at the both of them, Mr. Sivley went off in the other direction.

Eza grabbed Tavarra by her clawed nail, unafraid, and yanked her toward her old home.

Tavarra's shoulders relaxed as she thought about how Eza must be feeling. Tenderly, she opened her palm and placed the bat on her shoulder.

"Are you all right?" Tavarra asked, passing another garden on the side of the shelter, this one filled with green bushes covered in purple berries.

"I'll be fine," Eza replied, pointing up ahead. Tavarra walked down a curved stone path and circled around two wooden homes that weren't fully built, but were getting there. A redheaded woman hammered on the side of the building, not looking up as they crossed to the next.

"Have you been to the Crimson Forest?" Tavarra hadn't heard of it before.

"I haven't been inside, but I know where it is."

"It sounds pretty."

"Well, there is a high chance that we could both end up dead if we go inside it, but we've survived worse." Eza tugged at Tavarra's ear. "Stop! This is it!"

At the sharp pain, Tavarra batted Eza away and pressed a hand against her ear. The bat might have small hands but she still had strength in them.

"This is where I was raised." It was one of the first times Tavarra had heard Eza's voice crack, but the bat held the tears back.

The left side of the shelter looked as if it had never been touched, while to the right, most of the roof was missing. Whole tree logs surrounded it and were still attached at one end, but on the side where the destruction had occurred, they were cracked off. Since years had passed, it looked as if the shelter had been built that way, but she knew better. "Do you want to go inside?"

"No, this is good enough." Eza rested her hands on Tavarra's. "Having you here with me to see it."

Eight

Rhona

A boot pushed at Rhona's thigh, waking her. "I'm already awake, just give me a minute," she answered, slowly opening her eyes. She was on her stomach, cheek pressed to the dirt, even tasted it as she hurried to spit out the granules. Her gaze lifted to Perin who was already up and ready.

He cocked his head. "You'd think you would be more in a hurry."

She scurried to a sitting position, still feeling the weight of sleep. For a moment, she'd forgotten why they were out in the forest. Then she remembered Belen and her mother.

Rhona sniffed the air. "Did you cook something?"

"Someone had to, right?" Smirking, Perin looked at the fire they had used the night before. A small animal fully cooked, rested there, ready to be eaten.

Pushing her sword and daggers aside, she reached for the food. Perin swatted her arm. "Say please."

"Rats. Please."

"No, it's not a rat, but you may proceed." She wanted to smack Perin for his terrible jokes.

As quickly as she could, Rhona ate the meat and drank most of the water from her canteen. She wondered if her mother was all right. Something in her gut twisted at the uncertainty of it all. The vision of Jasmine's wilted face—*what might the other villagers look like now?* She shook the thoughts away and finished eating.

Over the next two days, their routine stayed the same. They ate, slept, and continued to head north for the mysterious prism.

By the third day, Rhona stood by a tree, sifting through her pack. The edge of her book peeped out.

Perin scrunched up his nose and angled his head. "You brought your book?"

"Yeah." She stared at Perin as if daring him to say something else, and he did.

"Out of all the important things you could have brought, it was a *book?*" he exclaimed.

Rhona shot him a glare. "Pear, you—"

"Don't call me that. I'm not a fucking fruit." He glowered in her direction.

"Are you sure about that?" Tilting her head back, she released a loud laugh and couldn't stop. "If you must know, I felt it would give us luck. Luca and the people who followed him made it here to a new world. Sort of how Wendy came to a new place that was Neverland."

"Where kids didn't grow old… We're not kids anymore."

"We're not a hundred years old, either." She placed a hand on his shoulder and gave him a soft shake. "Sometimes, I feel like you act it."

Perin stared at her for a moment before speaking. "I need to finish what I was trying to tell you at the willow tree." Something in his facial expression softened and made Rhona feel a tad scared. She hoped again that it wasn't a love confession, but what else could it be? She tightened her hood around her face. "And no, it's not a love sonnet." His voice hardened with those words, like hitting a tree that wouldn't budge.

She scowled at him. "Can you hear my thoughts, Perin?"

"What? No!" He shook his head and took a step back. "I can just read your facial expressions well."

Before either of them could say anything else, two beasts flung themselves from the forest. The intruders swung their swords at Rhona. Perin shot forward with his weapon already in hand. She struggled to pull hers out since her hands were on the buckle of her pack.

Finally, she withdrew the sword and waved it in the air. As she found her focus, it wasn't beasts swinging their blades, but two humans in dark cloaks.

"Hey!" she yelled—they didn't stop. *Now, they're going to get very, very hurt.*

Perin was striking his sword between the two, not breaking a sweat. One of the intruders' hoods had fallen, revealing a woman with a black braid tucked into the back of her cloak. The other, most likely a man, was taller and broader. Rhona went for that one. Just as she lunged to strike him in the back, the man whirled around and his sword clashed against hers. The clang radiated throughout the forest, a sound of two metals coming together that could unite and become friends. *Too bad that chance is dead.* She struck again. Harder and harder, faster and faster.

The hood blocked Rhona's view of the face, but long black hair poked out. Having a good fight for the day was enough to cheer her up—especially one she would win. A loud grunt came from the man as she pressed her sword against his, lifted her booted foot, and struck his chest. He didn't slip, though, instantly regaining composure.

For a brief second, Rhona made the stupid mistake of glancing at Perin. He had the girl already on the ground, sword at her throat. Rhona swung her head back to the cloaked stranger coming at her. Right as the weapon came down, she whirled to the side. But it was too late. The sword slashed her bicep.

She let out a small frustrated groan. "You make me bleed, you die, bastard!" Rhona leaped forward, light on her toes, almost enough to where she thought she could fly like the boy from her children's book. Her body was small and lithe, and she found the space that the bastard had left wide open. With the sword, she swung her hand repeatedly and then swooped low, pushing her foot forward and connecting with his, then pulling it up.

The man fell on his back with an "oof," the wind kicking out of his lungs.

"You need to learn new tricks," Perin called as her boot connected with the stranger's arm, her sword at his throat.

"It worked, didn't it?" She glared at him for trying to disrupt her win.

Rhona pressed harder on the sensitive area of the man's wrist until he released the sword.

"Now," she said in a harsh yet playful voice. "Do you want to die for so rudely intruding, or should we play a game? A game that involves you being nice."

"Fuck off," the stranger growled.

"I'm sorry, what was that?" Leaning forward, she moved her blade to the middle of his throat and removed the hood from the man's face. A faceless person might haunt her dreams—better to have a face. She'd have given anything at that moment to suck the life force out of the bastard with her ability.

Two golden-brown eyes, full of hostility, stared at her, but she knew those eyes, *that face*. She sucked in a sharp breath. His hair was longer, his face older, and his body stronger. But it was undeniably Quil.

Despite the burn of her arm, she tossed her hood back and lifted the sword from his throat. It had already drawn blood— a thin line creeping down the right side of his neck.

"Quil," she whispered.

His dark eyebrows slid up and surprise crossed his face, but then immediately turned into a scowl as he arched up a little. "Rho?"

She ignored his expression and wrapped her arms tightly around his neck as her legs cradled his hips. There was a pause as she waited for him to put his arms around her, but he didn't. "Why aren't you hugging me back?" she murmured into his ear, ignoring the throb in her bicep where his blade had struck.

Right as she was about to release him, his arms slammed around her, pulling her in tight.

"You know I hate you, right?" he said softly.

"I know."

"Is this reunion fucking over?" Perin growled, interrupting Rhona's thoughts. She released Quil and stood to her feet.

"Is your *friend* going to release Lana or do I need to keep my weapon out?" Quil demanded, picking up his sword.

"Release her." Rhona motioned for Perin to let Lana go. "It's fine, Quil's a friend."

Quil's expression hardened, and she didn't understand why. She knew he'd be mad at her, but she hadn't just up and left two years ago, although she kind of had. But it was because of Belen. Everything was always because of him. An image of a knife in Belen's hand, lowering it down to her, popped into her head. She shook it away, as she always had to.

"Quil, this is Perin. Perin, meet Quil."

"You sure you don't want to say *troll*?" Quil spat. *What's wrong with him?*

Quil looked at Lana, who stood and sheathed her sword. He did a few hand gestures and Lana nodded and tapped her hand twice, then moved her fingers into different signs. Her last motion was something with a heart over her chest and Quil shook his head.

"In case you don't remember me mentioning, my cousin, Lana, can't hear."

"I remember." Rhona smiled. "I wish you'd brought her to the river."

Lana pointed several times at Rhona and nodded, agreeing with her.

"Rhona, we need to get going," Perin mumbled, his sword still not tucked away.

"What are you? Her *lover?*" Quil spat.

Perin's shoulders visibly stiffened at the same time Rhona's did, and he said, "No, actually I'm her brother."

Rhona couldn't even focus on what Perin said, only Quil's hostile attitude. The day Belen took her away, he hadn't been like that, and it was hard to keep that memory away.

Rhona hurried through the forest because she had a surprise for Quil. It had been eight years since they'd first met, and she wanted to make him something extra special.

When she drew closer to the river, he wasn't there, but she knew exactly where he was—near the clovers. He still hadn't found that four-leaf clover he was so desperate to find.

Cupping her hands around her mouth, she shouted, "Quil!"

He looked over his shoulder and ran a hand through his short hair. Over the years he'd gotten taller, but was still lean at seventeen. Biting his lip, he stood and strolled toward her.

"Still nothing." He shrugged.

"One day." She grinned. "Then you can give it to one of the girls in your village who's crushing on you."

"Nah. I'd give it to my cousin, Lana. Maybe she could finally hear."

Rhona took the pack from around her shoulder and sat it beside the tree. "Why don't you ever bring her here?"

"I'll bring her when you decide to bring your friend, Perin."

"I would, but he's a bit ... serious." She still hadn't told anyone about Quil. He was her safe place, and she hadn't wanted to share him at first. Then, as years passed, she felt it was too late to tell people.

"So we're even ... for now."

"Anyway, I brought you something." Rhona sat on the ground, opened her pack, and fished out a wooden clover on a thick black cord. It dangled from her fingertips.

"For me?" Quil lowered his head, and she placed her gift around his neck. With a smile, he lifted the clover to inspect it. *"You made this?"*

"Yeah, I know it's not perfect, but I tried." All the leaves were a bit crooked, and of different sizes, but it was unmistakably a clover. She wasn't an artist by any means, but she wanted to give him that four-leaf clover he'd yet to discover.

"It's perfect." Quil released the necklace, letting it bounce lightly against his chest. *"I don't have a physical gift, but I can play you something new."*

"That's even better." Her heart sped up with furor, waiting for the melody.

From his pocket, he slid out a small pan flute and brought it close to his lips. A song drifted around her that was much different than his usual ones. It was slow, with a vibrant tone. Closing her eyes with her arms spread open, Rhona spun in a circle just as slow, moving her hips to the invisible waves of the music. It was hypnotizing, and she wanted to release pandemonium on the world with her movements.

Reclining her head back, she opened her eyes to the pinkened sky. It was light in color with puffy gray clouds traveling in a southern direction. A laugh escaped her throat, and she didn't know why, except that she felt free out here— always with Quil.

Her head came back down, her eyes meeting his. He was watching her. Not in his usual way—not even like in the several times over the years when they'd shared secret kisses. The kisses that she wasn't sure had ever meant anything to him, the way they had started to for her.

It was all in good fun and had been months since the last one. He'd never spoken of other girls in his village besides his *cousin, and Rhona hadn't discussed any other boys her age besides Perin.*

Feeling adventurous, she wiggled a finger for Quil to come join her. In answer, he just grinned against his flute and continued to play.

When the song ended, she smiled. "I better go. I have some things to do." Rhona had promised her mother she'd help her sew new clothing, so she had to start sword practice earlier.

"Wait! I have one more gift for you." By the heel of his boot, he pushed himself forward from the tree. Her heart accelerated with each movement that brought him closer. She didn't want to let herself feel this way, but she knew she loved him.

His gaze locked on to hers, and he stopped mere inches from her.

"You've gotten taller." It was a pathetic choice of words, but she was too scared to say the other three words.

"You're still the same size." He tugged on her tight curl.

Before she could say anything, his lips brushed hers in a soft kiss. He pulled away and took a step back and whispered, "I'll see you tomorrow."

"Okay." She turned around, let out a heavy breath, and looked over her shoulder. He stood in the same spot, studying her. The kiss had been sweet and light, but she needed more. If she was late, she would just come up with another lie, like she always did.

She whirled around and fixed her gaze on his. He cocked his head, as if challenging her.

"You jerk, you knew I'd turn around, didn't you?"

Crinkling his nose, Quil tilted his hand side to side. "My thoughts were leaning more toward yes."

She dropped her pack and lunged for him as she leapt forward, wrapping her arms around his neck and legs at his waist.

A low grunt escaped his mouth as he stumbled backward,

but he didn't fall. "I'm happy you did."

Her lips crushed against his, moving them back and forth, tasting everything from that precious mouth that she could. She wished she could taste his music and breathe it into her, and in a way she was. If Rhona were a hummingbird, then Quil was her nectar.

His tongue met hers, and Quil lowered the two of them to the ground under a shaded tree, positioning himself on his knees. Rhona tightened her legs around his waist, wanting to get even closer. Letting out a groan, he wrapped his hands in her curls. "I love your wild hair. Always keep it down."

"Stop talking." She laughed. Yet she always wore her hair down for him. Not because he told her to, but because her curls seemed to be meant for his fingers when he playfully tugged on them.

Quil leaned forward, gently placing her on the grass, as if she might break. The part of him that she wanted to feel was pressed to her. As they kissed, she slid her hands down his back, to his hips, rocking him against her.

Rhona moaned at the feeling that was increasing between her legs, and she wanted more. Her fingers drifted to the edge of his tunic and slid it up for him to pull over his head. He was being too slow, so she helped him by lifting her own shirt, and he finally realized what she'd been hinting at as he smiled against her lips.

"We have all the time in the world," he murmured, running a hand up along the side of her breast. They had touched each other before in curious exploration, but never like this.

"But I want you now, Quil."

"Then you can have me." The tip of his finger caressed her cheek before he kissed along her jaw, to her throat, to the center of her chest. Rhona's heart sped up as his mouth latched onto her breast, his tongue flicking her nipple, causing a delicious heat to spread throughout her. She threaded her hands through his hair, and when he released his mouth, she

pulled his lips back to hers.

When they were completely bare to each other, he stared at her. "Tomorrow I may just dance with you."

"I knew you eventually would."

He softly bit her lower lip, then brushed his mouth to hers once more. When he buried himself in her, she knew he was her "forever."

Somehow, after being together, they had both fallen asleep. As she opened her eyes, Rhona's insides filled with panic. She had only planned to rest her head on Quil's chest for a few moments.

She bolted up as he continued to sleep. Throwing on her clothes, she hunched down beside his ear. "I love you," she whispered, not yet brave enough to tell him to his face, even after all they had done.

His face looked so peaceful, angelic. "I have to go," she said a bit louder.

"See you tomorrow." He rolled to his side. "I'll go home in a bit."

Smiling, she covered his lower half with his tunic and rushed home.

After she made it back to the village, chaos greeted her. People were taking down tents and packing things up. She didn't know what was going on. Gripping the straps of her pack, Rhona hurried home as fast as she could. Her mother was loading things up in one of the carriages.

"What's going on?" Rhona asked, out of breath.

"Oh, thank goodness." Thea pulled her into a hug. "I didn't know where you were. We're leaving. The northern village is planning an attack tomorrow morning."

"What?" This can't be possible. I can't leave! *she thought.*

"We're leaving."

"I'm not leaving." Rhona took a step back.

"We are." Thea's expression fell. "I'm sorry."

"Let me find Perin. Then I'll help pack."

"We have to hurry!"

Rhona didn't look for Perin—she ran straight back to find Quil. She had to tell him she'd come back for him.

The two suns beat down on her as she moved quickly, pushing branch after branch out of the way. It wasn't fast enough. She let her body liquify and slide against the grass, moving at a rapid pace. When she came to the spot where she'd left Quil, she took form as herself again.

Shutting her eyes, she let out a frustrated sigh. He had already left.

Rhona took out a note to scrawl on and wrote:

Quil,

I know this is short notice, but we have to leave because of threats of an attack from your village. I'll come back for you. I'll always come back. Just, please, wait for me. I'll think of you every single night.

Rhona

She pushed the note on the sharp edge of a tree branch, knowing he'd find it in the morning.

When she re-entered her village, two strong arms grabbed her shoulders, and two icy blue eyes stared down at her. "Where were you?" Belen asked, his tone angry.

"Nowhere."

"You're lying." His grip tightened around her shoulders, squeezing too hard.

She let out a choked sob, and her head started to pound. The intensity increased more and more—everything around her blurred into splotchy images. Then the world around her expanded into a thick shade of white, and she fainted.

Nine

Tavarra

Tavarra walked back to Mr. Sivley's home with Eza on her shoulder, and they found him gardening again.

Eza leaped from Tavarra, pumping her wings. "Did you find out anything?"

He scratched the side of his head. "No, the people I asked don't have any idea. The Crimson Forest sounds like your best bet—maybe it's possible to find answers through there."

Eza nodded and glanced back at Tavarra. "It's a long journey to try to get there today."

Mr. Sivley swiped a gloved hand over his sweaty forehead. "You two are welcome to stay the night, or however long as you want. Your home still needs rebuilding, but it's vacant."

Eza was about to say something, but Tavarra fiercely shook her head. She didn't want to risk staying in this village near these humans if there was a chance she could change into the wild monster. Although, she was surprised the man had offered shelter after she had practically frightened him to death earlier.

"Maybe another time." Eza smiled.

"Don't wait another seven years before coming back, you hear?" He smiled in return.

Eza patted the man's head before she and Tavarra wandered back over the hills. In the distance, the stone mountains seemed grayer under the light of the suns. A flock of squawking birds flew over Tavarra's head as she hiked down the hillside.

"I'm going to head to the Crimson Forest tomorrow morning." Tavarra peered down at Eza. "You don't have to go." She didn't know what kind of things lurked in the forest, but from what Eza had mentioned earlier, it seemed dangerous.

Eza huffed. "You know my answer."

That, she did. Tavarra's body could be engulfed in flames and Eza would still try to blow air from her small mouth to help her.

"Now, to the west." Eza flapped her wings and flew ahead. Tavarra adjusted her heavy pack to make it more comfortable as she pushed forward and followed Eza through the forest.

After walking for a long while, they came upon rows and rows of peach trees. Pink and orange fruit dangled across the branches, plump and perfect. Eza became antsy as she dug her fingers into Tavarra's skin. Shaking her head, Tavarra lifted a shoulder. "Go. I'm not sure when we'll come across this many peaches again."

They were Eza's favorite fruit and a rare treat in certain parts of Laith. Whenever they found them, the little bat thundered with excitement—it was a dream for her. Eza clapped her hands and dove for a tree. Scanning the area, Tavarra didn't hear anything besides the wind swaying the trees' branches and leaves. The only other noise was her own slow movements.

The bat flicked her braids behind her shoulders as she arched her back, craning her neck for a dangling piece. With a tilt of the lips, Tavarra plucked a ripe yellow and pink one, placing it into her mouth. The sweetness didn't fill her, but it satiated her taste buds. A line of juice dripped down her chin, and she swiped it away.

The night's curtain was quickly drawing closed around them. She cursed herself for not being ready for it. As she looked around, the trees didn't appear strong enough to hold her if she transformed. *Maybe I'll be fine.* The night before, she had been. However, she couldn't risk it. She removed her boots and worried about Eza, despite the many conversations they'd had about it.

Tavarra sat on the edge of a log. Below her, the river flowed almost elegantly with its miniature ripples over the piles of chestnut-colored rocks.

It had already been a few years since her sister's death— she would have done anything to reverse that day and bring Nezarra back to life. But she couldn't bring something back that was already part of the earth.

The previous night had been a horrendous one. She couldn't remember it, but the dead sarilla bodies had been scattered everywhere. She felt more like the jovkins—a killer without mercy. If it wasn't bats that they had tried to kill, it was the sarillas. The sarillas were a small creature with loose pale-yellow skin and long floppy ears.

Tavarra had woken curled up with a sarilla's head ripped off from one of the bodies, as if it was her lover. She threw the head as far as it would go and spat out any remaining blood that had lingered in her mouth. That morning, she had spent hours trying to get clean from what the beast inside her had done.

"What would you do if I ever murdered you like these helpless creatures, Eza?" Tavarra whispered, terrified by the thought.

"Well, I'd be dead, so not much I could do." Eza shrugged.

Leaning her head back, Tavarra stared up at the darkened blood sky, no longer pink. It would be raining soon. The clouds were growing a dark blue, almost black.

"I'm serious."

"So am I." Eza sighed. *"If it happens, it happens—it wouldn't be as if the Tavarra I knew did it. So please don't dwell for me the way you do your sister. Even though I didn't get to meet Nezarra, I know for a fact she would side with me. From what you told me, she wasn't as stubborn as you."*

"Just promise me that no matter what, you always stay to the skies or somewhere high, and away from me while I'm on a rampage."

"I'll try." She smiled.

As Tavarra shrugged away the memory and reached into her pack to pull out the chains, a loud noise startled her. Her body froze, and her heart shriveled when the sounds came—heavy beating, earth shifting.

"Eza!" she yelled. "Hide!"

When she frantically searched the trees, her friend was nowhere to be found. Above her head, she finally spotted black wings on a branch—Eza stood in a warrior's stance.

If Tavarra wasn't so nervous, she would have rolled her eyes and laughed. She pulled two daggers from her waist that she rarely used since she preferred the claws, but the sounds rattled her this time. The weapons were now out and ready as she slowly spun in a circle. Holding her breath, she stopped when heavy footsteps started again.

From her right, a rustling and a movement came, then something charged for her. She threw one of the daggers as hard as she could straight at the gray skin. *Jovkin.* It struck the creature directly in the chest but missed the one organ she needed to hit.

Four curved horns decorated the jovkin—two in the front of his forehead, and two on the sides near his temples. As he ran for her with a rumbling grunt, Tavarra aimed her other dagger for him, penetrating his shoulder. He didn't miss a beat and knocked her to the ground.

"Where is it?" he seethed, his voice deep and breath hot against her face. "I can *smell* her."

Tavarra used her monstrous strength to shove him away, but he was immovable—as strong as her. Grinding his teeth, he held her down by the shoulders.

A buzzing sound came from above, and Tavarra silently cursed when Eza came flying with a small limb from a tree in hand. With a quick shove, Eza rammed it into the jovkin's eye. Howling in fury, he swiped at her, missing.

Giving a loud cheer, Eza flew back up.

"Stay up there!" Tavarra barked.

She rolled to her side, reaching for one of her weapons, but she had already thrown both daggers. A strong hand enfolded around her leg and dragged her back. All she had were her hands, so before he could pin her down again, Tavarra kicked her leg out as hard as she could into him. He fell back, and she rushed forward, wrapping her hands around his throat while squeezing tightly.

The moons had fully risen in the sky, and she could *feel* it. This time, Tavarra would welcome the change. Her body expanded and twisted in ways that would kill any normal person if they didn't have the curse. She held back the scream and used the pain to make her squeeze the jovkin's throat harder. Thick hair sprouted over her entire body, and her snout smelled something achingly delicious.

The only thing on her mind now was hunger. Tavarra stared down at the throat she clenched, and dug her claws in. The creature let out a raspy cry. With one hard thrust, she flipped the thing onto its back. Opening her jaw and baring her fangs, Tavarra dove into the soft spot between the neck and shoulder.

The aroma of blood rose into the air as it drifted to the surface and into her mouth. She lapped it up and wanted to drain the creature dry until there was nothing left inside it. Then she planned to rip the flesh and muscle from its bones, saving the glorious organs for last. A treasure to satisfy her desire.

With a savage roar, she followed through on the delicious

plan.

"You saved the day!" a small voice yelled. When Tavarra finished this creature, she would hunt down that one, too. And then another and another until all that surrounded her was blood. Her hunger would never vanish.

Ten

Rhona

"I'm her brother," Perin repeated. His words broke Rhona from her reverie. He was not her brother—*could not* be her brother.

"Perin," Rhona started. "Quil knows you're my *friend*." She emphasized the last word much more than she needed to, since Quil had used the term lover.

"Traveling alone in the forest together…" Quil shrugged. "I don't know, seems pretty lover-like."

"I don't know, *Quil*, couldn't I say the same about you and Lana?" The moment the words were out of her mouth, Rhona looked at his cousin and mouthed the word '*sorry.*'

"She's my *cousin*."

"And dare I repeat myself again"—Perin stepped forward, jaw clenched, sword at the ready for Quil—"I'm her *brother*."

Rhona shoved her sword to the side, blocking Perin's path to Quil.

"Perin, just stop, you're making things worse." She'd grown tired of the charade and wanted to move on.

Exhaling sharply, Perin locked gazes with her. "I wanted to tell you earlier—*was* trying to tell you—probably should've told you years ago, but yes, it's true."

"Wait here," Rhona said to Quil and his cousin. She latched onto Perin's tunic and pulled him to a space that was several trees away. "What are you doing?"

He frowned for a moment and ran a hand along the back of his neck. "I'm going to finish what I tried to tell you under the tree, and a moment ago before those two idiots came bouncing in."

"They aren't idiots."

"Whatever you say, Rhona. Anyway, your father wasn't from another village—he's from ours."

"Okay, you seem to be making this more dramatic than it has to be." Every fiber in her being zeroed in on Perin, on his features that seemed much too pained for her liking. It was as if the two of them were in a village play.

He stopped avoiding her gaze then. "Belen's your father."

Rhona's eyebrows lowered, and she poked his chest, hard. "No, Belen's *your* father."

I'd rather have my children help me. He had said *children*, not child. She shook the sound of Belen's voice from her head.

"Look, your mother wanted a baby. She asked Belen to help her. And he did…"

"If what you say is true, then how did he help her?"

Perin stared at her and blinked repeatedly.

Rhona cringed and almost threw up her food from earlier. She held up her hands. "That's gross, and for you to even say it did…"

"Belen told me. He offered to help her himself since my mother was already gone. Your mother knows that I know. She's *known* I knew for a long time. My father wanted to make sure I was aware when we became close friends in case … something was to happen between us."

"Then why didn't my mother tell *me*?" Gripping the sides of her head, Rhona glanced at Quil and Lana—who were signing to each other. This whole story didn't make sense to her, not one bit. She didn't believe her mother would have been with Belen like that. She would have told Rhona.

"You'd have to ask her that. I can't read her mind."

Rhona glared at him. Her thoughts flashed back to Belen slicing her flesh to see how fast her wound would close. It had started out as a daily thing, and as the years progressed, her cuts and bruises healed faster. There was no way that bastard could be her father. Her head became a jumbled, twisting, and twining thing of confusion as the trees around her seemed to feel like an enclosed barrier. Just thinking about him being her blood was going to make her throw up.

"You'd have to prove it." She shook her head. "I don't believe it."

"I don't know how you weren't able to see it, Rhona. I can see parts of my father all over your face. The same blue eyes, cheekbones, the way you clack your teeth when you're annoyed. The same way you're doing it now."

"I do not do that." She held her teeth together to prevent the habit from starting again.

"And if you think I'm the only secret holder here, what about you? I already know about Quil." He held up a hand. "Don't worry, I didn't tell your mother or Belen."

"*What?*"

"I followed you a few times over the years. You're not as good at lying as you think you are, but apparently, I am." His expression was unreadable, and she couldn't tell how he truly felt about it.

She shoved him and stormed off.

"I'm going to apologize in advance for what's going to happen, but it's always been my job to protect you, *sister.*" What was he rattling about now?

Quil was still signing to his cousin. He didn't look at either of them when they stopped in front of him.

"Quil, meet my possible half-brother, Perin," Rhona said with sarcasm.

"We need to continue, so good day." Perin tugged Rhona

in the northern direction.

"Wait, where are you going?" Quil asked as Rhona wriggled out of Perin's grasp.

"Do you remember Belen? The town leader I told you about?" Rhona started and continued before he could respond, "Well, he has this magical ivory prism and wants us to find the dark counterpart, but we're going to use it against him. Oh, and my ability has been shut off for a while."

"Rhona, you need to stop spilling secret details to these people," Perin growled.

"Quil's not a stranger."

The scowl on Quil's face withered away as his gaze fell to her bicep where blood was leaking out. "You haven't healed!" He shot forward, taking her arm in his hands.

Rhona pulled it from his grip. "No, I can't do that anymore." She didn't want to discuss that right now, either. "What about your neck?"

Quil touched the cut. "It's barely a scratch. We're not far from home, let me stitch you up." He reached for her again but must have thought better of it because he dropped his hand back by his side.

Rubbing his chin, Perin studied her arm intensely and nodded. When Rhona pulled the torn cloth back, the cut looked deeper than she'd expected.

Her heart thudded as she followed Quil and Lana back to their village. They circled around a cave covered in stringy dark moss and green shrubbery while stepping over fallen branches.

In the distance, logged houses peeked through the forest, unlike the tents Rhona's village used—besides Belen's large cabin. This had more of a permanent feeling—she liked that idea.

A part of her kept going back to what Perin had said. He was her brother… If her mother was all right, Rhona needed to ask her questions, find out if it was true. Her mother had always talked about how much she had wanted a child, how she would have done anything to have a daughter like her. And now Rhona supposed that maybe she had … by sleeping with that demon of a man.

Rhona's eyes met Perin's blue ones—like hers—like Belen's. Her jaw clenched, and she tightened her fists. It was true, she knew it… Somehow, she had always known it.

Quil stopped in front of a logged house with a wide porch. He turned around to sign something to his cousin.

Lana shook her head and tugged at Perin's tunic. "Come on, I'm going to take you to my home and feed you. You look hungry," she said, her voice sounded a bit muffled, but Rhona could understand her. Perin tried politely to pull his arm from her grasp, but she held on.

Quil rolled his eyes, and Rhona said, "I'll be fine, and I'll meet you after."

Perin gave in and let Lana lead him away.

Sounds of swishing greeted Rhona and Quil up ahead. A few women washed their laundry in wide buckets, while two men hung shirts to dry. Rhona turned around to follow Quil into a house. "Is this your home?"

"Yes." He opened the door and motioned her inside.

"Where is everyone?" Four wooden chairs sat in the living room—two on one side and the matching set facing them. A fur rug was sprawled out in between the furniture in front of the fireplace. Several paintings were hung around the room, and one wall was covered with pan flutes wrapped in decorative strings.

"This was my grandparents' place," Quil said, not looking at her. "When they both passed away last year, I took over the responsibility of it."

"Oh." Rhona hadn't been there for Quil in the forest when that happened, and it made her stomach fill with guilt.

He didn't say anything else. *Why is he being so distant?* Maybe he'd found someone else. Expecting him to wait for her was a selfish idea, especially when it had been two years.

"Come." Quil gestured at a wooden bench. She moved to the edge and sat down, while he straddled the opposite end and scooted closer to her. She got a whiff of the outdoorsy scent radiating off him, same as it always had been. It was as if his skin was made from the river, a smell that gave her comfort. He swept a lock of hair behind his ear.

"You grew your hair out," she said, tired of the quiet.

Quil rolled up the sleeve of her tunic, careful not to hit the wound. "Didn't feel the need to cut it."

"You grew taller."

"You stayed the same size." He threw her a look. "And before we talk about everything that's grown on me, let me clean this. Wouldn't want you losing your arm from an infection." She expected him to smile when he said this, the way he always had in the past when he'd seen her. But he didn't.

"I'd still have my other arm." Her tone was serious.

Quil stared at her, trying to fight a smile, and shook his head. At least he almost smiled, and that made her insides shine.

First, he cleaned the area with a clean rag and some water, then poured another liquid from a bottle over the wound. She sucked in a sharp breath and let out a loud curse, and then another and another.

He set the bottle down behind him. "I guess you haven't had to do this before."

"No, but I've had plenty of wounds." She stared down at the floor, not wanting to say any more about her supposed father. Quil had probably already seen her scars anyway.

"I'm going to start now, but if you need to squeeze my leg through the pain, you can." His tone remained calm, as if trying to tame a wild beast.

"I survived the cut, I'll be fine. A little needle won't be bad." Oh, how wrong she was! The little sting of the needle

sliding from one piece of skin to the other—over and over—
threatened to make her pass out on the floor. Blood seeped into
her mouth from her teeth clamping onto the inside of her
cheek.

Quil cut the string and tied the end. "There. Good as new."
He got up and left her there in a way that made her feel as
though she was a stranger. It was as if she'd been seen by a
village doctor since the entire transaction had been clinical and
impersonal. This was not the boy—*man*—she'd known.

When Quil didn't say anything or even look at her, she said,
"Well, I'm going to go find Perin." *Or should I start calling
him brother? No, it's too strange.*

"Three houses down with a rocking chair on the porch." He
seemed to speak to the walls, or the pan flutes, instead of her.

Shoulders slumped, she moved for the door and opened it
halfway. Before she could leave, Quil rushed forward and
slammed it, keeping his hand on the wood. He looked down at
her, eyes blazing. His skin took on an almost red hue. If he was
trying to blend in with his surroundings, it wasn't working.

"*Why?*" he asked, defeated, the sides of his lips tugging
down.

"Why what?" She wasn't sure what he was asking exactly,
or why he hadn't said anything when they were seated on the
bench.

"Why did you just leave?" His words were a whisper, as if
he was afraid to ask.

"My village was leaving and—"

"You could have stayed with me," he interrupted.

"Belen had told everyone that your village was going to
attack ours. He did something that night that knocked me out.
I know now that it was the prism's doing."

"Our village was never going to attack yours!"

Rhona slumped against the door. "I know… And I left you
a note saying I'd be back for you."

His eyebrows furrowed together, lips set in a tight line.

"That's not what you wrote."

Quil was starting to make her as angry as Perin had. "I *know* what my letter said." She pointed at her chest. "*I* wrote it."

With a frustrated sound, he released his hand from the door and stormed away. Rhona wasn't sure if he was coming back. She didn't know how long she should stand there. Two years was a long time, but she would've waited an eternity for him if he'd left her a letter.

Moments later, he came back with something folded in his hand. *Her letter.* She tried to backtrack to figure out which part she'd written that could have offended him, but she couldn't think of anything.

He handed her the paper, and as she unfolded it, she could tell it had been opened and closed numerous times over the years. Parts near the edges had already torn. That meant he *had* thought about her, but apparently not in a good way.

> *Quil,*
> *I wish I could tell you how I feel in person, but there's someone else. Our village is moving today, so don't come looking for me because I'll never be looking for you. You were a great friend for the time being, and I shouldn't have led you on.*
>
> *Sorry,*
> *Rhona*

As she reached the last word, Quil muttered, "I mean, you left me naked in the forest and then ran off with someone else?"

She barely heard what he'd said as she read the letter over and over, finally meeting his fiery gaze. At least his skin was back to its normal hue. "I woke you in the forest, Quil. I told you I had to go, and you said, 'see you tomorrow,' and that you'd go in a bit!" Each word got louder and louder.

"I don't remember that!"

"Well, you did!" she bit back.

He ripped the letter from her hand and shook it an inch from her face. "It doesn't matter because you still wrote me this!"

"I did not, you jerk! That's not even my damn handwriting. It looks as if a bird scribbled the words with its beak!"

"What?" He brought the letter closer to his face, even though the written words were barely even legible.

"Give me a piece of paper and ink." Rhona stalked the room, willing herself to calm down, all while she searched for something to use.

Wordlessly, Quil left the room again and brought her back a sheet of paper and ink. She dipped the quill in the bottle and quickly wrote the letter—*her* letter—word for word, handing him the paper. "This is what I wrote."

His lips silently moved as he read it over, then looked down at her. "Then who wrote the other one?"

Rhona didn't have to bounce around the idea in her head for long. "I think I know who." Frustrated, she took both notes from Quil and ran out of the house, straight for Lana's home, barely able to breathe. She heard the shouts of her name as Quil ran after her, but she didn't stop. The rocker on the porch slid into view, and she banged on the door, not even sorry for disturbing anyone outside. Quil strode up beside her.

With a confused expression, Lana swung open the door. "I could feel the vibrations—what's going on?" She pointed at her ears, the house, and then at Rhona.

Perin came to the door, carrying a meaty bird's leg.

"This is *your* chicken scratch!" Rhona hissed, taking a step inside and throwing up the note in Perin's face.

He casually lowered the bird's leg after taking a bite. "I knew this was coming, but I have a good explanation."

There were no good reasons or answers he could give. As hard as she could, Rhona slammed her fist against his jaw. Perin staggered backward, almost dropping the piece of meat while clutching his jaw.

Her knuckles ached from the collision, and she was about to strike again when Quil pulled her back.

"Why?" Rhona yelled.

Perin still rubbed at his face, but looked content, as if he was perfectly fine with her hitting him. "I suppose it's now time for *that* story."

Eleven

Rhona

Without a word, Perin handed over the bird's leg to Lana and brushed right past Rhona out the door.

"Where are you going?" Rhona turned around and marched out of the house, passing Quil. His lost expression registered, but she had to get some answers before they went any further. "Perin, you're going to talk to me about this right now!"

"I said I would, but we're done here. We need to get moving." Perin adjusted his cloak and kept walking.

"What?" Rhona screeched with annoyance. "You just acted like it was time for us all to circle around to hear your damn story, you ass!"

Rhona had almost forgotten about Quil when he suddenly hurried around them, then placed a hand on Perin's chest, stopping him from moving.

Perin looked down in a way that made it seem like the hand was corrupting him, his frown deepening. "Move your hand or you may lose that—and a leg." His tone bordered on dangerous.

"Are you in love with her?" Quil asked. For a moment, Rhona thought about punching him, too.

"Fuck!" Perin barely moved his mouth as he spoke. "If you

ask one more time if we're lovers, if I'm in love with her, or something equally disgusting, you'll lose every single one of your limbs and have to skulk around by pulling your body with your chin. How does that sound?" Rhona knew he meant it, too.

"In all honesty, it sounds a bit disturbing." For some reason, Quil stared at Perin for a beat, then snorted and patted his chest, before removing his hand.

Lana hurried and signed while she said to Quil, "The letter was probably for the best."

"What?" he shouted and motioned at the air. "You've known him for like two seconds, *feeding* him bird legs. What's next, marriage?"

"Fuck"—Perin shook his head—"is it Rhona or Lana that you think I'm swooning over?"

"I'm with Emma," Lana said, dismissing him.

"I'm done with this bullshit." Perin's tone meant business. "I'll just go look for the prism in the Crimson Forest by myself."

"*The Crimson Forest?*" Quil's deep voice went up an octave. "You didn't say you were going in there."

"Yeah, that's where Belen told us to go to get the prism," Rhona said. "He has my mother hidden, but what he doesn't know is that I'm going to find a way to destroy him." As much as she wanted to have this reunion with Quil, it would have to be postponed.

"Wait here." With those words, Quil jogged up the steps to his house and went inside.

Rhona turned to Lana, so her mouth would be easy to read. "What's he doing?"

"I think you know."

Perin had his arms folded across his chest. Moments later, Quil strolled out of the house with a pack on his back and sword and daggers at his narrow hips, looking prepared for battle. She knew what he was doing. He appeared powerful as he took long strides toward them. However, his face still had a certain sweetness to it that he'd never be able to get rid of, or so she thought.

Quil signed to his cousin, and she narrowed her eyes but nodded. "Lana's going to be ready here, in case we need her."

"He means if something happens to him," Lana said.

"Why would we need to do that?" Rhona asked, hands going to her sword. She knew nothing would happen to him with her protection.

"Look, I know where it is and have been near it before. This is just a precaution." She didn't like the sound of Quil's words.

Rhona and Perin had barely been around Lana, but she pulled them both into a hug anyway. Perin stood in a stiff position, while Rhona returned the embrace before leaving.

Once the three entered the outskirts of the village, Rhona turned to Perin. "Don't you think for a second I forgot. Now, tell me why you wrote that note?" She held her hands up. "Do I even know you? It's been lie after lie this entire journey."

"For one thing, these weren't lies. And for another, it was only a few accounts in which I didn't tell you the whole story." He pressed forward, moving a large limb from a bush with his sword.

"That's the same thing!" She took long steps to stay in sync with him. "A lie wrapped in silk."

Quil didn't say anything, but the way his eyes kept darting to the side told her he was listening to every word.

"Okay, well, over the years, I followed you a couple of times. Only because you *did* lie to me about where you were going. Picking flowers? *Please.* Give me a damn break." He gave her a condescending look. "So, if anyone's a liar here, then it's the person standing beside me."

Rhona's eyes narrowed, but he was right, she had lied to him. A lot. Maybe too much for one friend to do to another.

"Anyway," Perin continued, "the day our village was leaving, your mother told me you had gone looking for me.

When I went searching for you, I found you with my father as he knocked you out. I knew exactly where you'd been. So for you, dear *sister*, I rewrote the note and left it behind. It was better that way—*safer*."

"Safer for who? *You?*" Her entire body shook with rage. If she had her ability at the moment, Rhona didn't know if she would be boiling with fury or freezing with a harsh storm waiting to be unleashed.

"He wouldn't have stayed behind. *You* may have been able to stay away"—Perin's frown lessened as his gaze shifted to Quil—"but he would have come to the village searching for you. What do you think Belen would've said about that? He would've said 'someone's dead,' that's what. And it wouldn't have been you."

Perin was right. When she thought about it, Quil would have come looking for her. With that magic prism of his, Belen could have ended Quil in seconds.

Quil stayed quiet but finally glanced up, scowling. "Well, you changed the course of everything, didn't you?" He put a hand on his sword and took a step toward Perin. The idea frightened Rhona because she knew who would win at the sword game.

Perin shrugged. "Pull out your weapon, and you'll wind up on the ground. Ask Rhona, she'll agree."

Quil didn't listen and released his blade from the sheath. *Big mistake.* Before Quil could even clash their swords, Perin had him down on the ground, flat on his back.

The past few hours, Rhona had felt indifferent about everything that Perin had revealed—as if it wasn't real— hadn't happened. But something sparked in her then, anger so fierce she wished she'd had her ability to boil him for a second. Despite knowing Perin would win, she lunged at him with her blade anyway. As he raised his own weapon, she clacked hers against his.

A bout of sorrow seemed to form in his eyes, but she didn't

care, she was pissed. There were two people she trusted in her village—Perin and her mother—and both were liars. Or in Perin's words, kept things hidden.

Staying focused, she swung the sword harder than she ever had, beads of perspiration gathering on her upper lip. Birds chirped in the tops of trees as though they were watching and enjoying the show. Rhona made her next swing as if she was going to aim high, but she quickly bent her knees. Perin's sword arm was still up in the air, and she took the opportunity to slice at his thigh. With her boot forward, she then kicked his leg out from under him like she had with Quil earlier, knocking him onto his back.

This time she felt triumphant, her eyes locking with Perin's. But then she remembered something. *You need to learn new tricks.* Her anger came back. "You let me win, didn't you?"

Not a word escaped his mouth, and his gaze remained steady on hers.

"You could have blocked that easily." Rhona leaned over him, fury coursing through her that Perin had let her win. "Is that your way of saying you're sorry? Because it sure as hell isn't a good way—now your leg's bleeding and we'll only be slowed down."

"I'm fine." He stood from the ground and sheathed his sword. "I couldn't give a fuck about your friend, but it was about protecting *you*. What if, in the process, you'd ended up dead while trying to protect him?" *Protecting her?* He could have at least told her, and she may have understood. Yet he hadn't.

"I'm done talking about this, and I'm done talking to you. You can go fuck yourself." Rhona turned around and started walking north.

Quil didn't say anything, and Rhona took his silence as agreement—with her. She kept walking past moss-covered trees and large birds peering down at her. She needed to get away from the two people who were messing with her mind—

of course they both followed. But what was the point of Quil even coming if he wasn't planning on talking to her?

He now knew she'd written him a different letter than the one he'd received, so she was confused as to what the problem even was.

The terrain became denser with vines and bushes, and they used their swords to get past the area. When they pushed through, small furry animals scampered away. Rhona kept a look out for anything that could be dangerous, but there was nothing yet. *Maybe this will be easier than I thought.*

There were stories about people going into the Crimson Forest and never coming out, but were they even true? People made up lies all the time so others would stay away from danger, trying to keep them safe. She watched Perin as he released a dagger at a furry creature digging in the dirt. Even if Perin thought he was doing something right, he still should have told her the truth about her father. Maybe she would've understood, or maybe she would've run straight back to Quil. Either way, Perin should have told her, regardless of her lies to him over the years—because her lies hadn't been hurting him.

Or had they?

Closing her eyes for a moment, Rhona took the creature from his hands and started to skin off the fur. It wasn't her way of accepting his apology, but her way of saying, *let's move on for now.*

"That's not the right way to skin those," Quil interrupted her movements.

"Meat's meat," she replied, stabbing a dagger through the tough belly.

"Here." Holding out his hand, he waited for her to give it to him. She didn't. "You'll lose more meat cutting it that way. Let me see the drogwai." He gestured at her again, and this time she placed it into his hand.

"Show me your ways."

Quil propped the dead animal over his knee and turned it so its back faced the sky. Using gentle precision, he pushed his dagger into where the neck met between the shoulders. With back and forth motions, he sawed his way down, peeling up the skin as he worked.

"The head actually has more meat than you'd probably think, especially in the cheek area." He lifted the oval face and pointed at the two cheeks with his bloodied knife.

"How do you know all this?" Rhona's lips parted as she watched him. "You've never told me any of this stuff before."

Halting for a few seconds to look up at her, he said, "Over the past few years, I've been hunting outside the village. I've learned more about Laith, and it's been a good way to clear my head."

A large part of her wanted to ask him if he still went to the river each morning. She secretly hoped he did. Every morning after Belen took her away, Rhona would pretend she was there. If he had been at the river, in a way it was as if they were there together. But she didn't ask, afraid of the answer—and the hurt it could cause her.

She would have come back sooner, but whatever Belen had done to her scared her, and she'd been frightened that he would've had someone follow her. She should have been stronger.

Their canteens were already filled from the lake they'd passed earlier, so they were still good on water. As they set up camp for the night, Perin got the fire going to roast the drogwai.

The meat was one of the best she'd ever tasted. It slid right from the bone as though it wasn't connected.

After she finished eating, she found that Quil had already turned to his side to drift off to sleep. When he'd shown her how to peel the creature, she'd fallen into the trap of thinking things were back to the way they had always been.

She nestled down into the dirt and made herself as

comfortable as she could. The fire still blazed while Perin lay beside her. The flames highlighted his eyes—their hue matching hers. And she now knew why.

"Are we past this now?" he finally asked.

"Are you serious?" *What part of "go fuck yourself" does he not understand?*

"Yes." He tapped the dirt between them with a pouty expression on his face.

Pampering dirt wasn't going to make her feel sorry for him. "Maybe you haven't been around enough people to know when someone is pissed. It doesn't just dissipate. Also, you *let* me win."

He ignored the part about the sword fight. "We were friends first, but when I found out you were my sister, that I had someone else I was connected to besides my bastard father, I knew I always wanted to watch over you and make sure you were okay."

Rhona tried to steel her heart against his words. She was supposed to be mad. "Well, I'm not past it."

"Do you hate me then?" In all the times she'd known him, he never sounded truly wounded until that moment.

Rhona thought about it for a long while. "No." She sighed. "I don't hate you. But you need to be honest with me. Is there anything else you need to say? That you're *hiding*?"

"No."

"Then we'll take it from here."

For the following days, the journey was a repetitive cycle. The only thing that changed each day was Rhona desperately wanting a bath. Her scent was akin to that of an animal. They had found small rivers to collect water, but nothing deep enough to bathe in, so she had only splashed a bit of liquid on her face.

"We should be at the forest soon." Quil pointed up ahead.

Rhona nodded and glanced toward Perin. His face appeared weaker and weaker as time passed—pale with beads of sweat on his forehead, and his shoulders hunched a bit. It was enough to set her on edge. Perin never showed weakness.

"What's wrong?" she asked as they trampled over small rocks, leaves, and twigs.

"Nothing," he mumbled. "I'm fine."

She grasped his arm and stopped him from moving. "You're not *fine*."

"My leg hurts a bit."

Rhona peered down at his leg and the dried blood staining his pants. Through the visible tear from her sword, she saw the wound.

Before he could move away, she shook his arm. "Roll it up."

"I said it's *fine*."

She had to plant her feet in the ground to keep him from going. "And I said, roll it up!"

Relenting, Perin pulled at the fabric near the cut, exposing the wound that was *not* healing. It oozed a yellow pus, and the skin looked more than angry with red inflamed edges.

Rhona sucked in a sharp breath, and even Quil let out a low whistle.

"Did you not clean that with anything?" she seethed. They had been by the river, but maybe she should have offered to wrap it for him. She didn't know he wasn't doing *anything* about it.

"I said I'm fine. It's fine." Could he not see his leg? How pale he'd gotten? Even his movements were weakened—sluggish.

Stepping away from him, Rhona dug through her pack to see if she could find anything. To her side, a loud thrashing came. By the time she glanced up, a tall woman—*or something*—with orange hair, claws, and sharp teeth had Perin pinned on the ground.

And her fist was wrapped around his throat.

Twelve

Tavarra

Tavarra bared her teeth at the human in front of her. He wasn't Brice. She thought it had been him again. But this pathetic human just resembled him: strong jaw, straight nose, short hair, broad shoulders. However, his face wasn't as welcoming as Brice's had been. The weakling stared up at her with a hardened expression, but he didn't take his eyes away from hers for a moment. Blue eyes, not green. Brown hair, not black.

Two swords pressed against her—one positioned at her back where her heart was buried, and another at her throat.

"Release him," a high-pitched female voice demanded.

She didn't—she squeezed harder. Something about young males like Brice bothered her, as though all of them could break hearts like hers. Yet she knew anyone was truly capable of shredding a heart.

"Wait!" Eza yelled, out of breath, finally catching up. "Don't hurt her!" She landed on Tavarra's shoulder with a soft thump. "Release him. It's not Brice."

The annoying voice of reason on her shoulder had Tavarra grinding her teeth, but she let go, not taking her eyes off the pathetic human.

Once she released him, the swords still didn't come down from her flesh. She might not be the beast at that moment, but she had her claws ready to tear the intruders apart.

"Calm down, everyone. It's all going to be fine," Eza said, holding up her hands. "*Trust me*, she's not a beast right now."

"If you so much as make a move toward him again, I'll slit your throat," the female holding the sword growled.

Slowly turning to the side, not caring about what the female said, Tavarra came face to face with a small wisp of a human, freckles sprinkled across her nose and cheeks. At the nape of her neck and cocked to the side, the girl's blonde hair was pulled into a low bun—blue eyes matched that of the human she had just choked. She wanted to rip the girl's eyes out, but instead, she balled her hands into tight fists, her claws pebbling blood to the skin's surface.

The sword released from her back and another male voice spoke, "If you look at her like that any longer, you may end up losing those eyes."

Tavarra's gaze fell to a lad who stepped to the side of the girl. He was tall, with warm brown skin, and black hair to his shoulders—she hated him as much as she did the other male. Hated all three of them really.

"He looks nothing like Brice." Eza stroked the side of Tavarra's face, attempting to calm her down.

"He is still a fool," Tavarra ground out.

The blonde girl's eyes widened. "Do you know Perin?"

The girl must think me to be a scorned lover, and maybe I am, but not with him. "No… I just know what I see."

"I like them," Eza whispered to Tavarra. Her words didn't surprise her—the little bat liked almost anyone she encountered. What did stupefy her was Eza craning her neck to see the people better, and asking, "Where are you three heading?"

"You're a bat?" the girl said in awe, taking a step forward to Tavarra's shoulder.

From her hip, Tavarra pulled out a dagger to halt the girl from getting any closer.

Eza flew down and attempted to push Tavarra's hand away. "Stop, you beast! I think this girl is my new favorite human. For once, someone didn't think I was a fairy."

"No, I've heard about your kind, and somewhere down my long line, I'm descended from one," the girl said in awe. She looked nothing at all like Eza—it was probably a lie.

"Mmm, but you have no wings." Eza paused. "And no fangs or pointed ears."

"No, none of that, but I can turn into water." The girl stepped closer but didn't sheath her sword. Tavarra flexed her hands with her claws ready.

"Do it." Eza edged closer.

Shutting her eyes, the girl sighed. "I can't."

Eza pouted for all of two seconds but her mood didn't dim. She pressed onward with more questions. "Do you know where the Stone of Desire is?"

Tavarra was anxious to get away from this trio, but it was hard to do that when Eza kept being inquisitive. They didn't need these people—they could figure things out on their own.

The girl and the dark-haired male standing beside her both shook their heads, but then another voice spoke up, "I do." All eyes were on the fool she had choked, who was now standing, yet looked as if he might fall back down.

"You know how to get there?" the girl asked. "I just know Belen plans on taking the prisms there."

"Your mother told us. Remember in the story when Luca crossed over? The Stone is mentioned in it. Plus, I've been there once."

"What? *When?*" The girl's eyes widened.

"A long time ago when Belen sent me to survive by myself in the forest for a few weeks."

"And?" Tavarra interrupted.

"And nothing. I just came across it." He shrugged.

"I remember the story, but I'm not sure how to get there exactly." The girl shook her head.

"Ah, so you are looking for the prisms?" Eza said with a sly expression. Tavarra knew nothing about the prisms.

"This man from our village, Belen, already has the ivory one, so we need the dark prism to stop him," the girl said.

"Mmm, that is a tricky situation." Eza tapped her chin. "No one needs to have either prism."

"In order to get the other one back, we do." The girl sounded determined.

"How about a trade?" Eza smiled. "You tell us how to get to the Stone of Desire, and I'll tell you how to find the prism."

"Deal." The girl stuck out her hand to shake.

"No!" the fool bellowed.

Tavarra straightened her shoulders and stepped closer to the fool—they were the same height, so she was eye to his pathetic eye. "You *will* tell me how to get there." Fury consumed her heart as it kicked up notch after notch.

The girl stepped forward and pushed the fool back. "We need to go ahead and tell her, and then we're going to have to go back to the village. If we don't fix that infected wound, you're going to die." The girl turned to the other male. "Can you take us back?"

"No. That's just wasting time," the fool growled in frustration. "And I'm not telling them how to get to the Stone. Not if we don't get the dark prism first."

"How about I make a deal?" The girl didn't look at her, probably because she knew Tavarra would say no. So she faced Eza. "You tell us where the dark prism is. I'll get it and meet you all back at the village. Then I'll let my *brother* tell me where the Stone of Desire is, and I'll take you there myself."

"No," Tavarra and the fool said at the same time.

"Dammit, so help me, Perin, if you want me to forgive you!" The girl shook her small fist.

The fool—Perin—let out a deep sigh. "I'll take her with you to the Stone, but only after getting the other prism back from my father. *And* only if Quil goes with you, because you aren't going alone."

"No, I don't trust you to be alone with this woman." The girl pointed her sword at Tavarra.

Tavarra wasn't a woman, not even close.

"He won't be alone," Eza said. "I'll have his back. Trust me, she won't do anything." Tavarra liked how Eza left out the part about her changing into a beast most nights—she kept silent on that matter, too.

"I don't know about this…" Perin's sister rubbed at her lower lip.

"I'll be fine, all right? But if something happens to you, and Quil comes back, he's dead."

"If you touch a single hair on his head, I'll haunt you from the grave." The girl turned to face Tavarra. "Oh, and if he dies, the deal's off."

Smart bargain.

Tavarra couldn't let the girl have the last say. "And if *you* don't fulfill your end of the deal, I'll eat his heart in front of you."

"She's only jesting." Eza laughed and shooed them away.

"Deal," Perin said, not seeming the least bit worried about her threat. It only infuriated her.

The girl moved forward and pulled Perin aside. "I don't trust this situation. Maybe I should just take you back to the village."

"No, you'll be fine with Quil. And if my father finds out—"

"Finds out what?"

"That we're working against him, then he may do something about it. So we can't waste time." He swayed for a moment before steadying himself.

The girl narrowed her eyes at him. "If you die, I really will

111

hate you."

"By the way," Eza intercepted. "This is Tavarra, and my name's Eza."

The girl nodded. "I'm Rhona, that's Quil, and that idiot"—she pointed at her brother—"well, you've already heard Perin's name."

Eza shifted forward to rattle off the directions for the mysterious dark prism. "First, Quil and Rhona, you will need to pass through the Crimson Forest, circle around a lake, and then enter a deadly wood where you will need to find a tree with a hole that is the shape of a heart. That's all I know." She quickly held up a hand. "But fear not, if you need to take rest at the lake, nothing mysterious can venture out from the Crimson Forest."

It sounded too easy, and Tavarra knew Eza was leaving out a few pieces, most likely what was lurking in the forest and woods.

Rhona told Tavarra and Eza to look for Quil's cousin, Lana. Then she shot forward and wrapped her arms around her brother's waist. He patted her back. "You'll be fine. I can't say the same for Quil. He seems to be shit with a sword, so I wouldn't trust those hunting skills he thinks he has."

"If that were true, then you wouldn't let him come with me. Maybe I should just go with you."

"No, Rhona, I trust your skills, and I know you can do it. The sooner we get the ivory prism away from my father, the better."

"We'll see you again," Eza shouted, waving.

Tavarra didn't wave, only grunted and turned around.

"Lead the way," Tavarra said, not looking over at Perin. He started moving at a stiff pace, and she could tell his leg was bothering him, but she didn't care. *Let him lose the leg.*

"You could always offer to carry him on your back," Eza whispered. "It would be a much faster process."

"I don't want that filth touching me." Her hand had already

touched his throat, and that was plenty enough.

They walked and walked, at a pace that seemed to match Tavarra if she were to crawl. A small river slid into view, and they stopped beside it. Or she did. Perin kept moving past a large tree.

"Where are you going?" she shouted.

"Can I not take a piss?" he growled.

"He may need help with his pants so it doesn't rub the wound," Eza purred.

"He's *fine*." Tavarra sighed. "I think we made a mistake, Eza. We should have gone to get the prism ourselves, so we'd have something to bargain with."

Eza placed her hands on her hips. "Did you think I didn't consider that? That man needs our help more, and you're not really qualified for what lurks in there." She shrugged. "I'm not sure they are either, but they seemed quite good with swords."

Tavarra groaned and knelt at the river, splashing water across her face and hands. After finishing off her canteen, she filled it up with more water.

Eza hovered over the river upside down and dunked her head all the way in, taking long drinks. Tavarra laughed and shook her head.

"What's so funny?" Perin asked as he stepped in front of her, blocking her view.

"Nothing's funny." Her laughing stopped, and her voice became hard.

"With an attitude like that, I may have forgotten where the Stone of Desire is," he taunted.

"With an attitude like that, I may rip your intestines from your stomach," she bit back.

Perin didn't say anything after that, only turned around and started walking—or hobbling.

As they wandered through the forest, he pulled out dried meat from his pack and nibbled. He didn't offer her any, and she didn't ask. She could find her own meat.

"Can I have some of that?" Eza asked, landing on his shoulder. *The little traitor.*

He kept quiet but handed her a small piece. With a smile on her face, she ate it and stayed perched on his shoulder.

Ahead of them, a white rabbit with half its fur coated in mud appeared. Tavarra barreled forward, digging her claws into the throat and biting straight into the furry flesh. *Who needs dried or cooked meat?*

Tavarra lifted her eyes to meet Perin's, and instead of the disgust she expected, a bit of what might be a smirk was present. She ripped the fur from the body as she walked, stuffing bits and pieces into her mouth. When she finished, she discarded the body and sucked the blood from her fingers.

After pressing through the forest for hours, the suns lowered in the darkening sky, ready to set. "We have to stop." Tavarra reached around and pulled her pack to her chest.

"No, we can go for a while longer." Perin looked as if he'd roll over dead in the next second. There was no way he could go any longer.

"No! We have to stop *now*." There wasn't time to argue about moving—she had to stop.

Eza flew from his shoulder and watched Tavarra remove her boots, then opened her pack to pull out the chains. Perin's eyebrows knitted together in confusion. In front of her sat a thick and sturdy tree with a leafy red vine snaked around its trunk.

Stopping in front of it, she placed one manacle around her wrist. Eza grabbed the other end and looped it around the tree. Tavarra locked her other wrist while Eza held onto the key.

"What the fuck is this?" Perin asked with a scowl, lifting the chain.

"What the fuck does it look like, fool? I'm chained to a tree." Tavarra rolled her eyes. "It helps me sleep better." She wasn't going to tell him about it—he would have to see for himself.

Perin narrowed his gaze, not believing her, yet not saying anything, either.

"I'd suggest sleeping somewhere else." Tavarra nodded up ahead to a thinner tree drooped to the side.

Instead of listening, he crouched near the tree, directly next to hers. That wasn't what she meant. A sharp inhale came from Perin as he lowered himself to the ground.

"What if he gets worse?" Eza whispered in her ear.

"Then it wasn't meant to be." Tavarra wanted to find the Stone of Desire, if it really did exist, but not if it required having to be at the beck and call of this human.

Instead of flying up into the tree, Eza flew over and landed on Perin's shoulder. Eza was feeling sorry for the man—the bat sure did gather sympathy easily for people in need. She should probably stop that.

Tavarra sank to the ground in an uncomfortable position, but one she was used to. She twisted to the side, avoiding them both.

Right when the night had taken shape, she sighed in relief that nothing was going to happen. No beast tonight. But then a prickle slithered up her spine, and she knew she had been hopeful too soon. Moments later, she felt the shift, her body stretching. A howl of pain slipped past her lips, and her entire body ignited with internal flames.

She barely heard the shuffling sound, when a face appeared in front of hers. A face she couldn't focus on, nor realize who it was.

"What's wrong?" the male voice asked with a weary tone.

"Go!" she managed to grind out.

Hunger took over next. She was so hungry. A smell permeated the air, and what a sweet scent it was. A smell which led to flesh that would fill her entire stomach.

"Get away from her!" a voice shouted.

"What's *wrong* with her?"

"I'll explain that later. For now, you need to find higher ground."

Hair sprouted on Tavarra's arms, body twisting, fangs lengthening until she needed to eat the bones of the creature she had smelled. With a ferocious growl, she shook the chains, trying to crack the tree in half. Gathering all her strength, she roared at the two moons in the darkened sky.

Thirteen

Rhona

The remainder of the journey to search for the dark prism had been uneventful, and Rhona and Quil now stood in front of the Crimson Forest. The moment she looked toward the trees, she knew she'd made a mistake. She'd left Perin alone with two strangers—a bat and a creature that wasn't quite a woman, who had already tried to kill him. Perin was good with a sword, but those skills would be dimmed if his condition worsened on the way back.

"He'll be fine," Quil said. It was only the third time he'd spoken to her on the way, and he'd said the same thing every time.

"I don't think you can predict the future, Quil." That was one thing she knew for sure—the future was an unpredictable one.

"No, I can't, but once he gets to Lana, she'll help him. I do know that." He held up a finger. "And don't ask 'what if he doesn't make it.'"

She thought that maybe she shouldn't have been so hard on Perin, that she shouldn't have taken it out on him with the sword.

The letter and Belen being her father... Finding out about

those things had caused her to not think straight. Belen was the root of everything wrong—not Perin.

Rhona looked from Quil's face, then back to the trees. The entrance presented a dark aura, even though the day was still colored in brightness. Limbs of crimson trees folded and swirled around each other, creating a barrier of sorts. There were tiny holes that she could barely see through, and an opaque darkness stared back. A metallic odor wafted in their direction, coming from within. Outside it, birds and insects made their usual noises, but from inside, she couldn't detect any sounds. Yet.

"Do you happen to have any candles with you?" Rhona didn't have any in her pack.

"No, but I have a solution that Lana made with fireflies and fairy wings." He pulled out two glass tubes and handed her one.

She took the glass filled with pale blue fluid, her fingers brushing his, and a shiver ran up her spine. It could have been from his touch, or the thought of going into the forest, or maybe a mixture of both.

They shook their glasses, and the blue color became brighter, giving off the perfect amount of glow.

Drawing out her sword, Rhona swung it against one of the branches to make way, but it didn't pass through. Something howled, akin to a person's scream, causing her to flinch. It came from the branch, as if she'd wounded the tree.

"Did you hear that?" she asked.

"Yep." Quil didn't seem frightened by it, but he had been near here before.

At the base of the entrance sat a large opening—she didn't know if either one of them could fit through, but she would try.

"Let me crawl underneath," Quil said, pressing forward. Somehow, even with his broad shoulders, he shimmied his way in. Rhona blinked for a moment, and he shot a hand out toward her, wiggling his fingertips.

She pushed the glass tube inside to give him more light—then she grasped his hand, and he helped slide her through. A sharp piece of the branch scraped her back, but she ignored the small stinging sensation.

Rhona grabbed the lighted glass and held hers up. Since Quil was taller, he could hold his up higher and give off better light as they scanned the area. It wasn't completely dark in the forest—there was just enough dim light to be able to see.

Shadows danced around Rhona and Quil as the trees creaked and moved without even a smidge of wind blowing. Breathing deeply, she steadied herself, but still felt her bones shaking beneath her skin as fear crept in.

"Hey, it's all right," Quil murmured.

She clenched the blue light tighter. "You've been in here before?"

"Well, no."

Her voice went up a bit, practically a shriek. "Then how do you know it's *all right*?"

"Okay, I don't. Just trying to calm you down." His hand shook as he held up the lighted glass.

She cursed inside her head, wishing Perin was with them. He wasn't afraid of anything, and if his confident self had been around, she would have tried to compete with him. If nothing else, it would have been a good distraction from being afraid. With her free hand, Rhona pulled out a dagger from her hip, just in case.

In front of them sat a towering tree with a thick trunk, one of the largest she'd ever seen. She could probably join hands with six of her selves wrapped around the tree and still barely encompass its width.

Something wet caught her eye. "Hold your light more forward," she suggested, walking closer to the tree with her own glass out. A dark red tone colored the trees, but something slick seemed to be dripping from it and pooling at its base.

Sap?

After tucking her dagger back at her waist, she stuck out a finger and swiped at the thick liquid, holding it to the light. Crimson. *Blood.* The hint of metal filled her nose. This was the odor that had been drifting outside the entrance. She took several steps back, quickly wiping her bloody finger on the side of her pants.

"The trees are bleeding," Quil whispered in bewilderment.

"Crimson Forest isn't the proper name then—it should be *Blood Forest.*" All around her the drip, drip, dripping echoed and grew louder. Her head spun, her heart thundered, and her ears roared. A howling came again in the direction of the tree, pulling her out of her trapped moment. "Let's go."

Quil nodded, and they hurried down a rocky path, past several large bloody trunks. From the tops of the trees, glowing eyes watched them. The sounds of liquid slapping the earth continued to fill the forest.

More blood. Rhona tried not to feel faint.

Whoosh, whoosh, a flapping of wings came from her left, then something flew by her face. She caught a glimpse of clear, sparkling wings.

"Fairy," she whispered. One could be all right, but if a hoard of them was around, that would be a different story.

"Shit." Quil slapped the side of his neck. "Watch out, one just bit me." That made two.

Rhona looked around and didn't see any more, only the glowing eyes above them. She really hoped those were harmless birds.

A creaking noise came from her right, disrupting her staring spell. Quil whirled to the side, the glow from his lit glass highlighting the scarlet tree. The tree was *moving*. She squinted her eyes, and something in the middle of the trunk flicked open, revealing two silver eyes with a black center. When the thing pushed forward, a creak sounded again, as if being born from the tree. A bald creature made of bark stumbled closer, with twitching arms and legs.

"Move!" she shouted, yanking Quil in a direction that she prayed was the right way. They continued on the rocky path as more and more tree things left their homes. Blood dripped from their cracked, scarlet bark, their moss-infested movements slow. The forest reverberated with the creaking groans that escaped the bark creatures' mouths.

Distracted with the creatures, Rhona almost didn't see it. Then she caught movement out of the corner of her eye and came to an abrupt stop, Quil slamming into her back. Quickly, she tucked their two lights into her pack.

Up ahead, a bloody bark creature blocked their path. With desperation, Rhona swung her sword to get rid of the thing as Quil slid through another one at the side, making a revolting scrunch. A creaking howl of pain pushed out from the creature's mouth.

Rhona swung her sword through the creature's chest to finish it off. As the ghastly thing snapped its teeth at her, Rhona could see they were also made of bark. Another came at her, and then another. She whirled in a circle, swinging her sword, decapitating them both, thick blood oozing.

Each time they struck one, the creatures crawled back to their tree. *They better not be going in there to heal and come back out!*

A buzzing flowed through the air and glows of white lit up the darkness. It was almost beautiful until clear wings lifted from the tops of the trees.

"I think we better run," Quil suggested. "I don't know if I can kill all of those, and two people against them, well, let's just say our odds don't give me much comfort, either."

"Agreed." Rhona took off running down the trail as the buzzing grew louder, fiercer, and *closer*.

When she glanced up, a cloud of angry fairies swarmed above them. They flew in a vicious manner with their bodies straight and arms tight at their sides, yet the fairies' sparkly wings made them appear alluring. The fluttering of wings reminded her of the bat they'd met earlier. It was strange that Eza had looked so similar and a bit intimidating, but hadn't thirsted for Rhona's blood.

Rhona thrust her sword forward as the flock came after her and Quil. She pierced some while stinging bites from others came at her legs and shoulders. One angelic-looking fairy with flowing black hair hit the tip of her sword, and Rhona flung it to the ground. Before the fairy could make a hasty leave, she smashed the creature with the heel of her boot, while continuing to wreak havoc on the others.

"I've got an idea." Quil darted to the side, vanishing from her sight.

"Quil?" she asked, frightened. "Quil!" Then something pulled her to a firm chest, and she almost screamed.

"Shh!" Quil whispered in her ear.

"They might not be able to see you, but they can see me!" She couldn't alter her coloring the way he could. His camouflage could always appear more like invisibility.

"Not true. But they'll hear you if you don't stop talking!" Moving to the side, he hauled her back, his arms wrapped around her middle. She could smell his sweat from days of walking, but the scent of the river that carried with him still lingered. The familiar smell helped her relax into his touch— at least for a minute or two. The nuisances flying around still had her on edge. She wanted to go back and finish them off, but there were too many fairies. She wished she had her ability, too. Everything would be easier if she did.

A loud rumble came from farther up ahead. Just over the trees, she could hear heavy footsteps collapsing into the dirt as they moved. The ground shook beneath their feet, and she and Quil stumbled but maintained their balance. Sliding into view, near the treetop, was something that resembled dark gray stone. A volach.

When the stone-like beast shuffled forward, a cracking

sound came with each movement. Too-long arms fell at its side, a long mane of gray hair cascaded down its back, and at the top of its head, horns protruded—resembling a crown. Its stomach jutted forward as the creature's disfigured feet continued to inch closer.

The volach released a deep roar and jolted for the cloud of fairies, managing to swipe a few in his hand, shoving them into its mouth. Blood dribbled down the creature's lips and chin as it chewed. Rhona held Quil's shaking hands around her waist and didn't move or close her eyes.

Somehow no one was seeing her, the same way they weren't seeing Quil. She watched as the fairies flew off in the direction they'd originally came from, with the volach lumbering after them.

Tapping his hand, Rhona pointed up ahead, silently asking him to leave.

"Not yet. Remember when you let me become water with you?" Quil whispered near her ear.

Why was he thinking about that now? "Yeah?" It had only been for a split second, but she could never forget that moment.

"Well, this is sort of the same thing, except we're camouflaged."

"You never showed me this before." Her younger self would've loved to have tried this.

His voice remained a soft whisper. "We were never in this kind of predicament."

"So you could have done this way earlier then?"

"No, I'm not strong enough to camouflage and move myself and someone else at the same time."

"Okay, so what now?" She didn't want to encounter any more gigantic stone people that could stomp on her the way she had done to that fairy. Her skin stung from the small fairy bites, but it hadn't been as bad as it could've been.

Quil released her, his normal color appearing back to his

face and clothes. "I guess stay on the trail. Hopefully nothing else comes out."

"Mmm, horrible plan, but all right."

Smirking, he ran down the trail like they were playing a game back in their childhood.

"You little shit, you should have told me you wanted to race." She ran after him, taking more time to get her short legs to catch up.

"Who are you calling little?" He chuckled, slowing his pace for her to catch up.

"If I grew another head, we'd be the same size."

"I'd say two heads."

They continued in silence until they couldn't run anymore, and the rocky path stayed quiet besides the dripping noises from the trees. Up ahead, they neared a possible end where tree limbs tangled into each other, creating an almost-enclosed wall, similar to the entrance to the forest. This time, they could see out the holes where sunlight shone.

The booming sound of thunder came from above, and sprinkles fell to her skin. *Red.* She swung her sword, and it cut through the limbs. Each strike of her weapon filled her with tiredness. She tried her hardest to avoid hearing the cries from the wounded branches. As the thunder continued, she knew she needed to get them out before the rain really started to pour.

Quil grunted while he worked with her until there was enough room for her to shimmy through. She helped pull him to her, a piece of limb cutting his neck in the process. His shirt snagged on another branch, and she yanked him as hard as she could, knocking them both to the ground. He rolled off her onto his back, and they watched as the limbs grew and curved back together.

She twisted to her stomach and gazed at a lake straight ahead—a radiant blue body of water with a waterfall on each end, the splash of liquid filling her ears.

Pushing herself to stand, she turned to face Quil—he had a few red stains from the rain on his tunic. She inched forward to inspect his neck. The cut wasn't deep enough to need stitches, but it was bleeding.

"Are you all right?" she asked, pulling up her pants to inspect the bites. Small raised red bumps freckled her skin, but the blood was dry. The fairies hadn't latched on hard enough to make the wounds too deep.

"Yeah."

The fact that she hadn't tried to come into the forest alone made a wave of relief wash over her. Her thoughts turned to Perin, and she hoped he was okay, because—at that moment— she didn't even know if her mother was alive. From what Quil said about Lana, she would know what to do.

He rolled down the sleeve of his shirt. "I think we should camp here for the night."

"That's probably a great idea." The suns would be setting soon, and she was starving. A dip in the lake to clean off would be perfect, too.

If they had needed to spend the night in the Crimson Forest, she wouldn't have been able to sleep a wink. And if the forest was like that during the day, she wondered how bad it was during the night.

Stomach rumbling, Rhona reached into her pack and pulled out a couple pieces of dried meat and handed Quil one. As they walked together to the lake, she kept her eyes peeled for a small animal that she could cook, but they weren't that lucky.

After she took a swig from her canteen, Quil rubbed the side of his jaw and asked, "So, do you still like to dance?"

The last time she'd danced was that day in the forest with him before everything had changed. She wished with her entire life that it hadn't. "I do, but I haven't danced in a while."

"I brought a pan flute, just in case." His expression looked almost sheepish.

"So you still play?" She smiled.

"It's been a while." Biting his lip, he looked out toward the lake. Rhona knew, without him saying it, that since she'd left, he hadn't played every day like he'd used to. The thought made her heart feel as if it had been axed in two, and she had to fight her eyes from welling up with tears.

Fourteen

Tavarra

"Rise and shine, beastie," Eza cooed against Tavarra's ear.

Groaning, Tavarra cracked open her eyes and met two narrowed blue ones that *did not* belong to Eza.

"I see you have quite the secret there." Perin rubbed at his chin, his tone not one of the happiest she'd ever heard. "When had you planned on telling me this on our newfound acquaintance journey?" It was only morning and he was grating on her nerves. Could he go back to not speaking?

"I left that up to the beast to tell you, and if she never came out, then there would be no need to know." At least he was still whole—otherwise, the bargain between them about going to the Stone would be called off. And she wouldn't want his corrupted flesh in her insides anyway.

After Eza handed her the key, Tavarra unlocked the manacles. She rubbed at her wrists, relieving some of the soreness before folding and placing the chains back in her pack.

"Sorry, Eza didn't let me know anything—I only saw a lot of growling and baring of teeth." Perin arched a brow, his voice arrogant. "Come to think of it, that version isn't so different from your current one."

"Fuck off." Tavarra got up and picked up her pack, ignoring him as best she could.

Breathing rapidly, Perin tried to stand, but his back collapsed against the tree. He pushed himself forward and held his body up with his hand.

"Are you all right?" Tavarra asked, giving him a hard stare. Eza shot forward and placed her palm to his forehead.

"He's burning up!" Eza shouted.

Tavarra scratched the back of her neck—she didn't think he would make it back to the village.

"You're going to have to carry him." Eza hurriedly waved Tavarra to move forward—she didn't.

"I've got it," Perin growled, stumbling.

Tavarra hesitated. If they went another day at a snail's pace, they wouldn't get far, and she was certain he'd be dead. That meant no Stone of Desire. Tavarra's gaze went skyward because she knew what she would have to do.

"Either you get on my back," she mumbled, "or I'm going to carry you like a babe. And if you fight me, I'll chain your wrists together." She shook her pack at him for emphasis, letting the iron rattle.

"She will, too." Eza grinned, swinging her tight little fist.

Clenching his jaw, Perin moved toward her, not saying a word as he wrapped his arms around her throat. With a grunt, she picked him up. Before the curse, she never would have been able to do it. Even though the monster inside her was stronger, her almost-human form still contained a high amount of strength. Sometimes she didn't want it, either, but at that moment, she was glad she had it.

Perin rattled off the directions, and she picked up her speed. She would get them to the village that day. There was no point in sitting and poking around, leisurely walking.

She ran for a long while through the forest—too long—until she needed to relieve herself. She released Perin, taking much-needed breaths. "Go do your business, and then we're not stopping the rest of the way."

He didn't even nod, only wandered off. Eza flew in another direction, while Tavarra headed behind a tall tree next to several round bushes covered in small red berries. Once she had relieved herself and pulled up her pants, cool steel hit her throat after she stood.

"Move and you die, monster," a deep male voice growled from behind her.

The blade caressed the thick vein at her throat. The poor pathetic bastard thought he could track her down and outwit her because she wasn't a monster at that moment—he was wrong.

"You murdered two friends in my village, and now it's your turn." Right when she was going to ram him backward into a tree, he let out a loud grunt. The blade slackened from her throat, and Tavarra spun around to find Perin pulling out his sword from the man's back with a sickening squish. The man slumped to the ground—his face filled with lines, teeth missing from his gums, and dirt coating his skin.

She stared at the man on the ground, then at a swaying Perin. "You killed him," she breathed. Her eyebrows arched up, trying to find more words to say.

"Yeah?" With his shirt, he wiped the blood from his sword and sheathed it with an unsteady hand.

"His chest was connected to my back!" Her surprise turned into anger. He might have just killed a man to save her, but in his condition? "You could have driven the sword in too far!"

"I knew how much I could go," he stuttered. "Are you all right?"

He should be asking himself that! Surely the fever affected his brain to be asking if I'm all right. There was no other rational explanation for the fact he had not only saved her but did this despite not really needing her. After all, Rhona and Quil were already out to get the prism, so what use did he really have for her? She couldn't say she would have done the same for him if the Stone wasn't involved.

The confusing emotions swirling inside her head turned out to be too much. "I can save myself," she finally snapped and picked up her pack before her gaze fixed on his.

"Your eyes have a bit of gold in them when you're angry." Then his knees buckled, and he collapsed beside his victim.

Tavarra blinked and blinked again.

"Shit. I think Perin might be dead!" she shouted for Eza, not moving toward his body.

A few seconds later, the sound of Eza's wings swishing through the air echoed. "He died?" The bat hurried down and placed her small finger against the side of Perin's throat. "No, he's still good." She looked over at the other body and pointed. "However, it seems that one is dead."

"Yes, Perin *saved* me." *The fool had wasted all of his energy in doing so.*

Eza flapped her wings toward Tavarra. "He's quite the valiant hero, isn't he?"

"I think you like him."

"Yeah, he's nice, not too wordy. Too bad he isn't a bat because he'd make a good lover." She paused with a sly expression. "But he is *your* size."

Tavarra wrinkled her nose as if she smelled something rotten. "No, thank you. I'm fine staying celibate." Although she missed the feel of someone's body against hers, *inside* her, she was all right with sticking by herself.

"You're going to have to carry him, because I obviously can't." Eza flew down near Perin's ear.

With a sigh, Tavarra awkwardly scooped Perin into her arms. "Do you remember how he said to get there?"

Eza pointed in the direction to her left. "Yeah, we just have to head that way."

Tavarra looked back at the dead human's body—at least he wasn't from the village where they were heading. She didn't need any other problems or any more deaths on her hands.

As she hurried through the forest, Perin wasn't heavy, but it was hard to hold him because his shoulders were so broad. He kept sliding out of her arms. At times, she wanted to throw him down. But then he would let out small grunts of pain, and she knew she had to get him to this village so they could try and heal him. She probably should have figured out a way for him to tell her where the Stone of Desire was.

Tavarra blew a lock of hair from her face that she couldn't get out of her eye. "Hey, so how do we get to this Stone of Desire?" In Perin's state of delirium, she hoped he would confess his secrets, but his lips remained sealed.

"Good try," Eza chirped.

She had been running for what felt like days, for sure, almost the entire day. Her muscles ached, her strength waned, and she was starving. She hoped it wouldn't be much longer since she'd still have to go back out into the forest for the night once she dropped him off.

Just ahead, the trees became less dense, and log shelters appeared scattered throughout the area. Her tired heart took a satisfied pump at the same time her lungs breathed heavily. She shook Perin a little, maybe a bit too much because his head rattled and he let out a groan. His lips were chapped, but she didn't have time to feed him with the canteen like a babe.

"Wake up!" Her voice came out a bit louder.

His eyes fluttered open, and his glassy gaze locked onto hers. "Most beautiful thing I ever did see."

"You really are sick." Tavarra looked at the nearing shelters and hurried. "Do you know where Lana lives?"

"Who?" And then he passed back out, his head lolling to the side.

She glanced up at Eza. "Can you go and see if someone can help you find Lana? I need to try and get some fluid in him."

"Sure." Eza flew away while Tavarra glanced back at Perin. His face and neck were covered in more perspiration than before. She was, too, but his clothes looked as though they had been submerged in the sea.

Tavarra knelt, pulled out her canteen, and propped him up at a strange angle. "Perin. Here, you need to drink." She splashed some water on his face. Then she opened his mouth with her finger against his bottom lip and poured some water in. He choked and coughed.

"Sorry, but you need to drink—unless you want to die." Tavarra put the canteen to his lips, and he sipped with his eyes shut, just like a babe. She couldn't wait to see the expression on his face when she told him that she had carried and fed him.

It had been several long moments before she heard running feet, and the soft swishing of bat wings. A woman with black hair falling past her shoulders sprinted toward them. Something in her features reminded Tavarra of the other man, Quil.

The woman dropped to her knees in front of them. She made a series of hand motions and asked, "What happened?" The way she spoke sounded different than others, but Tavarra could still understand what she had said.

"Lana can't hear," Eza said, diving down to them. "Make sure you look at her when you speak."

Tavarra focused on the young woman's face—Lana—Quil's cousin. "His leg got infected from a wound, but I'm not sure what happened. I ran into your cousin and his friend, and they told me to bring him back to you for help," she said, her lips and words a little slower than necessary.

"Follow me." Lana didn't look the least bit afraid as she stared at Tavarra. She leaned forward to help carry Perin, but Tavarra waved her off. While scooping him up, Tavarra hoped the shelter wasn't too far.

Lana moved at a quick pace, and Tavarra kept up with it as Perin bounced lightly in her arms.

"Did it take a while to find her?" Tavarra asked Eza as they hurried along.

"No, but it took her a long time to understand what I was

saying. My lips are a lot smaller than yours. Finally, Lana got a magnifying glass and that did the trick. I didn't even have to repeat myself."

They approached a small shelter with a rocking chair on the porch, and several flowers in clay pots decorated the area. Lana swung open the door and helped them in.

"You caught me right in time. I was about to have dinner at my partner's house." Lana waved them into a room down the hall with a small bed. Gently, Tavarra lowered Perin and his head fell to the side as soon as it hit the pillow.

"What now?" Tavarra asked, looking at Lana and pointing at Perin's leg.

The young woman moved closer, pulled back the cloth at his thigh, and inspected the wound. Lana let out a small hiss. "Remove his pants while I get the supplies to clean and help with the wound." She hurried out of the room, leaving Tavarra frozen in place.

"You going to remove his pants, or just stare at him all day?" Eza pressed her lips together in amusement. "I'm too small to take them off."

Tavarra had done worse things in her life—she could do this. Reaching forward, she rolled up his shirt to his belly button, exposing a thin line of dark hair leading to the one part of his body she did *not* want to see. Pursing her lips, she hurried and unfastened his trousers and lowered them, careful not to rub at the wound. The deep gash had a rancid odor wafting to her nostrils, and a yellow substance oozed out—it was bad.

She covered his lower half with the blanket, then tugged off his boots so she could fully remove the pants. As she tossed them on the floor, Lana ran back into the room carrying a bowl full of water and a cloth. She lay the things by the bedside and dipped the rag into the liquid. Turning his leg to the side, she squeezed the cloth over his skin. Next, she rubbed a bar of soap on the rag and cleaned the cut.

Perin let out small groans, but his eyes remained closed. Once Lana finished cleaning the wound, she picked up a glass jar and spread a generous amount of ointment over the infected area. Then she lay strips of white cloth on top to keep the gash covered.

"He'll be okay. I've seen worse." Her tone radiated confidence, but it soon changed to a hint of panic. "Are my cousin and Rhona all right?"

"They *were* okay." Tavarra looked at Eza. She wouldn't dare say the full story of how she had choked Perin. "Eza knew the way for them to find what they seek and gave directions."

"Thank goodness." Lana sighed in relief. "Sorry I didn't introduce myself with everything going on. I'm Lana."

"Eza mentioned your name. I'm Tavarra." Several floral wood carvings hung on the walls, a chair in the corner, a bed, a side table, and a dresser. Her eyes darted to each object, antsy and wanting to return to the forest.

"You two are welcome to stay in here as long as you'd like, or I can take you to Quil's cabin."

"I'll be back in the morning," Tavarra said in a hurry. "Is there a lake somewhere near here?" In the morning, she would need to find somewhere to wash off.

"There's a large one to the west, and if you go a little more south, there's a long river." Lana scanned her up and down. "Do you not have any other clothing?"

Tavarra peered down at herself, the ripped shirt, the torn pants, both from her change into the beast the night before. She shook her head because she had already used the ones from her pack.

Lana exited the room and came back with a new set of clothing—a loaf of bread, dried meat, and two apples—setting the things on the bedside. Eza waved her hands, and Lana pulled out the magnifying glass from her pocket and held it up in front of the bat's face.

"You didn't have to do all that," Eza said.

"There will be more tomorrow. If you need anything else, I'll be a few houses down. But I'll come back after dinner to check on Perin, right now it's best for him to sleep." Lana smiled before she left.

Tavarra turned back to Perin. She pulled out his canteen from his pack and set it beside the bed. As he slept, he looked so helpless.

Picking up a dry cloth from the table, she dabbed the sweat from his forehead, face, and neck. She couldn't help recalling how he'd saved her. *Why?*

His eyes fluttered open, focusing on her—she hurried and yanked her hand back. "Sorry, just wiping away your sweat … and filth. Lana cleaned your wound, so try not to move too much."

"Are you staying?" he rasped.

"No, I have to go to the forest, but I'll be here in the morning. I'll leave some food and water in case you're hungry, and Lana will be back to check on you later."

"You can stay. I'll watch over you and make sure you're all right." Then he closed his eyes and passed out.

"No, I don't think you could." For some reason, she smiled at that and left the room.

Fifteen

Rhona

After Rhona finished eating the last bit of dried meat, she stared in the direction of the Crimson Forest. It was strange that it had thundered and rained inside there, but outside of it, the sky was bright pink and filled with sunshine. Swallowing, she turned to face Quil. "I'm going to bathe because I smell worse than an animal."

"Maybe a bit." He chuckled.

She smacked his arm and looked past him, her gaze settling on a field of glistening clovers. "Hey, did you ever find a four-leaf clover?"

Quil shook his head. "Nope."

"You know, I searched for one for you every day." There were several meadows near her home, and patches stayed there year-round—even during the winter. Her hands had been on the verge of frostbite, but she'd still dug through the freezing snow to try and find a four-leaf clover.

"Would you have brought it to me if you'd found one?"

"I would have wanted to, so you could have finally given it to Lana." Rhona would have found a way—one she should have found much earlier.

Biting his lip, he gave her a small smile as he locked gazes with her. Her heart beat rapidly as his smile widened.

"So, yeah." She couldn't think of anything better to say even though she yearned to.

"Yeah," he echoed. "Back to the clover, I may not have found one, but Lana did. And guess what? She didn't use it on herself. She gave it to one of the children in the village who was blind. Lana had said to actually hear would be too distracting for her—she likes the silence."

That act of kindness was something that Rhona found worth looking up to. "I already like her—she's nice."

"Yeah." He smiled. "So while you go bathe, let me see if I can have better luck finding a clover here."

That wasn't the answer she'd been hoping for. She silently wished he would've joined her in the lake, so they could talk more about what he'd been doing over the past two years. His cousin had a partner of her own. What if Quil had found someone else?

With her head down, she walked closer to the lake and pulled off her clothing. She thought about what Perin had done with the note, and she'd obviously been pissed about it. But what if Quil had *been* with other women? What if he had a lover waiting for him at home right now? His house was large enough.

Maybe she had been the only one in love because it wasn't as if he'd ever spoken the words to her. *What if it was just the two of us having fun? Why's my head spinning with such annoying questions?*

Rhona dunked her head in the freezing water and almost screamed when the liquid brushed her skin like icicles. She expected the lake to have been warm—where she could float around for a while—but no. Teeth chattering, she hurried and cleaned herself as thoroughly as she could before hopping out. She used her cloak to dry off as best she could while goosebumps prickled up across her arms and legs.

More thoughts swirled through her head about her mother

and Perin, but she pushed those sinking feelings aside. Hurriedly, she tossed on her undergarments and dragged the tunic over her head. Her hair was wet, but the curls were already growing wild. She wanted to leave her hair unbound, the way she used to wear it, but tied it back up into a low bun anyway. Sometimes wearing an armor, even if it was something as minuscule as styling her hair differently, helped her forget about who she used to be.

Right when she was about to pluck up her pants from the ground, Quil jogged to her with a smile on his face. He froze when his gaze left hers and fell to her legs. She scurried and grabbed her pants to cover them up.

"What happened?" he whispered.

Over the past two years, Rhona had wondered if he'd seen the unraised pale scars when they'd been together under that shaded tree. He hadn't mentioned anything that day, but his face had never ventured below her waist.

"They're just scars." They were more than that—they were reminders.

He marched forward, stopping directly in front of her, his voice worried. "Did you do this to yourself?"

"No!" Although, she had thought about doing them to herself instead of Belen performing the task.

"These can't all be accidental."

"No, they're not." She pushed to the side and shoved on her pants, not wanting to talk about it anymore.

The way Quil looked at her made her feel as if she was something foul. "I know I'm vile." She turned away from him and sat down, but he came and perched beside her.

"No! You're not. I'm just ... why didn't you tell me? Or are they new?"

"They aren't new, so just stop!"

As if knowing she didn't want to talk about it, he clasped her hand and pushed something into her palm. "Here."

Rhona glanced down at the piece of green in her hand. A

clover. One, two, three, *four*! She stood from the ground and screamed, "You found one!"

"Yeah." He smiled almost shyly. "It's for you."

"No. No. No! All these years searching for one? It's definitely yours! I couldn't."

"You can." Softly, he reached forward and closed her hand into a fist around the clover.

"Is it because you think my legs are disgusting?" Rhona tore her gaze from his and stared at the grass and dirt.

"No, stop saying things like that! It's meant to heal. I was thinking you can get your ability returned to you, the way the girl from the village got her sight back after she ate the clover."

If she could get her ability back, that would help out so much. "Are you sure? It may not work."

He reached out and clasped her other hand. "Just try it. Worth a shot, right?"

At those words, and his hand anchoring her, she dropped the clover into her mouth and chewed—it didn't have a grassy flavor. The taste was sweet, almost like honey. Closing her eyes, she thought of skin, muscle, and bones melting, followed by liquid moving as she swallowed. She released his hand when she felt a cooling sensation flow through her body. It was as though the liquid inside her was coming alive, out of hibernation. Her skin became a soft blue as her physical traits softened, turning clearer, and she descended to the ground, becoming a puddle of water. Like the liquid inside her, she felt alive, too. Quil hovered above her, grinning. Despite the wondrous feeling, she wanted to change back. She gathered her inner strength and let all her body parts take shape and form once more.

"Thank you." She wanted to wrap her arms around him but instead gave his hand a quick squeeze.

"Eh, I'll find another one again."

She rolled her eyes. Maybe sometime in his next nineteen years, he'd find one.

"I'm going to rinse off."

Before he could leave, she owed him something for his selfless gesture. She reached for his hand as he got up to leave, grabbing him by the wrist. "It was Belen, Perin's father … my father."

He bent his knees so they were eye to eye and leaned forward, his brows almost becoming one. "Did he *do* something to you?"

Rhona knew what he meant, and it was nothing like that. "No, only using my ability on things, or cuts to my legs to see how quickly I would heal over the years. I don't know why he did these things, except that I'm one of the few that has an ability. My wounds haven't always closed as quickly, so they used to leave scars behind. The healing kind of grew as I did— to the point where they started to heal rapidly."

"He's dead." His jaw worked back and forth.

"Don't worry. I'll do it." It was something she should have tried harder to do a long time ago, even if her ability didn't work against him. *But then, the prism protected him anyway.*

"How's your arm?"

Rhona had almost forgotten about the stitches when she pushed up her sleeve—it had already healed. "Good as new, thanks to your sewing job and the clover. I'll get the stitches out. Go get cleaned up, you smell like an animal."

"Some people like animals." He chuckled and walked away.

She stared down at the small pebbles beneath her feet and bit the inside of her cheek as her thoughts turned to Belen and her mother.

"Where are we going, Mama?" six-year-old Rhona asked. The morning suns had just risen into the sky.

Thea let out a heavy sigh. "We have to see Belen."

Rhona closed her eyes, and let out a whimper. "I don't want to go."

"What is it?" her mother asked.

"Nothing. I just don't like talking about things," she lied.

"We all have weekly sessions with him for guidance."

Her mama walked her to the large tent, and Perin stepped out. He was only a year older than her, but she didn't want him to leave.

"Can Perin stay with me?" Her eyes opened wide, desperate.

"No, he has to come with me. Just as when any of us are here, we may only speak with him alone."

Rhona put on the bravest face she could. "Play after, Perin?"

"Sure." Perin shifted closer to her side as if he didn't want to leave. He handed her a doll that looked more scary than comforting.

"I know it's not the best, but I want you to feel better."

She tugged the doll closer to her chest since Perin had made it.

"Come on," Rhona's mother said, pulling Perin away.

Rhona lifted the flap of the tent back and walked inside. She moved the next one aside to go into Belen's office. On the other side of the room, he was seated at his desk, sorting through papers.

"Hello, Rhona. It's good to see you today." His voice sounded warm, yet his eyes were as cold as ice.

She didn't say anything, only bit the inside of her cheek to keep from crying when she sat in the chair across from him.

"Are you ready?"

In her lap, she squeezed the doll from Perin and shook her head. She wanted to go home.

He tilted his head, his tone deep and steady. "You don't want to make me angry, do you?"

She shook her head again.

"We wouldn't want something to happen to your mother, would we? Or perhaps even Perin?"

Her head shook even harder.

"It will only take a few moments." He paused. "Now—can you roll up your pant leg?"

With shaky fingers, she sat the doll beside her and rolled up her loose trousers. From the knee and above, her legs were already growing a collection of scars, some lighter than others.

Belen pulled a small knife from his drawer and moved toward her. She stared at the blade, already knowing how it would feel when it entered her thigh.

This time she wanted Perin's gift to protect her.

"Here, I'll hold your hand." His bright blue eyes met hers as he held out his palm, pretending to offer her kindness.

Rhona didn't move, and his face fell into a glower as his eyes narrowed. She didn't want to make him madder, so she placed her small hand in his.

"Remember to be quiet." Belen stuck the blade into her thigh, and she let out a gasp of pain. He made a small stroke, dragging it only a few centimeters before lifting it out.

Tears slid down her cheeks as she stared at the blood. Hurriedly, he grabbed a cloth and dabbed at the scarlet wound. "You're all right," he said, like she'd only fallen out of a tree and gotten cut. "The bleeding has already stopped. Each week, it appears you're healing faster. I'm sure this one will be lighter than the others, and eventually you might not scar at all." He smiled as if he was the one gifting her this ability, when he wasn't the one responsible.

She grabbed the doll's hand and squeezed it harder, but she felt no comfort at all.

Rhona found herself gripping her thighs. It had been years since Belen had cut her. Once she didn't scar anymore, he'd stopped, and they'd moved on to her dehydrating plants.

A small flower lay a few steps away, so she crawled forward and closed her eyelids, thinking of draining water. When she opened her eyes, the flower had wilted. It felt good to have her ability back. Pure anticipation settled in the pit of

her stomach when she thought of going back to her village—
and finding Belen. He'd have far worse than the scars he'd
given her—Belen would be gone.

From behind her, a soft sound interrupted her thoughts,
followed by a fast melody playing through the air. She
whipped her head over her shoulder and got up so she could
see. Around the bush, Quil sat facing the lake, playing his pan
flute. It reminded her of the first time she'd found him when
he'd been a small, lanky boy—he was neither of those things
anymore. She glanced to the Crimson Forest, and as Eza had
said, nothing came out, even with the music playing. But if
something did, she had her sword. She'd rather risk anything
to hear Quil play the pan flute anyway.

The only clothing he wore was his pants, even his feet were
bare like they always used to be. She crept closer to get a better
listen of the music, the notes increasing in their enchantment.
He claimed he hadn't played in a while, but it sounded as if he
hadn't missed a day.

"Is that a new song?" she asked when she stood directly
behind him, her shadow covering him in a soft touch to get a
better listen, too.

Quil stopped playing and turned around to look up at her.
Beads of water dribbled off the ends of his dark hair and onto
his chest.

"No, my grandfather used to play this one." He pushed
himself up so that he was now hovering above her. "Dance?"

She stared at the water, catching a small glimpse of a fish
coming to the surface, as if it wished it could breathe the air.
"Not tonight." Her heart yearned to dance, but her head was in
such a place that she still couldn't bring herself to do it.

He lowered his hand with the flute, and she clasped his
wrist. "But I don't want you to stop playing." No matter where
her thoughts had drifted to, she always wanted to hear him
play—always would.

"Then for you, I won't." Quil lifted the pan flute back up to his lips and blew several soft breaths, creating a low tone that became something much bigger. Rhona tried not to focus on his lips and the way they curved and moved with each air of breath he puffed out. Instead, she concentrated on the world around them—the waterfall, the boulders, the mountains in the distance.

The night was taking its place around the two of them, and Quil let out a yawn as he tucked the flute back into his pack.

Rhona laid back and placed her sword and daggers at her side in case she needed them. At the moment, there weren't any thunderous sounds or any heavy stomping, but she needed to be prepared in case things could really come out of the Crimson Forest.

Her cloak had mostly dried, so she tucked it behind her head and stared up at the sky. The whole area surrounding the lake was filled with small flickering lights that resembled stars. Around them, the fireflies blinked on and off.

"If you hold up your hand like this"—Quil grabbed her fingers and opened her palm, then straightened her arm in the air—"one might come to you."

At night, when she had been younger, she'd always chased them with Perin. But they never came to her.

"I don't think they like me," she said with a laugh.

Quil held up his hand beside hers. "You just have to be patient."

A small speck of light landed in the center of his palm, blinking rapidly as though it was conversing with him.

"Well, I'm being patient and had mine up longer than yours, but I still don't have a little light friend, yet." She smiled, feeling almost antsy because her hand was still empty.

Slowly he rolled to his side, careful not to jolt the bug. With his empty palm, he softly held her wrist and joined his hand—holding the speck of light—next to hers.

Waiting, she blinked in the dark several times, and then the light creation took measured steps from Quil's hand to hers.

The fragile legs tickled her palm. It seemed to flicker a small, "hello," then, "goodbye," before flying off to meet the others once again.

Finally, Quil released her wrist, and she already missed his warmth. She ached to tell him how much she missed him and even wished that she'd danced earlier. But sometimes, she didn't feel she could do the things that had once made her happy. And Quil had always made her happy, yet there was so much uncertainty between them now.

"Good night," she said and rolled to her side, hiding the tears sliding down her cheeks.

Sixteen

Tavarra

Tavarra hadn't gotten a wink of sleep that entire night. This was the part she hated because she could have stayed inside instead, cozy in front of a fire, relaxing on a fur rug. She didn't know what that was like, and most likely never would.

Stepping out from the lake, she slid her clothing back on. Eza had already gone back to Lana's after taking a quick dip to clean herself.

As she brought an apple to her lips, Tavarra was in no rush to get back to the village.

With not much sleep during the night, she had thought about Perin—more than she probably should have. A minor piece of her hoped he hadn't died overnight. It was the part of her that thought about him rescuing her, even though he had really put himself in danger. What if the man had spun around and stabbed Perin? It wouldn't have been hard to do with him having been so wobbly.

After she finished the apple, she chucked the core near a tree and pulled out a leather strap from her pack. She tugged it around her thick hair, taming it in place. The sleeves of the shirt Lana had given her weren't long enough to cover the tangerine fur along the sides of her forearms, but they would have to make do. Like everything else … she always made do.

Before heading to Lana's, Tavarra wandered through the waking village. In front of one shelter, there stood a small boy around the age of ten, blowing glass and shaping it into a bird. Outside another shelter was a woman chopping meat and a man waiting to barter with her. As Tavarra passed, the people stared a bit too long, but each gave her a friendly smile. She didn't smile back.

When a woman with shorn hair called Tavarra over to learn more about the sick lover that she had allegedly brought into the village to be saved, she turned around and left, knowing Eza had already started gossip, trying to create a sob story so everyone would *feel* for Tavarra.

Fuming as she marched up the steps to Lana's, Tavarra didn't even bother to knock when she headed inside.

No one was in the front open room, only a desk with a needle and thread resting on top—across from it was an empty sofa. Inside the bedroom, Perin was stripped naked except for a towel draped across his hips. His eyes were closed, and she stared a little too long at his chest. It wasn't the defined muscles that caught her eye, but the crisscrossing scars above his navel and below his neck.

The beat of wings came from another room, and Eza skirted around the doorway to come in. "There's honey in the kitchen and bread. The utensils are a bit big." She held up a sticky hand and looked toward Perin. "As are other *things*."

Groaning, Tavarra exited the room and avoided looking at Perin's other *things*. "Where's Lana?"

Following behind her, Eza sang, "Hunting for the day. She said his fever's gone, so I told her you and me could keep an eye on him throughout the day." That meant Tavarra would be pampering Perin… She could have killed Eza.

Tavarra found the loaf of bread and sliced it into smaller pieces. She handed an extra small one to the bat after putting a dab of honey on it for her. When Tavarra finished eating her slice, she took two more pieces and spread honey inside it to make a sandwich.

On the way out of the kitchen, she opened the front door for Eza to go outside and explore. Once back in the bedroom, she stood in front of Perin. With her index and middle finger, she nudged his shoulder. "Hello!"

His eyes flew open, and he shot up, reaching his hand out for something. Then his blue eyes caught hers, and he froze. She tried to avoid his gaze because the towel had shifted a bit. Eza's words repeated in her head, *as are other things.*

"Where's my sword?" he asked. Her eyes fell to the crisscrossing scars that lined his entire back as they did his upper chest.

She toed the metal with her boot beside the bed. "Your salvation is right here if you need it."

Peering down at himself, he raked a hand through his hair. "What I *need* are my clothes."

"No, you *need* to lie back down." The stubborn man didn't listen to her. "Okay, well, you at least have to eat." She handed him the honey sandwich, and he took it from her, eating like a starved jovkin.

The canteen still sat by his bedside, and she gave that to him, too. Lana must have filled it because it was already full once more.

His fingers brushed hers as he grabbed it, and swigged the water down. "Thanks." He reached to put it back on the table.

Perin's eyes met hers and he frowned. "So, where did you go last night?"

Why is he so worried where I went? "In the forest."

"Chained to a tree again?"

"Yeah, but don't worry, I was fine." She held up her claws. "No beast last night."

Perin didn't look impressed as he continued to frown. "You going to fill me in on that?"

"No." A black smudge of dirt was on his right cheek—she

almost stretched over to wipe it away, but only because it was bothering her to look at. "You've got something black on your cheek."

He reached up and swiped the wrong cheek.

"The other side!"

He completely missed it.

Sighing, Tavarra picked up the cloth from the table and pushed the tip into the bowl of water. She turned around and washed the smudge from his face. "It looks like you're going to be treated like a babe all day today." She smiled, her fangs protruding.

His lips tilted at the edges, not in annoyance or embarrassment as she expected—she made her smile disappear. She had felt the old Tavarra slipping in for a moment. The one who was intrigued by humans—the one who *trusted* them.

If she was going to travel with him and his friends, then she might as well tell him a part of her story. "Sometimes at night, because of the curse, I become a beast. I don't know what I'm doing during that time, and I don't remember what happens afterward. If someone dies because of me, all I know is that there's a dead body and that I did it..." Tavarra thought about her sister, and she could feel her eyes start to water. She didn't want to cry in front of this man—or anyone—ever. So she turned around.

It took him a few moments to say anything, as if he was trying to solve a riddle. "When I saw you the other night, you appeared to be some sort of werewolf."

"*Werewolf?*" She spun back around. That word was not familiar to her in the slightest.

"Do you know what a *wolf* is?"

Tavarra shook her head.

"Haven't you ever heard the story *Little Red Riding Hood?*"

She shook her head again, trying to remember stories that Eza or Brice had told her. There had been a lot of tales, yet that one didn't strike a chord.

"*Okay*… Well, that story doesn't have a werewolf, but it does have a wolf. Back from Rhona's and my ancestor's world, there were stories passed down from one generation to the next. Vampires with sharp fangs who drink blood and never grow old, werewolves who are human but become a mix between a wolf and a man—*or* woman—when a full moon rises, and zombies who are buried dead bodies but come back to life from the ground and eat other humans."

"All the dead things I've seen here have stayed dead, and no one lives forever." At least she thought so.

"And you don't become a beast under only full moons either, but it is at night…" He didn't appear smug as he told her this, but she didn't like talking about it.

"I'm finished discussing this."

Perin maneuvered himself to the edge of the bed. With his hand draping the towel tighter around his waist, he stood from the bed and took a deep breath.

"What are you doing? Sit down!" she snapped, stepping in front of him.

"Lana left some of Quil's clothing." He moved around her toward the chair in the corner. "I'm going to go get dressed."

"No, you aren't." Her hand was pressed at his scarred chest. She could shove him back to the bed with a flick of her finger.

His brows lifted, and he blinked at her.

She grimaced. "I mean, you're staying in here until tomorrow." Turning around, she found the folded clothes on a wooden chair.

"Well, I need to take a piss." He scowled.

"You can sit your ass back down and continue using the bowl."

Holding the tunic up, she tugged it over his head. With a frustrated groan, he sat back down and pushed his arms through the sleeves.

She placed the bowl on the bed beside him. "Now, relieve

yourself, then I'll change the cloth on your leg. You will have to leave your trousers off and continue to use the towel for now. We can't let that wound become infected again, now can we?" That would put a damper on getting to the Stone.

He narrowed his eyes at her but snatched up the bowl. "Are you going to watch me urinate, too?"

"No!" She hurried out of the room, shutting the door behind her. Her cheeks grew hot. Was she blushing? No, she was only doing that because she was annoyed.

Throughout the rest of the day, she changed the cloth and reapplied healing cream after inspecting the wound. It looked much better, no longer oozing pus.

She fed them lunch, which consisted of a basket of meat, pie, and pears. One of the young men, who Eza had already befriended, brought it over—the bat hadn't stayed since Tavarra had the situation with Perin handled.

She had to push Perin down numerous times when he tried to get up to relieve himself, reach for his sword, eat, or just try to sneak out. It was truly like taking care of a babe, except he was a rather large one—and listened much worse.

"Tell me this *Little Red Riding Hood* story," she finally said, feeling bored and constricted inside the shelter. This was the longest she had been inside one. But she was also a bit curious about the tale.

Working his jaw, Perin pushed himself up so his back was higher against the headboard. "This girl, Little Red, ventures out on a journey with food in a basket to bring to her grandmother. On the way, she bumps into a talking wolf. She tells him that she's going to visit her granny. The wolf then leaves her and hurries to the house before the girl comes. When the wolf arrives at the grandmother's home, he eats the gran and pretends to be her when Little Red arrives. Something feels off to the girl, and she tells 'her gran' what big eyes, ears, and teeth she has. Then the wolf in disguise tells Little Red that *'they are better to eat you with,'* and leaps up from the bed…"

"Then what happens?" She shifted closer and craned her neck to hear more.

Perin cocked his head and popped his neck. "There are three endings that I know of… One, he eats the girl. Two, the girl kills the wolf and rips open the stomach to find her gran alive. Three, the girl kills the wolf, but the gran is truly dead." He paused, his blue eyes meeting Tavarra's. "Which ending would you choose?"

She rubbed her chin and thought about it. "If this wolf is anything like my beast… I've never swallowed humans whole before. There wouldn't be any way that a wolf could swallow a person, and for them be able to live in the stomach. I'd go with the first or third ending, but most likely the first one. I don't know a lot of happy endings."

"My favorite was always the third one—a girl being able to take down a wolf on her own." Something that might be considered the start of a smile formed on his face, and confusion washed over her at first. "It could also be a metaphor—that the girl was the wolf. There had never been a separate beast—the girl in her wolf form had eaten her own grandmother but found a way to rid herself of it." And at that moment, Tavarra knew Perin was talking about her. *Does he mean I can defeat the beast?*

The front door creaked open, and Tavarra hurried out of the room to find Lana, carrying four furry rabbits. "I'm going to cook dinner if you want to help."

"Yes, I'll help." She would take the distraction over her wayward thoughts.

Tavarra looked back into the room, seeing Perin staring down at his hands. She didn't want to talk about tales of beasts that made her think and wish and hope anymore. She knew what her life was, and she would go to the Stone of Desire, and it would either help her, or it wouldn't. Most likely, she would always be the way she was now.

Seventeen

Rhona

Rhona woke on her stomach, her eyes meeting Quil's back.

He was stooped over a small fire, cooking something. Her tired body yearned to fall back to sleep. But then she thought that wouldn't be fair, so she lifted her head and asked, "Need help with that?"

"You're late on that front," he said. "It's already finished. I caught two squirrels."

"You?"

"I told you I've been hunting more." His tone sounded as if this was a usual routine—she was proud of him. When they were younger, it was mainly she who would retrieve fish from the river.

"I'm impressed." Pushing herself to her knees, she stretched her arms, then arched her back.

He shifted toward her and bent down to hand her the meat on the stick, steam rising from its belly. With his lips pulled together, he softly blew on the meat.

Her gaze moved to his shirt, where the collar shifted, and she could see a black string around his neck. Her heart soared in her chest as she reached forward and withdrew it from beneath his shirt. A misshapen wooden clover rested in her hand—the one she'd given him years ago.

She stared down at the piece, not taking her eyes away from it. "You still have this?"

"I wear it every day, only take it off when I bathe." His tone was soft, sad.

"Oh." Rhona dropped it as if it burned her hand. *I should've come back sooner.*

When she met his gaze, a frown had crossed his face, but he kept his words unspoken. They ate in a cloud of quiet and filled their canteens with water from the lake. A rainbow was at the center of one of the waterfalls, rising into the pink sky, painting its wonder above.

Rhona pulled on her cloak in silence while Quil did the same. She smiled to herself when he tucked away the pan flute into his pack. When she thought about the previous night, wishing she had danced, her chest seemed to fill with fireflies that sparked on and off inside of her, creating a lightning storm.

Continued silence spilled between them as they gathered their things and headed around the lake. Rhona wanted to say so much, but the words were stuck in her throat. She'd never had that insecurity around him.

In front of them, trees with sharp thorns slid into view—the deadly woods that Eza had mentioned. The trees were of a charcoal color, with leaves blacker than the darkest of nights.

"Are you sure you want to go in? It's fine if you want to wait here." Rhona didn't want Quil to think he really had to go in there. She could lie and tell Perin he had.

Perin. Thoughts of her brother made her heart clench in pain. *He's fine*, she told herself. *He has to be.*

"Of course I'm going with you. How will you ever survive without me there?" Quil chuckled.

"You mean the other way around," she teased back. Relief washed over her, but not enough, because she didn't know what would happen in these new woods—or if they'd encounter worse things than in the Crimson Forest.

With her sword in one hand and the dagger in the other, Rhona edged forward. A strange sort of hissing diffused around them. It stayed consistent—one hiss, two hisses, three hisses, and on and on. The air felt heavy and weighted against her skin as she moved, smelling a tad like the after-effects of heavy autumn rain.

Whirling to her right, a wide tree with gnarled and twisting limbs covered in large razor-sharp thorns stood tall.

A slow and jerky movement caught her eye as if the tree's bark was crawling around itself. However, it wasn't the tree's natural skin—a black snake blended in with the bark, slithering around its trunk.

Oh, it can't be just one snake, Rhona thought. There were hundreds and hundreds of them swirling and traveling over and under one another, letting their dark tongues release to sniff the air. *Smelling* Rhona and Quil. She held back a shudder.

The trees they passed all had the dark snakes as their personal little pets, but none of the reptiles tried to advance toward them. Rhona and Quil were both ready with their swords if they did.

Inhaling deeply, Rhona searched the tops of the trees for fairies or volachs, even checking to make sure none of them had birthed any bark children. "How do we know where to find the prism? It could be anywhere." She needed to find a trunk with a heart-shaped middle. But she didn't know how she could do that if the damn trees were wrapped in slithering snakes.

"You forgot something, Rho." Quil tapped her shoulder and gave her a smirk. *This is no smirking matter.*

"What's that?" she asked, more than a little annoyed.

His smile became a wide grin, until she could see the one tooth that stuck out a bit farther than the others. "Remember how you showed me what you could do with a flower?" He ticked each one off on his fingers. "Drain, freeze, and boil."

"Yeah?" She paused, thinking. "*Oh!* You want me to do it on the snakes!"

"Unless you'd rather us cut through all of them. We can always try that, too." He shrugged with a chuckle. "Might take a while, though."

"You know, I'm not going to reprimand you, since you did find that clover, after all." The situation didn't feel like a loss now. There was a lot of hope, but also a whole lot of trees and snakes.

Stepping toward the first midnight-colored trunk, Rhona lifted her hands to give herself balance as she studied the snakes. She closed her eyes and thought about pulling the water from inside them, dehydrating their scaly bodies. There were so many to focus on that weakness consumed her.

She opened her eyes to concentrate harder. Tugging. Tugging. Tugging as much as she could. One by one, snakes crashed to the ground, their blackened color now pale with a brown hue. Snake after snake fell and fell and fell—their bodies didn't jerk or wiggle. When she was finished, the tree had also withered and shriveled in on itself—died. She watched as it stiffly fell backward to the ground with a loud whack, a cloud of dust rising from the impact.

Quil let out a low whistle. "Might not want to kill all the trees because this might take a while."

Stepping over dead snakes as she peered underneath, Rhona inspected the tree but couldn't find a heart-shaped hole around the base. She should have known the first tree she encountered wouldn't be the one she'd need.

They headed to the next tree with what seemed like more snakes, or maybe that was only in her mind. This time, instead of dehydrating them, Rhona boiled the reptiles from the inside out. Though she held out hope for the tree, that was lost when the trunk fell over in a slumped position, as if its body was made of skin and muscle. There was no hole on that one either.

"Sorry, tree," she mumbled.

"Try freezing them this time. Most trees seem to survive winters pretty well." Quil's thoughts oddly aligned with hers.

Holding up a hand, Rhona thought of water freezing to ice. To increase the cold, she imagined a blizzard on their insides, snow blowing through them. Finally, snakes fell from the tree, the smoky coolness of their frozen bodies drifting up into the air. She hurried forward to examine the tree—it was cold to the touch, yet still alive. No hole.

Tree after tree, she killed more and more reptiles. At number twenty, when the snakes struck the ground, Quil vanished to the back of the tree. His head peered around it. "It's your lucky day, Rho." A wide smile spread across his face.

Anxiously, she leaped over the corpses and pushed him over a little so she could see the hole. It was indeed in the shape of a heart, as though it had been perfectly carved with two symmetrical sides. A blackened dandelion bloomed from its center.

"Where's the prism?" She searched around, waiting for it to appear.

Quil whistled and called, "Come here, dark prism."

She rolled her eyes and stared at the pitch-black sphere inside the hole. With his long fingers, he plucked the dandelion and handed it to her. She took it from his hand, her fingers lightly touching his.

"Should I blow?" she asked.

"You should definitely try blowing." He smirked.

Shaking her head, she took a deep breath and blew onto the fragile seeds. In a rush to leave their home, they gracefully floated through the air. She repeated the same motion until the flower was only a stem.

Trying to be patient, she waited for a prism to appear in the hole. The weighted air seemed to grow heavier while they watched. A sizzling sound filled the air. Instead of the object appearing, the branches from the tree started to sway back and forth. Rhona took a step away, and another, while pulling Quil along by his tunic. The bark of the tree became even darker—the color of a thousand ravens' feathers melted together. The thorns up and down the trunk and limbs slid together, combining to create one large thorn from the center of the trunk.

All of Rhona's nerves thumped in sync—she kept her sword ready, still holding the dandelion stem in her other hand. The limbs churned and twisted, two forming new front legs, while two more created back ones. The top of the tree jutted forward as it lowered, the large thorn now at the center of a beast's head. Bark became fur, and black eyes that could hardly be seen stared at Rhona and Quil. In front of them stood a stallion of midnight with a horn the color of the night sky. The creature was dark and beautiful.

Rhona didn't see a prism anywhere. Was she supposed to defeat the stallion now in front of her?

Quil reached forward.

"What are you doing?" she shrieked.

"Searching for the prism." He held her stare. She yanked his hand back, not knowing if he'd have one at all if he touched the stallion.

Her eyes met those of the creature. She didn't know if the stallion would understand her, but she tried anyway. "May we borrow the prism from you? I promise to bring it back along with the ivory prism once we retrieve it."

The large beast knelt before them, and when they didn't move, the stallion cocked his head toward his back.

"I think he wants us to get on." Quil motioned to the creature with a shaky hand.

Rhona's hands twitched as she straddled the horned-stallion. She preferred to keep her feet on the ground—she could always trust her own legs. Quil slid on behind her and brought his arms around her to thread his fingers into the stallion's hair. His strong chest pressed against her back, and her body heated at his closeness. She mirrored his movements, placing her fingers into the dark locks.

"Do you have the prism?" she lowered her voice and asked the creature in a gentle tone.

In answer, he let out a loud whinny as if to say yes.

"Can you take us south to Quil's village?" She wanted to arrive there as fast as they could to get back to Perin.

He grunted. She wasn't sure what it meant, but it could have been more of an *I shall try*. "Take us out through the Crimson Forest."

The stallion jerked forward, and Rhona gripped onto him tighter to prevent herself from falling off his back. They flew by the trees and the snakes she'd destroyed before entering the suns' bright light. The stallion passed by the lake, hooves pounding and striking the earth until he came to a stop in front of the Crimson Forest.

A huff of air came from the dark stallion's nostrils, his right leg stomping and kicking the dirt. Before them, the branches untwisted and pulled apart from the stallion's unspoken demands. The fresh metallic scent struck Rhona's nose once more.

As the beautiful black beast galloped into the unlit forest, Rhona placed her hand on her sword, prepared to fight off anything she could. In the dark area, bright white eyes blinked all around them, blood splashed to the ground, and a rock giant peered at them from a corner—volach—but nothing came for an attack. The forest creatures moved backward, appearing fearful of the dark beast who seemed to be protecting Rhona and Quil. At the outskirt of the forest, the tree limbs unraveled with slow creaks and groans, exposing brightness on the other side.

Once out of the Crimson Forest, the dark stallion pummeled the land as it galloped. The world around Rhona was all a blur of color and trees, the wind beating heavily at her face and body. The stallion leaped over logs, and she and Quil ducked under low-hanging branches. After hours and hours, the stallion finally slowed to a stop, collapsing to the grass. Rhona and Quil hopped off him, and the creature fell to its side, exhaling and inhaling heavily.

Gently, Rhona placed her hand on the stallion's back, touching its soft fur. He curled up on himself—shriveling, withering, falling into a shrunken state, practically dying. She jerked her hand away, wondering if *she'd* done this with her ability and drained his insides of any water that was there.

The stallion shrank in size until he folded into a small dark object on the ground. Rhona's lips parted, and she sucked in a sharp breath. Quil scooped up the dark prism and held it up to the suns. Inside it, she could see two eyes peering out.

She knew what she had to do.

"I promise to bring you back." Rhona's tone was gentle to the stallion as she tucked the small object into her pack for now.

"Let's hurry back." Quil handed her a piece of jerky after hearing her stomach growl. "We should only have to stop for one night."

She ate as they walked, thankful the stallion had brought them back this far. "Do you think I'll be able to do this?" Belen had knocked her out easily before—she hoped with this prism that he couldn't do it and that she could get closer to him.

"I've always thought you could do anything." Quil's words made her shoulders and chin both lift, helping to give her a boost in confidence—one she desperately needed.

"I'm sorry I didn't come back—I had planned to in the next few months." Even at the price of her life, she would have tried to leave. It was his *life* she was always worried about.

"Sometimes things change." His gaze avoided hers while he shrugged nonchalantly, yet his shoulders remained stiff.

Without another word, no matter how much she wanted to say something else, they trekked as far as they could until the night had grown too dark. They stumbled upon a small cave and decided to stay for the night as they headed inside. Rhona scavenged a few twigs to start a fire and pulled her cloak tighter. A shiver escaped her—the air around them had grown cold and damp.

"Did you ever think about me?" Quil asked, as if he'd been holding onto this question for the entirety of the day. She'd already told him she'd planned on coming back for him. *Wouldn't that mean that, of course, I'd thought about him? I looked for clovers for him every day.*

"From the moment I woke up each day, to the last suns' rays when I passed out at night." In truth, he had always been on her mind, in her heart. "Did you think … of me?"

"I tried not to." He stoked the fire. "I hated you for a while, but even then, while I thought you were happy with another, I knew I could never hate you."

"So you found someone in your village?" The envious feeling bit at her insides, constricting them.

A loud rumble of laughter pushed past his lips as though she'd said the funniest joke in the world.

In return, Rhona glared at him.

Licking the center of his bottom lip, Quil said, "I did find someone who kept my lips company from time to time."

Her heart dropped, her skin and muscles shattered. She didn't know why he had to word it like that.

"Sometimes she was my salvation, sometimes I had to rotate to a new one because she wasn't enough." He opened his pack and pulled out his pan flute. "But she's the one that fits my mouth the best without me even having to touch her body with my lips." He placed the flute to his lips and blew a musical note.

"You…" Rhona's fists clenched at her sides, barely holding back the impulse to shove him.

"I think it's time you dance, unless you're too *tired*." Quil arched a brow in challenge, and with a smile on his face, he blew again into the flute until the sounds became a song.

The irritation left her as the notes filled her soul. Rhona stared at him a beat longer, her anger diffusing with each note that passed his flute.

With slow movements, she released the hair from her bun, setting her wild curls free, the way she liked—the way Quil liked. Standing from the ground, she spun in short circles and held her hands up to the roof of the cave, wanting nothing else than to feel the song. He played several—one after another until they both grew tired. But never did his eyes waver from her dancing form.

By the end of the night, Rhona lay on the floor, shivering from the cold air despite the fire still going. Quil shifted nearer and wrapped his arm around her, pulling her body closer to keep her warm. She slid her arm around his waist and held him tightly to keep him warm, too. Their cloaks draped over them both, creating a thicker barrier.

Her head was tucked to his chest, and he lowered his face, kissing the top of her scalp. "There's never been anyone else, only you."

In her chest, Rhona's heart beat faster, thumping its own music. She had the prism, she had Quil with her, and she would defeat her father.

Eighteen

Tavarra

Once Eza handed Tavarra the key, she unlocked the chains that bound her wrists.

Eza perched down on her shoulder and took a seat, crossing her arms. "You were loud last night."

The night before, Tavarra had felt the change, and she'd hoped she wouldn't have to deal with the monster while staying near the village for the few days. Alas, that hadn't happened—she had turned into the beast.

"No one came out here?" Tavarra asked, searching around the trees, worried that villagers may be coming with weapons.

"Oh, *someone* did," Eza sang and brought her hands together in a small clap.

Crinkling her forehead, Tavarra rubbed at her wrists that would bear the scars from the chains forever. Each time she changed, it only became worse. Frantically, she looked around for a dead body. There wasn't any around her, and she didn't appear injured anywhere else.

"No one was killed." Eza pushed off from Tavarra's shoulder, flapping her wings. "And no one from the village came. You were loud, but you aren't the only ruckus-causing creature at night. Humans are used to it."

Her shoulders relaxed. "Oh, so it was a traveler?"

"I said no one from the village." The bat ticked her finger side to side. "It was Perin."

"*What?*" she growled. That fool came outside when he was supposed to remain in bed like she had told him to do.

Eza held up her hands. "I told him I had it handled, and he asked how I would be able to hold you down if you escaped. I didn't have an answer for him, so he stayed."

"He wouldn't be able to hold me down either!" she shouted. His body was still weakened, and even then, she was much stronger—more so when she became the monster.

"It's … possible." Eza knew it was not possible.

Tavarra didn't know if she was more frustrated that Perin had brought his nosey ass into the forest to watch her as a monster, or because she had told the imbecile to stay in bed until morning. It was the latter.

"Go help him bathe." Eza smiled. "I'm going to go and visit Jonathan."

"The boy with the basket?"

"You mean *man*, and yes, he's nice. If only he were a bat." The *man* she had seen looked rather small and stick thin.

Tavarra raised a brow, and Eza zoomed off to visit *Jonathan*. She tightened her fists at her sides, her claws biting into her palms. Quickly, she replaced her old ripped clothing back with the shirt and tunic Lana had given her. She didn't want to have to ask Lana for new clothing or have her see the ones she had gifted Tavarra ripped.

Inside the village, Lana was seated on the porch in her rocker, fiddling around with her sword. She glanced up and immediately gave a genuine smile. "I'm about to leave and go hunting. If you need me to stay, I can."

"No, I have it handled." Did she? The fool didn't seem to listen to her.

"Quil and Rhona should hopefully be back soon." Lana didn't seem fazed in the slightest, as if there wasn't any possibility that they could die. Tavarra knew that death could come at any time.

She studied Lana's ears and wondered what it would be like to not be able to hear anything. At times, she felt like it could be a blessing. "How did you lose your hearing?"

Lana stood and sheathed her sword. "When I was younger, I caught an illness."

"So you weren't born this way?" she asked, surprised. "Do you miss it?"

"Not really. I like the quiet, and when I hunt, I can *feel* the vibrations." Lana looked in awe—perhaps it was possible the vibrations sang to her. "Except for the one time in the forest with your friend in there—he got me on my back with a knife at my throat rather quickly." Perin wasn't Tavarra's friend.

"Don't worry." She smiled, feeling it was now okay to mention her first encounter with him. "I got him on his back by the throat one time."

Chuckling, Lana shouldered her pack. "I'll see you tonight. This morning Perin said he felt good all last night and slept like a baby."

Oh, I bet he did.

Tavarra gritted her teeth and headed inside, finding Perin asleep on his side, the towel poorly draped over him—exposing his backside. His shirt was off again, and she couldn't help but admire the shape of his body, even with the flecks of scarring. It was as if someone had taken a knife and sliced him in random spots.

For a moment, she had a sinking feeling at the idea—then her anger came crawling back. "Perin!" she barked, hands on her hips.

With a hard jerk, he sprung forward, his eyes lining up with hers. "Fuck! Second day in a row you come in here like a banshee."

"Banshee?" Another mysterious word she didn't know—like werewolf.

"Never mind." He ran a hand through his short hair.

"Didn't sleep well?" she asked as sweetly as she could muster. Then she slammed her hand down on the bed. "Trying to catch up on sleep after risking your leg? You just had to come and stay up all night in the forest?"

"I told Eza to keep quiet," he mumbled.

"Always remember, Eza is on *my* side. She's *my* friend."

The sides of his lips twitched, almost becoming a smile. "Someone is a bit possessive."

"Sit still." She lifted the bandage to check how the wound was doing, her eyes then meeting his. "You're lucky you didn't make this worse." It looked much better than it had been. There were now fresh stitches sewn in since the injury was no longer infected.

"Lana said I'm fine now. Just keep it bandaged for a few days and go about like normal."

Tavarra picked his clothing up from the chair and threw the shirt and pants at him. He easily caught them—she had hoped one would have hit him in the face.

"Get dressed. We're going to the lake." She hurried out of the room and grabbed the food Lana had left for them. A few moments later, Perin came out. The shirt looked a bit too tight, and he rotated his shoulders backward, then forward, trying to loosen it.

"Quil's shirts are a little too small," he said.

Tavarra handed him the basket of food and turned away.

They trudged their way through the forest, not even the slightest of breaths from the wind blew. Birds chirped from the branches of trees, and insects sang to one another. Everyone and everything seemed bright and happy—except for her, and maybe Perin.

When they stopped in front of the lake, he turned to face her. "I can bathe by myself."

"Oh, I'm not going in there with you. I'll be off in the forest, so let me know when you're ready, and we'll go back." She left him to strip down and walked off. A minuscule sliver of something inside her wanted to turn around and take a glimpse of his naked form, but she didn't. It had been too long without being skin to skin with another, that was all.

Quietly, Tavarra found a small rock, took a seat on it, and gathered in her surroundings. This place was different than the rest of Laith that she'd visited—she'd never seen such green landscape and vegetation in her life. She wondered if it resembled the world where the humans had come from, and maybe that's why most of them stayed out here.

Her gaze fell to her claws. No matter how many times she'd tried to cut them or file her teeth down, they always came back by morning. So she left them as they were—a burden.

Uneven footsteps trampled through the forest, crunching leaves. "Why can't the fool listen?" she grumbled to the trees.

When he drew closer, she didn't even turn around as she spoke, "Didn't I tell you to let me know when you were finished and I would meet you there?"

"Tavarra, I'm fine."

Her body stilled, and she slowly twisted around. That was the first time he had called her by her name. The young dweller that still lived somewhere inside her heart was thrilled by how he made it sound.

She hated that dweller.

"You want to go hunting? I've been stuck in bed for too long—I'm feeling antsy," Perin said.

"You sure you're okay?" She hadn't known him for that long, but apparently when Perin set his mind to something, he didn't back down.

"I didn't have a limb torn off, so I'm all right."

She couldn't tell if that were meant to be in jest or if he was serious. "I might have had to carry you again if that happened."

"Don't ever remind me of that." His eyes drifted away from hers. "But thank you." If she didn't know better, she would think he was embarrassed.

Together they spent the remainder of the day in the forest, hunting. Using her dagger, Tavarra had struck a large bird hiding in a tree with a single throw. Perin had hit a squirrel, even though he claimed to not be that good with daggers.

They wandered in the forest until Tavarra looked up and stopped—darkness would be falling soon. She turned around and headed back for the night.

"Where are you going?" Perin called.

"To the tree I've been sleeping next to."

With a brief nod and not even a goodbye, he left. She didn't quite know how she felt about that.

Per usual, she placed her manacles around her wrists and waited to give the key to Eza. Moments later, she heard the swoosh of wings and the stomping of feet.

Glancing over her shoulder, she found Perin following behind Eza. "No! Turn around and go back."

The fool didn't listen as he sat down beside her. "I had to grab a few things."

Eza landed on Tavarra's shoulder. "He does have a point. We're close to a village, and you wouldn't want anything to accidentally happen to make our trip to the Stone of Desire go awry."

Her insides filled with frustration, and she wanted to disagree, but she knew her friend was right. Keeping quiet, she handed Eza the key.

"Does it always happen right when the moons rise?" Perin asked.

She and Perin had kept their conversations to a minimum in the forest, but now he seemed in the mood for questions. "No, sometimes it can be moments after they've settled into their nightly home. But never too long after."

The moons had finally taken their place, and Eza was curled up on Perin's shoulder, already asleep. Tavarra rested her head against the tree and stared up at the sky.

There had been times, at first, when she had wished Eza

would leave her alone, go and find someone better to be around—someone who wouldn't destroy her life. It was as if Eza had no life now besides sticking by Tavarra, making sure she was all right. It wasn't fair for her.

"She loves you," Perin said softly, careful not to disturb Eza as he glanced down at the bat.

"Maybe a little too much. It terrifies me at times." She studied the ground. "I'm afraid one day something will happen to her because of me."

He nodded. "Can you tell me how this curse came about?"

The only other person she had talked to about the curse, and exactly what had happened, was Eza. It had been their secret, maybe because no one else had ever wanted to know. No one had been around her long enough to ask.

"I didn't always live on land." She paused and took a breath. "I was born a sea dweller, and had a tail the color of my hair. No scars on my wrists, no fangs, no claws, and no fur. But my heart was never in love with the ocean, and it wanted *desperately* to be part of the land. It was my one true desire, my dream, my fantasy. Even when I was small, I would go to where the water met open land and lie there while the water tickled my tail."

Nezarra had always found her and dragged her back by the tail, telling Tavarra she was scared she had gotten lost. Tavarra couldn't mention her sister, though, so she left anything about her out. Brice was easier to talk about now, because there wasn't real love there—the love she had for her sister was real, only a different form.

"One day when I was almost seventeen, I met a boy a few years older than me. I fell in love with him. Eventually, a water sprite told me that when both moons are at their fullest, a sea dweller can become human for a day. Instead of returning to the sea, I chose to stay, and was struck with this curse."

"What happened with the boy?" Perin shifted and leaned forward. She knew what he thought—that she had killed him.

"I gave him my heart, and he broke it. He had a wife and a babe of his own, and I know I'm not the only heart he broke."

"Do you want me to kill him?" His brow furrowed, his lips pursed—he wasn't jesting.

Tavarra cracked a smile. "I recently had the chance and let him flee."

"Just let me know if you change your mind." Whether unknowingly or not, Perin's hand drifted down to his sword.

She couldn't take the grin off her face. As he studied her, a hint of a smile started to spread, the first she had seen from him.

Then she felt it—the throbbing and all too familiar pain. Her bones cracked and popped.

"Tavarra." Perin spoke her name in a calm tone, moving forward. Eza hopped from his shoulder, wide awake.

"Go!" Tavarra shouted, her voice raspy from the aching and twisting of her joints. Her jaw jutted forward, and she was so hungry. So, so very hungry. As hair sprouted along her flesh, she took a sniff of the air—the scent of fresh meat had her salivating. A loud howl released from her and reverberated through the forest.

Her head snapped to the creature in front of her—she yanked at the chains. He stared at her, unmoving while the winged thing beside him flew up into the trees. She would devour them both and grind their bones into dust, then eat that, too.

Stomach aching, she shook the tree she was chained to, growled, groaned, moaned, and roared. Still, the creature didn't run, as if he *wanted* her to destroy his flesh and insides. She would.

Over and over she pulled at the chains binding her wrists until finally, she could feel something start to give. She didn't hesitate, only kept ripping at the shackles, careful to not let the creature know that, in a moment, she would be free. The havoc would come. Indeed, it would.

Her heart beat for the blood to fill her stomach, and for the sweet taste to consume her mouth. With one hard final tug, she knew the bolt on her left hand would release. And release it did.

The creature already stood with a weapon in his hand, as though he had been prepared.

"Climb up in the tree! Now!" the winged creature yelled. Tavarra would rip the wings from her back and swallow them whole.

She lunged for the creature with the weapon, and he shifted to the side, her claws striking the tree where he once had sat. The sound of the chain still attached to her other wrist clanged behind her as she moved.

"Don't kill her!"

"Stay up there!" the male creature roared to the winged one.

Whirling around, Tavarra barreled forward—the creature didn't move out of the way in time, and she knocked him to the ground.

As she drove her head back and then forward to feed, he clenched his teeth. "I'm sorry."

Something struck her head, as if he had planned it all along.

And she felt herself die.

Nineteen

Tavarra

Opening her eyes to bright light, Tavarra lifted her head.

Yawning, she stretched her legs—the side of her head throbbed as if lightning had struck it.

"Finally awake?" Eza chirped, pumping her wings until she landed on Tavarra's knee.

When she looked down at her clothes, there were more rips and tears—she should have put on her old clothing. Another night of change, but she was still chained to the tree so everything was all right.

"Do you remember last night?" Eza asked as she handed her the key.

Tavarra unlocked the manacles around her wrists. "No? Should I?" There were no dead bodies anywhere near her.

She searched around for Perin, but he was nowhere in sight. *He probably got sickened by me last night and left. I would be, too.*

Folded on the ground beside her was a new set of clothes. "Thanks, Eza."

"You don't have me to thank for that." Eza darted up until she was face to face with Tavarra. "Thank your special gentleman. And you have another thing to thank him for after last night, so you better find a good way to make it up to him. I think it should involve less clothing."

Biting her lip, Tavarra rubbed at the tender spot on her head. "What do you mean thank him? For sitting out here for no reason?"

"Oh no, you, my dear friend, were about to go on a rampage… You broke one of the links on your chains."

In a rush, Tavarra looked down and picked up her chain, dragging it from around the tree. She inspected each and every link. "It's not broken."

"That's because Perin fixed it for you."

"Oh?" *What have I done?*

"After you knocked him down and tried to eat him." She smiled.

Tavarra wasn't smiling, her heart in an uproar, her voice a whisper, "What?"

"Don't worry, we can tease about it now. He's still whole and stayed up all night watching over you." Eza appeared worried as she studied her. "Only, how's your head? I did fear you wouldn't wake, but here you are now, so you're alive." She flew down and wrapped her arms as far as she could around Tavarra's neck.

No words—she had no words that she could form. Her heart had now practically stopped beating while she stared down at her reddened wrists. Tavarra had somehow broken her chains, almost eaten Perin, and he still brought her new clothing?

"How did he knock me out?" From the way other humans and creatures had ended up from her rampage, she didn't see how he could have come out of it unscathed.

"He let you push him down, then used the handle of his sword to do the work." Eza appeared impressed when she nodded.

Perin should have killed her—not taken a risk like that. "But I could have knocked the sword from his hand! I can do that even when I'm not a beast."

"The beast isn't as smart as you—it was too preoccupied with eating his face." Eza slowly shook her head as if she'd been ready for Tavarra to be buried. "For a minute there, I did think one of you would die. My heart stopped pumping."

Tavarra needed an escape, so she picked up her clothing and headed to the lake. Rinsing the dirt from her body, she let her hair float down her back into the water. She had confided in Perin the night before, and what had she done after? Tried to *kill* him. She didn't want to face him again.

After dressing and pulling her hair back, she stayed in the forest and ate. Eza didn't leave, even when Tavarra told her to go visit her new friend, Jonathan. The bat could somehow read how Tavarra felt.

A heavy sound of crunching came from behind her, and Tavarra peered around the tree with her dagger ready. She lowered it when familiar blonde curls and dark hair came into view—Rhona and Quil, covered in dirt, but alive, nonetheless.

"You survived!" Eza cheered.

"Here we are, and we found it." Rhona smiled warmly at them, even though she didn't know them at all. Even though Tavarra had almost killed her brother—*twice*.

"I need to go find Perin." Rhona's words were filled with worry. She and Quil rushed into the village, and Tavarra sat with Eza, feeling like an outsider.

To her surprise, after a little time passed, Rhona eventually came back after Eza finally left. Tavarra straightened her spine awkwardly.

Without a word, she plopped down in front of Tavarra. "Perin seems to be feeling better."

"Oh…" Tavarra wondered what he was doing at that moment.

"I told him I was going to bathe in the lake and that I'd come back in a bit."

Tavarra had waited too long to tell Perin, and she needed to tell this girl about the monster inside her. It would be wrong for her to travel with the group even farther and not say anything. "I should have told you before I left with Perin, but I have a bit of a secret…"

"Go on." Rhona's brows rose up a bit, but her eyes held Tavarra's.

"I was once from the sea, felt like an outsider, and when I decided I wouldn't go back, I inherited a curse." She started. "At night, on occasions, I can become a beast that could rip you apart. There's no controlling it, so I chain myself to a tree."

"And?" Rhona's tone didn't sound scared but interested.

"And that's it. Even now, you must be frightened of me. Perin said the monster is similar to a werewolf, but I've never heard of those until I met him."

Rhona shook her head. "Maybe the day in the forest when you had Perin by the throat, I was a bit frightened then. But now? He's safe, and all thanks to you bringing him here."

Perin must have kept quiet about everything, including her breaking the chain.

"I can change into water," Rhona began. "I can kill living things by taking life away from the inside out, so in reality, we're both monsters. With my ability, I can choose when to use my power—you can't. But don't be afraid, I've made several promises along this journey, and I promise I'll take you with Perin to the Stone of Desire. If the Stone doesn't work, we'll find a way."

"But you don't even know me," Tavarra whispered.

Rhona patted at her chest, then left her hand resting there. "Yet I can tell you have a good heart hidden in here. Whatever may have changed you, you still have pieces of who you were before inside of you. And maybe as we get older, we can't always find them, but they are still there, helping us."

Tavarra wished she could believe Rhona, but she couldn't.

"We'll be leaving in the morning." Rhona stared up ahead toward the village. "There's a gathering in there tonight if you'd like to come."

"If it's at night, I can't."

"Come until the suns set, then." Rhona's tone was persistent.

"I'll think about it." She was already done thinking about it, because the night was her enemy, not her friend.

Unafraid, Rhona grabbed Tavarra's wrist and set her hand on top. "I've never had many friends, and maybe something can come from this."

Putting on a fake smile, Tavarra nodded. She would have liked that, but not while she had the curse. Having to hide every night from her, or for Rhona to stay up to watch over Tavarra wasn't a life for anyone. It wasn't a life for herself, either.

☾

"Please come," Eza chanted beside her. Tavarra's younger self would have been excited about going, would have been the first one to dance and sing, but she couldn't bring herself to do it.

"Go have fun. I'll be fine." Tavarra looked out toward the village, past tree after tree, and could hear the sound of instruments playing. That was good enough for her.

"No, I'll stay here." Eza had come back after Rhona had left, and stayed with her all day. She had told her numerous times to go, but Eza wouldn't listen. Well, she would listen this time.

"If you don't go, I'll never speak to you again."

"Stop with the lies."

"I'm serious. Please go and tell me about how fun it is. You can let me know what I missed out on." For a moment, she imagined what it would be like to dance and listen to the music, and not have to worry about the suns setting.

"*Fine*," Eza drawled, "but only because you pushed me into it. I'll be waiting for you, though."

After Eza flew away, Tavarra pulled her knees to her chest and let out a small sob. She turned to face the tree, away from the world, and let herself cry hot tears of melancholy. Every part of her was tired—so tired of this. All she wanted was to go home, but nowhere was her home.

Footsteps came from a short distance, and she lifted her head from her arm. Perin was striding toward her, his muscles flexing beneath his tight tunic

"Go back to the party." She tried to hold back the tell-tale rasp in her voice, indicating she had been crying. But a loud sniffle came out despite her best efforts.

"It's not my kind of thing." He took a seat beside her, his eyebrows drawing together. "Are you crying? Eza told me you weren't coming, so I said I'd watch over you tonight."

A burden was all she was. "You never came today, and now all of a sudden you want to?" Why should she care if he stayed away?

"I was with my sister most of the day, and then I was hoping you'd come and see me." He leaned his back against the tree. "But *you* never did."

"Did you grow spoiled when I was taking care of you?" The shadow of a smile tugged on her lips as she thought about having to take care of him like a babe the other day.

"Maybe." His tone sounded a bit mischievous.

They stayed in comfortable silence until Tavarra finally spoke. "Eza told me what happened last night. You shouldn't have done that."

"I was protecting—"

"The village, I know," she interrupted. The things she could have done. The monster inside her had the potential to destroy that village, and if people had come out to her, they could have wound up dead.

"No, I was protecting *you*."

Something inside Tavarra froze as she stared at him. "You're lying." She didn't believe her own words as they fell from her lips.

"I'm not him." He picked up a small stick beside him and tossed it in front of them.

"No … you're Perin." From what she knew, he wasn't like Brice. But she hadn't known Perin long enough. She had known Brice for a full year, and all he had hidden was deceit.

"I know there's more to your story." His eyes met hers, waiting.

"I know there's more to yours." She couldn't tell him, so she thought about his back, his chest. "Tell me about your scars."

The suns were starting to set, and she hurried to reach for the chains from her pack. With quick movements, he stopped her from grabbing them. "No."

Tearing away from his grasp, she reached for them again—he pulled them away. "You're not going to do that tonight."

Fists clenched, she could feel her blood pumping with irritation. He wasn't in control of her—she was in control of herself. If she wanted to chain herself to a tree, she damn well would. "I can't risk not doing it."

"I'm fast, and if something starts happening, I'll chain you up." He lifted her chin to stare into her eyes. She couldn't move, her eyes ticking side-to-side from the too-gentle touch. Even on nights when she knew she wouldn't change, she still left herself confined to the tree because it felt better. A punishment she deserved.

"Promise?" she whispered, her breath mingling with his.

"I promise."

She stared at him, reading the truth in his eyes. Then, she nodded and wordlessly pulled back. After a beat, she murmured, "Now, tell me about your scars…"

Tavarra didn't think he would, until he finally did. "Rhona didn't know she was my sister until this journey—I kept it from her in order to protect her. My father would have punished her more if I'd told her because he knows how much I care about her, and it would have given him a sick pleasure to see me punished in that way for disobeying. The scars on my back and chest are from my father, Belen. I got them each time I'd try and protect Rhona, each time he'd given her one. She's able to heal quickly, but I'm not.

"I did go to the Stone of Desire once, as you heard, but it was to help my sister. Free her from my father. Maybe even free myself. But the Stone never answered me, just as it didn't answer my father. That's why my father needs the prisms because after a man named Luca came to our world, the Stone refused to answer human desires anymore. The good thing is, you're not human."

He would do anything to protect his sister, while I killed mine. "My sister's dead because of me," Tavarra confessed, fighting tears, helpless to keep her secret any longer. A huge chunk of herself was relieved to get it off her chest.

Perin's eyes showed a brief moment of shock when they widened, but then his expression softened. It was the second time he'd gone lax around her, and it lessened the panic at his next words. "Go on…"

Tavarra took in a deep breath. "The night I was supposed to go back to the sea, I asked my sister to stay with me for one more night. I wanted more than anything to stay out of the water, but for her, I would return. I just wanted that one extra night… In the morning, I woke up with her next to me—dead. I'd done it, and it could have been prevented if I'd only gone back into the sea. It wasn't even like with Eza where she knows the risk. My sister and I had no idea that this is what the curse would be. I shouldn't have been so selfish…" Tears streamed down her cheeks, but she didn't wipe them. Maybe he wouldn't notice the tears if she left them alone.

There were no words of comfort, but Perin shifted closer, which only made her feel worse for telling him.

"I'm not very good with words ... but whatever happens at night isn't your fault. It isn't like you knew what the curse really was or intentionally did it. So what happens, happens."

Tavarra stared at him and blinked several times. "You're right. You aren't very good with words." He made it seem as if murder was just a shrug of the shoulders.

The darkness was upon them, and she reached for the chains again. Perin grabbed her hand and intertwined her fingers with his callused ones. "Stop."

"Don't tell me what to do!"

Something about his features under the moons' lights made him seem even fiercer. A true warrior. If he had been a dweller under the sea, the others would have flocked for him—humans probably did, too.

"Do you want to go to the village?" he asked.

Tavarra shook her head, her early frustration leaving her.

"Me neither." He anxiously tapped his fingers against the dirt. "I'm not the dancing type, but would you care to dance?"

She had never danced on land, not once. Under the sea was an entirely different story. She'd been to dances since she was a little dweller. Sometimes she and the other sea folk would spin in circles and all hold hands. Other times, she would dance alone with another, sharing stolen kisses with the females and males—sometimes going further. But it was only ever for that night.

The moons were bright crescents above them, and she knew she most likely wouldn't be shifting because of how long the night had gone on already. Tavarra looked at Perin again, whose fingers were twitching as if he was embarrassed for what he'd suggested. Firmly grasping his hand to let him know it was okay, she drew in closer to him.

"I'll dance," she said. They stood, and he placed his hands at her hips while keeping a distance. She put her palms at his shoulders and didn't meet his gaze. "You've told me of your father, but what of your mother?"

"I never met her—she died during childbirth." He shrugged, his expression unreadable. "I don't even know what she looked like except that I have her same eye shape and cheekbones."

"I bet she was lovely." Her own mother and sister both were.

"Why do you say that?"

"Because most females are."

An eyebrow quirked. "There's a ring I carry with me in my pack everywhere I go, and it belonged to her. My father said it was handed down throughout her family. It's the only piece of her I have."

"I wish I still had a piece of my parents and sister." While on land, her sister hadn't brought anything special with her. And there was no way she could ever go back deep enough in the sea to find any trinkets. By now, they were probably all gone anyway.

"You do." Lifting his hand from around her waist, he lightly tapped the side of her head. "In here."

Tavarra smiled and her gaze fell to his lips. It was as though they were aching to be kissed. She wanted to lean in, if only for a moment just to see what it would feel like to press her lips against his. But she didn't have the courage to, because he may not even want to. Another voice inside whispered, *what if he's like Brice?* She pushed that ugly thought away.

"What makes you happy?" If he'd asked her that question in return, she wouldn't know. The one person who did, though, was Eza.

Cocking his head, Perin bit his lip in thought. "There's this hidden meadow that I like to go to, my quiet place. No one goes there, not even Rhona. Maybe after I take you to the Stone of Desire, I could show it to you one day."

"I'd like that," Tavarra whispered, wondering what possibilities would be open to her if the Stone of Desire did help her.

Twenty

Rhona

Rhona leaned against a large tree, mostly hidden from everyone laughing, dancing, and eating. Lana was signing with her partner, a woman named Emma who was a little older than her with an endearing smile every time Lana looked at her.

Perin, who should have been there to keep her occupied, had gone to watch over Tavarra. He didn't do things unless he wanted to, so she smiled to herself at the thought.

When she woke that morning, she and Quil had hurried back. She already missed Quil so much that her heart ached at the thought of parting from him again. But he didn't yet know that she would have to leave him here once more.

After Rhona had found Perin, she felt relieved.

Rhona knocked on the door to Lana's home, and when Quil's cousin opened it, she pulled Rhona in for a hug—then frantically looked around. "Where's Quilan?"

"He went to bathe in the lake."

Lana let out a heavy and relaxed breath that puffed up her cheeks.

"Can I see Perin?"

"He's not here."

"What? Where is he?" For a brief moment, she thought that maybe he had died. Everything inside her at once deflated while her hands shook with fear.

"He's in the field out back, doing something with my old sword." Lana pointed to the right of her house. *"If you go around there and keep walking straight, you'll find him."*

She left the front of the house and looped around to the back, passing a small garden filled with flowers of yellows, pinks, blues, and purples. After passing by several thick tree trunks and a banana tree, the clank of a sword striking something firm echoed.

Perin was facing a tree and using a sword against it.

"You've found me again, sister," he said without turning around.

"So you can call me that now, brother?" she said without sarcasm, actually liking the way it would feel to have him as her family.

He turned around with a small smile—she wasn't used to seeing that expression on his face.

"You're going to break the sword by doing that," she pointed out, stepping closer.

"It's one of Lana's old ones, and she doesn't use it anymore." He struck the tree as hard as he could again.

As she stared at him, her eyes filled with tears—it had hit her that he could have died without her getting to know him as not just a friend, but a brother as well. She ran for him and threw her arms around his neck, sobbing against his chest.

Perin patted her back and gently removed her arms. *"I'm not dead, Rhona."*

"But you could have been, all from acting like an idiot."

"You're the one who wanted to fight me!"

"And you're the one who let me cut you!" she shouted, shaking off the fright that still consumed her. *"Then pretended that you were fine!"*

"You're wearing your hair down again—I assume the

journey went well with Quil."

"Don't change the subject!"

Perin planted the sword into the ground beside him and leaned on it. "I missed you."

"I missed you, too."

"Can you do me a favor?" he asked, not quite meeting her eyes.

"Of course! What is it?"

"Will you check on Tavarra and talk to her a bit for me?"

"You want me to check on her?" Rhona was confused. The last time she had seen her before their brief encounter earlier was when she was strangling Perin. And now he wanted... "Can't you do that?"

"I will tonight if she doesn't come to me."

Tonight? She didn't know if something was going on between Perin and Tavarra, but whatever it was, she felt it was strange.

"Yeah, I'm going to go bathe. How about I come back and we practice for a while after I check on her?"

"Don't think I'll go easy on you." With a small smirk, he lifted the sword from the grass and turned around.

"I wouldn't expect anything else."

"You know... Quil's going to be upset when you leave him behind again."

"I know... He even helped me to get my ability back." And she hated that Perin was always so good at figuring out her plans.

Rhona's head lifted when she felt a tiny thump on her shoulder, pulling her away from her thoughts. She looked over to find Eza, swinging her legs up and down.

"Thank you for helping us," Rhona said.

"You're welcome."

"I promise we'll do the same for Tavarra." Thanks to Eza, she had the prism, and she'd do whatever she could to help the bat's friend.

"I like you already, and you know what? I bet way further down the line, we really are related."

"I bet we are, too." Rhona had only known Eza for brief moments, but she could see the bond between Tavarra and the bat. It was strong and tender—the same way hers and Perin's was. Only she hadn't known he was her brother, but even if he hadn't been, he still had always felt like one.

Eza's gaze followed a boy around Rhona's age, crossing the small field, and stopping to sit on the ground with a basket at his side. He had a head full of dark curls and was slender, the way Quil used to be before he gained the muscles.

Rhona smiled as she looked at Eza. "Go ahead. We'll have plenty of time to talk on the road when we leave in the morning."

"You sure?" She seemed hesitant.

Rhona nodded, and Eza flew off, landing on the boy's shoulder. He gave her a smile and pulled out a plum from his basket, and she dove right in.

Something sweet filled the air, and Rhona's taste buds came alive, wanting to eat whatever was being made. The mingling of different scents, like various meats being cooked over the fire, and the smell of the outdoors gave her a feeling of euphoria. It all felt lovely.

Something tapped Rhona's shoulder, and she whirled around to find no one there. Then another tap, but on her other shoulder, and again no one was there.

Biting her lip, she turned the other way, hurrying to reach out and grab what could be considered an invisible person. Quil's skin color changed from bark and turned back to his normal warm brown shade.

He smiled, almost shyly. "Hi."

"Hi." She grinned back.

From the other side of the tree, Quil bent down and pulled up a basket full of food. "I thought we could go to the river? Unless you want to stay here."

"Won't it be dark down there?"

There were two lanterns beside the tree that he pointed at. "I've got you covered."

Rhona kept the prism close around her neck, beneath the tunic, safely tucked inside a small pouch. She hadn't left it alone—even taking the small prism with her when she bathed in the lake. Afterward, Quil had given her a small pouch that she'd placed the prism inside before finding her brother for the second time. The prism had stayed quiet—if she didn't know better, she would've assumed it wasn't magical at all.

Quil handed her a lantern, and they pushed through the forest, shoving branches out of their way. They each held the lanterns in their opposite hands—it would have been so easy for her to grab his free one if it hadn't been holding onto the basket.

The sound of the river gave her the comfort it always had. This felt like home, her real home, even after these past two years. One day, she would come back, bring her tent, and live out here.

Sitting down on the bed of the river, Quil placed the basket between them. They removed their shoes and stared up at the sky together, watching as the crystalline stars twinkled above.

He handed her a sandwich, and they ate in silence until he finally spoke, "Tomorrow, we'll set out, find your father, help Tavarra, and then what?"

"Then home," she whispered. It was wrong for her not to tell him that he wasn't coming, but she couldn't bring him—couldn't risk his precious life.

"Home..." He bit his lip and looked at her as if he was unsure about what she meant.

She needed to show him.

Rhona angled closer, held out her hand, and pulled him to stand. Before she grew too cautious, she took a deep breath and tugged her tunic from her head, removed her trousers, followed by her underthings. He stared at her for a long moment with his lips parted, finally realizing what she was waiting for—hoping for. Watching her as if she was his world, he repeated her earlier movements, until they were both bare before each other. Holding her hands up, she waited for him to place his palms against hers. He did, trusting her. She spread her fingers apart, then interlaced them together.

"Close your eyes and think of water," she murmured, voice husky, imagining it already.

"I dream of water every night." He closed his eyes, and she watched his serene face for a moment before shutting hers.

Rhona thought about two liquid hearts beating as one, two bodies as close as they could get with nerve endings touching, and no barriers in the way. They both collided to the grass in one splash, each molecule finding its partner.

The one time they had done this when they were younger wasn't the same, their clothes had been on, and it had happened too quickly. This felt different—they caressed, they touched—it was the greatest sensation in the world. Instead of communicating with words, they chose to use tiny blissful movements, and each one she made, she knew he felt, too. She loved him, loved him so much, and she didn't know if he truly felt the same, but even if he didn't, her love burned brighter than all the crystalized stars in the sky, enough for the both of them.

When she brought them back up, she didn't release hold of his hands. "Before I left, before I came back with the note, I had whispered to you that I loved you. I just wanted you to know that."

The world was dark, but his eyes stayed locked on hers under the moons' glow, with the lanterns' light surrounding them. "I've loved you since the first time I kissed you," he said softly. "Why do you think I asked you that stupid question to kiss you?"

The smile on her face grew. Instead of saying anything else, she gently pressed her lips to his, creating their own magical starlight. He wrapped his arms around hers and pulled her close to where her skin was pressed to his.

His warmth heated her up, as if her own liquid inside her body was boiling. With an anxious tug, she dragged him to the ground, his body lingering on top of hers. His tongue swept across her lower lip, and he kissed down her throat until he got to her breast. He placed her nipple between his lips, and she moaned even louder when he pressed his hand against her other one. Then his wicked beautiful kisses traveled lower and lower until his face was at her center in between her scars.

"You're perfect," he murmured, kissing as many scars as he could before pressing his lips to the spot that yearned so desperately for him. The forest became hazy around her as his tongue circled, devoured, making her feel things she'd never felt before. Her back arched as he tasted every inch of her, a storm of emotions crashing through her, then he kissed his way tenderly back up her heated flesh to her lips.

She rolled him to his back and trailed kisses down his chest, his abs, until he was in her mouth. He growled and whispered her name as she stroked his hardness and licked his salty flavor. When they both needed more, she ventured back up to the tender flesh of his throat and stopped right at his ear, her chest heaving. "Don't ever think I don't love you." Then she lowered herself onto him and rolled her hips forward as he gripped tightly on her waist. She had never looked at anyone else, never dreamed of anyone else. It had only ever been him—would always be.

Rhona's pace picked up, both of them growing frantic with desire for one another. More and *more*. An invisible water wave crashed through her, a heightened emotion sending her over the edge—she groaned in pleasure at the same time Quil did. She collapsed on his chest, their bodies slick with sweat, their hearts attempting to catch their breaths too. He folded his arms around her and she grinned as she inhaled his river scent.

After talking and laughing for a while, he fell into a deep

sleep, but she stayed awake to savor the rest of the night. No matter how tired she'd be in the morning. As Quil's breaths came out slow and even, she sat next to the lantern and pulled a paper and quill from her pack.

Quil,
I know you're going to be angry, but I promise I will come back. I'll meet you here, and I'll dance for you every day as you play the pan flute. Please wait for me, and if for some reason I fail, know that I love you, and that's why I couldn't take you with me.
Love Always,
Rhona

She lay back down in his arms, feeling his skin against hers, and smelling the scent that was all him. Before the suns rose, she kissed his chest and whispered *I love you* into his ear. Gently, she covered his lower half with his clothing, and it felt like only a few years earlier. She placed the note under one of the lanterns that had died during the night. Then she pulled out the *Peter Pan* book from her pack and placed it there, too—so he knew she'd come back unless her life had ended.

Rhona hurried back to the village. She knocked on Quil's cousin's door, and Lana shook her head after Rhona explained everything. "Quil isn't going to be happy." But Lana let her in and filled up Rhona's pack.

"Thank you for everything." Rhona wrapped her arms around Lana, hoping to see her again.

"Stay safe and see you soon."

Out of the village, Rhona rushed down the stone path until she came to the spot where Perin and Tavarra stood. Perin looked like a warrior, patiently waiting for her.

Tavarra seemed tired with dark circles under her eyes, and Eza was sleeping on her shoulder.

"We need to hurry." Rhona looked behind her.

"You know he's going to be fucking pissed," Perin said, obviously not feeling sorry in the slightest.

"Better pissed than dead." If she'd brought Quil, he'd be too much of a distraction. And her father could try and use him against her if he got a hold of him. Perin, on the other hand, was Belen's son, and he had never truly hurt him.

Twenty-One

Tavarra

As Tavarra headed through the forest with Perin, Rhona, and Eza, she stayed lingering in the back. The night before came back in a rush—Perin dancing with her, her almost kissing him. Her *wanting* to kiss him.

The farther they went, the greener things became, almost making her squint. Rhona slowed to a measured pace beside her. "Are you all right?"

"No." Tavarra blew out a breath. "I don't think I've been all right in a long time."

Rhona clasped Tavarra's bicep and stopped her. "I've felt that way a lot over the years, but when you find that safe place, you'll know."

Everything was always an uncertainty, and maybe there wasn't a safe place for everyone. "What do you plan for us to do once we get to your village?" Last night Tavarra had decided she'd go with them inside the village, not wait behind. She didn't know Perin's father, but the marks he left behind on his son's back and chest made her want to tear Belen to pieces. And Rhona didn't even know he had suffered along with her.

Rhona let go of her and clutched the pouch at her neck,

glancing up ahead toward Perin. "*We?*" As she looked at Perin, she appeared hesitant. "Belen's expecting us to come back. But with Perin's sword fighting and my water ability, along with the prism, I hope we can do it."

"And my claws?" Tavarra smiled.

"No, you don't have to do anything. You and Eza have helped me well enough, and it'll be my turn to return the favor when we finish." Rhona attempted to change the subject, but Tavarra would still go. "So tell me what it's like to live down in the sea."

Tavarra would play along for now. "It isn't always a dark place of horrendous nightmares as I have thought at times. It's beautiful, and possibly even magical, but it's not like here. Even with the curse I bear, it's not home."

"And the land is?"

"I hope one day it can be." She really and truly thought about this, staring at the small bat perched on Perin's shoulder, and came to a conclusion. "But Eza is my home."

Rhona must have noticed her gaze drift from the bat to Perin—or the back of his head, at least. Her eyebrows shot up. "Do you like him?"

"No." She clenched her teeth but felt her face grow hot. "I need him to help me get to the Stone of Desire, that's all."

"That's all," Rhona echoed with a smile. Her blonde curls were untamed, and she looked freer, more so than the day they had met briefly in the forest. But her eyes were sad, and she knew it was because Rhona had left one person behind.

The four of them didn't stop to eat, only to relieve themselves. They ate jerky and fruit along the way—Tavarra held out a ripe plum that Eza devoured. With such a small mouth, Tavarra was surprised at how quickly the bat could consume such a prize.

The day had been hot and humid, the suns pounding their rays as hard as they could against her skin. "We're going to have to stop," Tavarra called as she peered up at the suns. She needed enough time to find a place to chain herself to.

Perin looked over his shoulder and continued walking. "We're not doing that."

"Not doing what?" She narrowed her eyes.

"You aren't going to be chained to a tree out here." He turned his head back over his shoulder, ending the conversation.

It wasn't over.

"Yes, I am," she argued back, folding her arms over her chest as if she was a babe.

"I told you, I have it handled." With a groan, Perin pivoted around and paced right up in front of her.

"I can throw you with one arm right now if I wanted to." It wouldn't be that difficult, but a part of her liked that he believed she wasn't a monster needing to be chained.

"Rhona has it handled." He inched closer.

Tightening her jaw, she moved to him, too. "I can throw her as well."

"Eza has it handled."

"Don't even." Tavarra pressed a hand at his chest, his warm breath striking her mouth.

"If I have to, I can drain you of a little water to slow you down." Rhona approached them, breaking the tension. "You aren't going to be chained to a tree unless you change." The girl hadn't seen Tavarra's monster, so maybe she wasn't frightened now, but she would be if it showed up.

Surrounding them, the trees looked more like twigs and wouldn't be able to hold her anyway. For now, Tavarra didn't argue.

As they stomped through muddy areas, a light rain started to pour from the sky. Brightly colored hills appeared farther in the distance—they looked to be made from rainbows. The wet sprinkles against her body and face felt good after the heated day. It didn't last as long as she would have liked, though, and the area beneath their feet grew more firm with each step, where rain hadn't touched down in what must have been weeks.

The day sky was starting to fall and would be dark in moments. They had to stop soon, whether the monster would choose to rise or not.

"Should we pause here?" Rhona asked.

Perin surveyed the area, his gaze falling on trees, ones full of fruit—peaches. He narrowed his eyes and continued to scan.

Eza, now on Tavarra's shoulder, perked up. "Peaches!" she cried in a bubbly and excited tone. Smiling at her gleefulness, Tavarra lifted her arm for the little bat to go fly to a luscious piece of fruit. She zoomed through the air, wings batting against the light wind. Tavarra couldn't deny her this moment.

"Stop!" Perin roared. "Don't!"

Tavarra was about to yell at Perin to mind his own business, when something twisted out from a large bush beside the tree. With quick reflexes, a gray hand snatched Eza from the air. Perin shot forward, but not before a tall body rose to great height. Two large horns at the front of a head, and two at the sides. Jovkin. A female one. Golden eyes glowed under the setting suns, and her flat nose took a stealthy inhale as it rapidly brought Eza to its dark lips, ripping her delicate head from her body. Eza didn't even have time to shout for help.

Tavarra's breath stopped, everything that had made her who she was seemed to not exist, and then the moment rushed at her. She screamed, longer and harder than she had the day her sister died. Because she was *seeing* this, the blood from the jovkin's lips.

Perin swung his sword and the jovkin went to ram him, with Eza's body still tightly in her grasp. The dark had almost completely fallen, and she could *feel* it.

"Perin's too close," Rhona shouted, holding her hands up. "I can't use my ability just yet."

"Don't," Tavarra growled at her, throwing down her pack.

"Don't! Get Perin out of here and let me do it."

"I'll rip your horns off and stab you with them, then make you feast and choke on your own blood!" Tavarra yelled to the jovkin.

The creature's head twisted to hers. "Your blood doesn't smell as sweet as a bat's, but I'll have to taste it to find out." The jovkin lunged at her, but Tavarra was able to throw the creature to the side.

Her hunger was growing—she was *starving*. Bones cracked inside her, and she howled with rage. Dead blood enveloped her, yet there were plenty of live things for her to taste. A tall creature with gray skin watched and shoved a tiny lifeless body into her mouth.

Hair sprouted along Tavarra's skin. A male creature jolted toward her with a sword as her jaw jutted forward, teeth growing sharper, longer. She would eat all his organs and cherish them all before sucking the marrow from his bones. A small female creature with hair of gold lunged at the male and knocked him to the ground. They vanished from her sight into liquid, no longer there.

Something shoved Tavarra to the ground. Her head whipped around, her hand closing around the throat of the horned-female creature.

"Your friend tasted delicious." She licked her lips. "I think she may have been the very last bat."

With a powerful flip, the horned-creature rolled to her side, causing Tavarra to loosen the grip on her throat. Tavarra had no friends—only the scarlet color she longed to devour.

Head pointed down, and horns forward, the creature lunged for her. Tavarra dodged out of the way and rushed ahead, leaping onto the creature's back. Despite wanting to sink her teeth right in, she held up a furred hand with claws spread and drove it into the female's back. The creature cried in agony, turning around and throwing Tavarra from her.

The heart she longed to taste wasn't beating in her hand,

yet a clump of skin and muscle fulfilled her for a moment—until she needed more. When Tavarra charged forward, diving her hand into the chest to pull out a beating heart, the creature weakly fell to the ground. Dead and ready for Tavarra to devour. She ate the still-warm organ that had already lost its pulse, but the taste made her own heart beat much, much faster.

Despite wanting to savor the moment, she ripped the beast in half, tossing out organs that weren't to her liking. Then she fed and fed and fed, relishing every moment of it.

Twenty-Two

Rhona

Rhona watched from her water form as Tavarra devoured almost all of the jovkin. She didn't let her just murder it, she let her finish it off as much as she could because Tavarra would have wanted it. Eza was dead because of the jovkin. She ignored Perin's rage and blocked him away.

When Tavarra rose on her haunches, she looked toward the moons and released a ferocious howl, her muscular body arched back. She was part woman, part wolf, like the werewolves in the stories. Thick orange fur, triangular ears coming to a point, long snout, two rows of sharpened teeth, and claws that could end Rhona's life in one swipe. It was a terrifying, yet beautiful sight at the same time. The thought of liquid becoming solid flowed through her veins until she and Perin stood before one another. Rhona pushed him to the side, right as Tavarra's head whipped around to face her.

A low, dangerous growl escaped the werewolf's throat as she stalked toward Rhona. *Liquid draining*, she thought, staring at the werewolf. Tavarra stumbled a bit.

Perin hopped to his feet. "Stop! You're killing her."

Rhona released her ability, and Tavarra swayed a bit before slumping to the ground.

"Hurry!" she demanded, her voice desperate.

Perin found Tavarra's large pack and pulled out the heavy chains. Rhona rushed forward and clasped one of Tavarra's large, furry arms while Perin grabbed the other. They dragged her to the nearest tree. Cuffing a manacle around her wrist, he drew the iron around the trunk to the other side, quickly bounding her other one.

"Don't ever do that to me again," he growled, his voice furious. "I don't want to feel confined."

"Don't ever put your life at risk like that again!" Rhona bit back. She would do it again and again if it would save him.

"I knew what I was doing." He stared at the tree, seeming uncertain that the trunk would hold Tavarra.

No, he didn't. He hadn't grown up around a werewolf, and neither one of them had encountered many jovkins. She thought Perin was being too rash, not using his head, always wanting to save people, when he needed to be looking out for himself.

Sliding down to one knee, he stared at Tavarra. "Is she going to be all right?"

"I don't know… I've never done it on a person before … only animals."

"My father…"

"*Our* father…" Rhona pressed her hand to his and clasped it tightly.

Neither one of them wanted to speak any more about Belen. She released him and sat against the tree beside Tavarra's. Perin took a seat next to her, dragging a hand through his hair. "I-I told Eza to stop."

"I know." The storm inside her had settled, and now she was left with thoughts of Eza.

"No, you don't know!" he shouted. And she knew for sure that Tavarra would stir, but she stayed asleep, her breaths slow and even. "Something felt out of place, but I couldn't put my finger on it, until it was too late."

"I know you had started to like her over the past few days." In just the short time Rhona had been around Eza, she had, too. But she didn't feel what Perin might have, nowhere near what Tavarra was going to. Tavarra had said Eza was her *home*.

Perin stayed silent, looking off somewhere in the distance.

"You're going to have to be there for her for a little while." She sighed.

"I know."

Rhona knew they couldn't sit around and mourn—she had to focus on Belen. This … this was all Belen's fault, the reason they'd been out there in the first place. She hated even thinking about him.

"You've done brilliantly with the plants and the trees, but this time we need to try something else." Belen held up a small kitten in his hand—her kitten, Peter. His long, curly ponytail swayed down his back as he approached her.

"No." Rhona shook her head—she wouldn't do it.

"No?" He ran a hand across his chin. "I can hurt your mother and Perin." His hand wrapped around the cat's throat. "Or even your dear Peter."

"I could kill you in a second." She threatened for the first time in her life.

"If I'm dead, don't you think I have someone who will kill your mother or Perin?"

"He's your son."

"He's a necessity until I say he isn't. But do try your best."

She conjured up an image of Perin's and her mother's throats being slit. He was lying about hurting Perin and she knew it, but he would hurt her mother and others. Holding up a hand, she focused on draining him from the inside out after he set the cat down. To her astonishment, Belen didn't wither as she'd hoped. Thankfully, he hadn't noticed she'd tried to use her ability on him.

Belen placed Peter on the wooden chair before her. One of the neighbor's cats had kittens a few months ago, and Rhona had instantly taken a liking to the feline. She turned her attention on Peter—she'd never stopped at the halfway point when she performed her ability, but she knew she could do it. The kitten let out a low purr, but she ignored it, focusing. She pulled the water out, and the fur became damp. Then she released the liquid, but it was too late, the kitten was already slumped over in the chair.

"That didn't go as planned." Belen shrugged a shoulder. "We'll have to try again tomorrow."

Each day there was a new animal, sometimes little mice, other times birds. Eventually, she was able to do it. After Peter, she never kept anything for a pet again. And she'd always been frightened that Belen would make her practice on a human. But he hadn't. After they moved, he had left her alone—until the day she was knocked out for the second time.

☾

The next morning, Rhona woke up, catching a glimpse of Perin moving what was left of the jovkin. Tavarra lay beside her, orange hair covering part of her face, still asleep.

After he hid the remains behind several large flowering bushes with thorns, he came back to grab two of the canteens and fill them up at the river. A few moments after he left, Tavarra stirred from her slumber. Her eyes caught Rhona's and she quickly sat up, noticed the chains, then stared up into the trees.

"Eza," she whispered. "Eza!"

Heart plummeting, Rhona shook her head. Pressing her hands to her face, Tavarra let out a wounded sob. Inching forward, Rhona removed the chains from her wrists.

Quickly, Tavarra sat up, her spine becoming straight. "Where's Perin?"

"He's fine." Rhona handed Tavarra her canteen. "Drink

this. He went to fill up some more because I had to use my ability on you, so you're going to have to drink plenty."

"What?" Where is the jovkin?" she growled, pushing the water away, more furious than Rhona had seen, more so than the werewolf.

"After you… Well… You took care of things, and I let you." Rhona couldn't keep her eyes on Tavarra's. She drew her attention anywhere else, her fangs, her nose, her forehead.

Tavarra hastily stood up and marched forward, her expression fierce. "I need to see it."

"No, you don't." Rhona pursed her lips.

"Show it to me!" Tavarra seethed, exposing her fangs. Perin had wasted time trying to hide the body. She should have known Tavarra would want to see it.

Releasing a huff of air, Rhona gave in. "All right, but it won't help anything."

"I don't care!"

Rhona nodded and led her past several trees until they stumbled upon the mutilated jovkin, partly hidden by several thorny bushes.

Before Rhona could stop her, Tavarra rushed forward and pushed her hands into the already torn-apart jovkin's stomach. Rhona reached to grab Tavarra's arm, but she yanked it out of her grasp. Blood had gathered on Tavarra's hands and arms, and Rhona let her continue to do what she thought Tavarra needed. Tavarra was angry, so angry, and she let out a loud roar that didn't sound the least bit human. More low growls came until she finally stopped sifting through the carcass and dropped to her knees. "Eza is…"

Rhona didn't know the right thing to say. There wasn't a good word for gone, dead, eaten, never coming back. "It's my fault for bringing you here."

"It's not your fault." Tavarra pulled at her long orange locks with bloody hands, while wet tears slid down her cheeks. "I should have made Eza stay back at the village with your friend.

She would have still been alive. I should have demanded her to stay!"

"She wouldn't have listened to you." The bat had seemed stubborn, wanting to protect Tavarra as best she could.

"I don't want to go to the Stone of Desire anymore." Tavarra pulled her knees to her chest and cried harder. Rhona hadn't imagined that Tavarra could ever seem so human, but at that moment, she looked so very fragile. "Just go. Leave me here to rot. Everything I touch turns to shit. *Every single thing*."

Rhona had awful experiences, but she had never lost someone to death—she'd barely talked to anyone. She'd thought she had a father who'd died, but that was never the case. In her village, she kept her distance from almost everyone. Grief was not her specialty. So she said the only thing she could, wrapping a hand around Tavarra's shoulder. "For Eza, you're going to go to the Stone of Desire—she would have wanted it."

Twenty-Three

Tavarra

Tavarra went to the lake with Rhona and quickly rinsed the blood from under her claws and the rest of her, scrubbing away every part of her she could. She wished she could have cleaned away until there was nothing left—not even a memory of herself.

Perin had handed her a spare set of clothes from his pack. Not only did everything die around her, but even her clothing did—every time. Her boots were ruined and ripped—she couldn't bring herself to care. Perin didn't question her about sifting through the dead jovkin's remains. If he did, she would have yelled at him. She had done it because of the *Little Red Riding Hood* story he had told her. She believed that maybe Eza could have still been alive in the creature's stomach, but she wasn't. The happy ending didn't exist, and Perin shouldn't have made her believe that there could be one.

She had pushed through their journey, up the colorful hills that gave her no cheer, down through ravines that only made her heart hurt. Perin and Rhona kept forcing her to drink, and she did, only to keep them off her back.

Eza, Eza, *Eza*. It didn't feel real—perhaps it couldn't be. Perhaps when she got back to Perin, Eza would be curled up on his shoulder, but her friend wasn't.

Perin's eyes met hers. "Are you—"

"I'm fine!" she snapped.

"We're going to come back for you after finishing at my village." His words left no room for argument.

"No! I'm going to help you, and then we'll traipse along to the Stone of Desire and have the world be covered in rainbows," she ground out. The anger helped to hide the pain, and she'd rather hold onto that.

"I get it, you—"

"No, you *don't,* Perin!" she interrupted. "I murdered my sister, and now I practically killed Eza. If she had never met me, she—"

"She might still be dead," he interrupted, making her stiffen until she grew livid. "Did you ever think about that? Did you ever think that maybe she wouldn't have lived quite this long without you around to protect her?"

His words, they ripped and tore at her tarnished insides. "But she's… She's…"

Awkwardly, he wrapped his arms around her as she sobbed into his shoulder, unable to hold onto that anger.

She had been with Eza every single day for seven years, spent more time with her than she had her own sister. Eza *was* her sister, and she didn't know how she would be able to survive this world without her. She wanted the anger to come roaring back again, but it just wouldn't because her heart felt as if it had been struck with blades. She couldn't help but hate herself for what had happened.

Light footsteps came from her left, and she glanced up at Rhona who avoided looking directly at them. Her eyes were the same unique blue shade as Perin's. How could Rhona not have known they were siblings? They may have different mothers, but they had the same features, only Perin's were sharper, jaw harder, and lips fuller.

He released her and they continued on like they needed to.

Tavarra did everything she could to avoid thinking of her friend, who she had been so close with.

There were no more jovkins, or any other dangerous creatures, that they encountered as they moved forward through a sea of vines. They walked over large grassy knolls and entered another part of a forest with weeping willows spread all around. The trees were lovely, cloaked in their own green clothing, and the beauty made her feel like a shriveled-up plum.

"We should stop here for the night," Rhona grunted. "We'll make it to the village in no time from here."

Tavarra reached for one of the straps of her pack.

"No," Perin said, shaking his head.

"I'm starting to get tired of that word from *your* mouth." But she left the pack on her back.

"I'm getting tired of *you* not believing in me."

Did he believe in her? Something told her that he did—otherwise, he would have demanded she be chained to the tree.

"So"—Rhona toed the dirt with her boot—"I'm going to keep watch a bit farther out in case I hear anything strange out here."

Perin crinkled his nose and lowered his eyebrows in confusion but nodded.

Together, Tavarra and Perin built a fire and gathered extra tree limbs to place in it. The night pulled down its blanket on top of them and Tavarra tried not to think of Eza.

There was still time for her to change into the monster, and she wanted more than anything on this night to become it. She didn't want to think, didn't want to feel, didn't want to be her—only wanted to forget. Tears streamed down her face and she wiped them away, careful to not make a sound.

Perin caught her weakening emotions anyway. "How about you talk about one of the happiest memories you have of Eza?"

Those thoughts should have made her even more upset, but she closed her eyes to think. "Oh, there are quite a few of those. I hadn't thought about them being happy until right this moment." She paused, letting the moment building up inside her come to life. "After Eza helped me bury my sister, and her following me around for days, she would leave small things in my palm for when I woke up. Sometimes leaves, pebbles, or small trinkets she took from humans. Most of the time, I was annoyed because I didn't want to be in this body, but then the gifts started to make me smile each morning. Not because of the things she brought, but because Eza had done it with care.

"She once took me to this secret cavern that has various-colored dragons—some as yellow as the suns at their brightest, or orange, the color of when they set, or even a blue that's almost the color of your and Rhona's eyes. The dragons were so small—they could fit in my hand. Eza kept trying to fly and ride one, but none of them were having it. She tried to chase them down, and when one shimmering yellow dragon landed in the palm of my hand, she threw a little hissy fit." A tiny laugh escaped her throat as more tears came, and she wiped them away. "I knelt in front of her, and the dragon stayed to let Eza pet its head, but still wouldn't let her ride it. She waved her fist in the air when the dragon flew off."

"I'd like to see that place one day." He stared at the ground, something like sadness crossing his face.

"If you really want to see it, I'll take you." She shrugged.

His eyes slid to hers. "Maybe."

Something in her chest fluttered, and she changed the subject when her thoughts turned to Eza. She needed a distraction before she fell apart again. "What other stories do you have besides *Little Red Riding Hood*?"

"*Peter Pan*."

"Tell it to me." Tavarra wanted to take her mind somewhere else.

He breathed out a deep sigh. "I've never been a storyteller, but here it goes. It's Rhona's favorite. In it, there's a boy who could fly and never grew old when he lived in this secret world known as Neverland. One time, he came to his old world and found a girl named Wendy who intrigued him very much. With him, he brought his best friend, a little fairy named Tink. She wasn't like the fairies here, though, she was feisty and always hung around him, flapping her wings and—"

Tavarra let out a rack of sobs. She couldn't control herself—the damn fairy already reminded her of Eza.

"Oh fuck!" Perin's eyes widened. "I didn't mean… I told you I'm not good with words. I didn't think."

"No, it's okay," she cried again.

Although Tavarra had hated her life at times, she never truly felt weak over the last seven years. But she wanted to stay brave for Eza—or at least try. "Please go on."

As he scratched the back of his neck, he seemed hesitant. Yet he finished the story about how the boy took Wendy and her two brothers to Neverland for an adventure.

"I'm sorry I tried to strangle you the first time I met you," she rushed the words out as soon as he finished the story. It was an apology long overdue. For a moment, she thought if she hadn't met him that Eza would probably still be alive, but she knew it wasn't fair to think that. She didn't really know anything. A large chunk of her thought if she hadn't met Eza, then maybe Perin was right, that the bat wouldn't have lasted long.

"Your grip was quite fierce." His voice sounded almost teasing as he rubbed at his throat.

"What other stories do you have?"

"Only ones that are too dark and may give you nightmares." He frowned, sinking back into how he had looked when she first met him.

She studied him then and wondered if he truly smiled, not the small glimpses she had seen. She didn't even know if he ever threw his head back and really laughed—not really—but she hadn't in a long time either.

Closing her eyes, Tavarra leaned forward, finding the

young dweller that was still hidden in her depths, and placed her lips lightly to his.

"What was that for?" he whispered, pulling back with his eyebrows arched up in surprise.

"Thank you." She brought her hand to the back of his neck and pressed her forehead against his.

"For?"

"Trying to save her." Tavarra hadn't scanned the area well—she hadn't noticed anything. Even though Perin was too late, he'd still called for Eza to come back.

"Thank you," he finally said.

"For?"

He ran the tip of his tongue against his lower lip. "I haven't…"

She stared at him.

"I don't get close to that many people, as you may guess." *He hasn't kissed anyone before? Is that what he was trying to say?*

If that were so, he needed something a bit better. Slowly, she leaned in again and pressed her lips to his. His soft mouth moved against hers, kissing her back. The caressing of their lips was gentle and delicate for long moments before she came back for air. It had been a long time since she had been with a human man, the only one besides dwellers—Brice. But it didn't bother her anymore to think about him. A massive part of her wanted to take Perin right there and now, let her hand drift into his pants to feel him, but this was the first time he'd even kissed anyone. She knew she had to slow things down. Not selfishly do things for her own needs. Besides, Rhona was somewhere out in the forest. Hopefully asleep.

A small smile tugged at his lips, not a full one, but it was something. She smiled back at him, not quite a real one either, but pretty close. He leaned back against the tree while she rested her head in his lap. Tears fell down her cheeks as Eza slipped back into her thoughts, until she finally drifted to sleep.

In the morning, Tavarra woke and found Perin gone. However, something lay nestled in her palm. A trinket. A ring with a blue sapphire in the middle—his mother's ring. Her heart beat quickened as a few tears gathered in her eyes—he had done this because she had told him of the gifts Eza had given her. This one was special to him, though. Why would he give her something so important?

With her chest feeling full of *something*, she tucked the ring away into her pack. He was *nothing* like the other humans.

Across from her, on the other side of the willow tree, Perin was talking to Rhona. His sister shook her head at him and looked back at Tavarra. Rhona's face turned into a smile, but not quickly enough to disguise the intense expression. "Good morning."

"Are you ready?" Tavarra asked.

"Of course." Rhona didn't meet her gaze.

The three of them gathered their things and ate fruit as they started walking. Tavarra approached Perin. "What was that about? With you and your sister?"

"Nothing." He shook his head with a frown. "Sometimes she doesn't want to listen, even though she knows I'm right."

"Sort of like when you thought you were right about leaving me unchained from the tree?"

"Precisely." Perin brushed her hair over her shoulder, his hand hurriedly falling back to his side. She smiled to herself because he could murder so easily, but a simple human touch seemed to have him in a panic. Perhaps she could help him through that. Eventually.

It didn't take them long to get to the village, and there it sat in the distance. Across the expansion of the area, large tents were set up in no particular order, except for one shelter built from logs.

"When we first moved here, that cabin was already standing," Perin said. "It's my father's."

"I'm ready." Tavarra moved her hands to the daggers at her hips. She would have Eza's strength with her.

Perin turned to his sister. "Do it now."

"Do what?" Tavarra asked in confusion, staring between Perin and the shelter.

"I'm sorry," he whispered, catching and locking onto her gaze.

Tavarra's insides tightened as if they were being squeezed and drained. She looked at Rhona, who pursed her lips while holding her hands up.

Tavarra dropped to the ground, and everything faded away.

Twenty-Four

Rhona

Perin caught Tavarra before she hit the grass. Rhona shook her head and watched as he gently laid her down. "She's not going to be a happy werewolf."

"It was necessary, just as it was with Quilan." Perin strode toward her, hand at his hip. "She'd only get in the way. Maybe if Belen didn't have the prism, but you and I *know* him."

That, they did. Rhona wasn't sure what Perin felt for Tavarra, but they'd started to build a friendship from the look of things. And because he was her friend—her brother—she didn't want him to lose anyone or get hurt, so she had agreed to do what Perin asked of her. "Let's go."

"Wait, one last thing." Perin stopped in front of her. "You're going to be angry."

"Spill it…" Nothing could be worse than Belen being her father. After that, she now thought she was immune to most things.

"I'm supposed to spill your blood and let you die so your power can be absorbed into Belen."

"*What?*"

"It was the only way I could get him to trust me to let us get the prism—for *you* to get it."

"I asked *you* if there was anything else you needed to tell me, and you'd said no." Rhona held up a hand because they couldn't waste any more time. Now that she was approaching the village, she worried about her mother, about finding her. "We'll talk about this later." Rhona couldn't even let herself be furious about it, but maybe once they were finished that would change. Her being immune to things would have to continue until after that discussion. "Come on."

She led the way through a lush field when they approached the village. The almost-silent landscape provided an eerie feel, raising goosebumps on Rhona's back and arms. Only the chirps of bugs could be heard here and there.

Rhona assumed the entire village must still be in a slumber, with Belen absorbing their lifeforce. Now she knew Belen wanted her dead, and that really wasn't a surprise. *I shouldn't have been expecting anything different. I'll just have to see if my mother's still alive,* she thought.

As they passed the tents that seemed to interweave with one another, Rhona peered inside hers to see if her mother was there—just as a precaution—but she wasn't. Belen wouldn't have given her a gift like that, anyway.

Perin clasped her arm and stopped for a moment. "I just want you to know you were my sister before I even knew you really were. I love you." He handed her a folded paper from inside his pocket that she read over quickly. "I wrote down the directions on how to get to the Stone of Desire. So we both know now."

She put the note away and placed her hands on his shoulders, gripping firmly. "You're not dying here, Perin. And I love you, too. Now, come on."

Taking the prism from the pouch around her neck, Rhona stuck it into her pocket. In its place, she pulled out a rock she had found in the forest the night before and tucked it into the small sack at her throat. She then pulled it over her head and handed it to Perin to fool their father. It wouldn't distract Belen for long, but it was the best she'd come up with.

When they came to Belen's porch, there was no use knocking on the door—he probably already knew they were there. *But what if he isn't in the village anymore?*

Perin reached for the knob and opened the door. Fur rugs lined the floor, and paintings decorated the walls. The sofa was missing any sign of life.

They walked through the rest of the house and checked all four rooms, but there wasn't anyone, only Belen's lingering earthy scent.

"Where do you think he is?" she asked.

Perin looked back at the front door. "Let's check the sword field."

They crept their way toward the practice area, careful to not make too much of a sound. Each and every day while they lived here, Rhona would practice swords with Perin. After this, she hoped they'd have the chance to continue and for her to finally beat him—just once. Withdrawing the sword from her sheath, she craned her neck forward at the sound of clanking metal. Perin's shoulders seemed to broaden as if he was ready to go right in and end this.

The clicking of swords clashing together echoed.

Up ahead, Belen didn't try to conceal himself, didn't try to hide. But why would he? He had the ivory prism—his two children had arrived. However, he wasn't alone—he caught Rhona's gaze and gave a wolfish grin. He lowered his sword from the person in front of him. It was Thea.

"Mother!" Rhona called, about to run forward. Her mother looked like herself, long blonde hair, no withered skin. Yet, Thea's eyes were glassy, and she didn't approach them or say a single word.

Perin placed a hand on her shoulder, stopping her, and shook his head. She trusted Perin, of course she did. With everything in her, she wanted to still go to her mother, but she met Belen's stare. Stealing her spine, she prepared herself.

"Father!"

"So my precious clover now knows the truth." Belen's smile only grew wider. "My son, the liar."

"No, you're the liar!"

"How could I be a liar if you never asked, my dear?" He produced the small white object from a hidden pocket—the prism. The suns' rays and color of the sky made it seem as though the prism was glowing. His gaze fell to Perin. "The time has come, my son."

In a single instant, Perin had a sword at Rhona's throat. The cool metal pressed in so tight that she wasn't sure if it was real or not anymore. But she trusted her brother—he'd never once asked her if he could hold the actual prism. He pulled the fake one from around his throat and tossed it to his father's feet.

"Now!" Belen shouted as he scooped up the pouch.

"Now, Rhona," Perin whispered, releasing her.

All that was around them were the field, trees, and tents—but she had her hands. Bringing her palms up toward Belen, she thought of draining him, freezing him, boiling him. But nothing worked, just as it *always* hadn't. She shifted her gaze to her mother who stood next to Belen, staring at her, dazed.

"Remember you don't have your ability," Belen said with his lips pulled into a sneer. But she *did* have her ability—she felt the liquid swirling inside of her, as if creating a tornado made entirely of water. Belen's gaze then fell to Perin. "I knew you would end up a traitor."

"Baby!" Thea ran for Rhona and Belen held up the ivory prism. With a flick of the wrist, Belen made her mother tumble to the ground. Thea grabbed at her throat as if she was being choked by an invisible leash. Her mother had to be under some strange control because of Belen.

"Don't be fooled," Perin whispered.

"Come to me, or your mother dies," Belen ground out, then his gaze fell on his son. "Last chance, Perin, tie her up."

"*No.*"

Quickly, Rhona fished out the dark prism from her pocket. It halted Belen, but only for a moment, when he realized she had the real one. She fisted it in her palm, and the object warmed—her ability growing stronger. It was as though it was waking to her when she needed it, the dark stallion inside answering.

A black plume of smoke wrapped its way around her and Perin. Belen brought up the ivory prism, and something inside her felt as if it was expanding.

Perin refused to stay safe, though, and lunged forward to protect her from Belen. Her father's focus turned to Perin, and her brother fell to his knees, letting out a groan. The world stopped for a moment—Rhona's hair rose around her, a static electricity forming and surrounding them. Everything got brighter and brighter, almost to the point where she believed that this could be what the inside of a star looked like.

Rhona raised the dark prism higher. The alabaster around them decreased as a night sky from her prism shot out and cloaked only the two of them—a white twinkling came from Belen's hand, lighting him up. That was all Rhona could see. She couldn't see her mother—she couldn't see Perin. Her heart thudded wildly in her chest.

"I've been searching for that one long enough, and my dear child has so graciously brought it to me. Your ability will now connect between the two. I created you to absorb your power when you reached full development. From the moment you were conceived, I knew the time would come that one day I'd consume your power. That day has come."

His words sickened her—they always did.

White can light up dark, and dark can conceal white, so how can one ever overpower the other? If her ability was so strong, then maybe her prism could work harder. She could do it.

Rhona focused on Belen—she tried again to take everything from inside him and drag it out. Her hands shook, and her entire body became drenched with sweat, as if she was pulling the liquid out of herself. Maybe she was? It was possible the ivory prism was reflecting her power. If she worked too hard, she might pass out, and Belen would end up with the dark object.

Quil. He wasn't there—she might never see him again. A realization hit her that she had done the stupidest thing by not bringing him—he could have cloaked and hid them both before she made a move. She was angry with herself—pissed for not trusting that he could help and not hinder her.

The one thing she knew that none of the villagers could do was be able to change into water. Rhona thought of Quil as though he was concealing her, darkening instead of clearing, as she drifted down with the prism in her hand. She blended in, becoming a chameleon, the color of her water staying a part of the darkness. The entire atmosphere was shrouded in a murky color, making everything appear the same except for that one person lit up like the brightest of starlight. He was stupid enough to hold onto the ivory prism that illuminated him.

Rhona didn't know if she could move close enough to him, but she had the prism this time, and it was worth a shot. She wouldn't be afraid anymore. She shifted toward Belen, the liquid staying silent. He backed up, trying to shine the light like a lantern.

He searched in front of himself while she crawled with liquid hands toward his back, forming to her natural shape and staying cloaked in darkness. While holding the dark object, she hoped it would counteract the protection Belen had from his, and not fling her backward. She grasped the prism in his hand—a bout of white electrical sparks contacted her palm, but she didn't yield as she ripped it away. With one prism in each hand, she held them out in front of her. Lightning from the alabaster prism connected to the black one and created a heady rumble of thunder.

With the power she felt radiating inside of her, she tried again to boil the water within him. Any way she chose for Belen to go would be painful, but this way would be the most. He let out a loud scream that echoed in the darkness, then he slouched to the ground, writhing in pain. Pus-filled welts formed across his skin, veins and eyes bulging, until no sound escaped his lips.

Rhona carefully lowered the prisms and let the pull of color slide around her once more. The darkness and light—gone. The village came back into view, along with her mother and Perin.

When she looked into the distance, Tavarra was there, already awake and running for them.

Rhona's shoulders relaxed, and her voice sounded small when she looked at her mother. "Mama."

Thea stood from the ground and stared at Belen, then moved toward her, no smile on her face. Just as she noticed a hidden object in her mother's hand, Perin shoved Rhona to the side. The hit made her arm ache, and when she glanced up, Thea's fist rammed into Perin's stomach.

It wasn't only a hand when her mother pulled back—a knife was tucked inside. Perin hunched over with a pool of blood blossoming at his stomach.

"No!" Rhona screamed.

"You did this. You killed Belen, and you need to die!" Thea shouted, eyes still glazed, glancing toward Belen's body before she moved toward Rhona. Thea held up a shaking hand with the still-bloody knife. If she had to, Rhona knew she would kill her own mother. Tavarra got to the woman before Rhona could do anything, and snapped her neck.

Rhona's lungs barely pumped—she didn't know what the hell was going on. Her mother… She… She didn't know if Thea was under a trance, or if she had been on Belen's side the entire time, or both.

When she turned to face Perin, he was slumped to his knees.

She hurried to his side, Tavarra already there, lowering him onto his back. Tavarra pressed her hands to his stomach. "You're okay."

Rhona stared down at the wound, the location, the amount of blood. It wasn't one that could be mended. The hottest of tears slid down her cheeks. What she needed was a clover—she needed the four-leaf clover that *she'd* eaten.

"A clover," she shouted. "We need a clover." Frantically she looked around, trying to find a patch. They were all over the field. So many that there had to be one. She crawled near Perin's head and ripped up a handful and shakily searched through them. Three. Three. Three—

Perin grabbed her wrist. "I-I suspected something was going on with her when she was outside. I didn't know."

"It's okay." It wasn't.

"But look at you, you finally won." He coughed. "You don't need me to look out for you, Rhona. Never did." She wanted to shake him for those words, because he could beat her for the rest of his life if that meant him living.

"Just hold on, *please*! I'm going to find a clover." She started sifting through them again.

Perin's head angled to Tavarra, who had her hands firmly pressed against the wound, still trying to staunch the blood. "The night in the forest when we danced under the moonlight, I should have kissed you then, too. A thousand times and more."

Tavarra pressed two fingers to his lips to keep him from talking.

"Do what I told you… You know how to get there," he said to Rhona. Then he stopped breathing, his eyes empty, lips parted. The clovers fell from her fingertips, and she sobbed harder, her head falling to his warm chest as she wrapped her arms around him, begging him not to leave her. He was all right—he'd always be all right.

"Why did you knock me out?" Tavarra growled, anger

laced in her tone. "*Why?*"

"He didn't want anything to happen to you," Rhona cried softly.

"But now something's happened to him because of it!" she snapped. "What did he tell you to *do*?"

"Make sure I protect you when I take you to the Stone of Desire, in case he wasn't able to." The note was tucked away in her pack, and she'd thought he'd be fine. But he wasn't fine, he was gone. *Gone.*

Perin had been worried about Quil being Rhona's distraction, but she had always been Perin's. A fierce and protective brother. Her thoughts repeated in her head—if she'd only looked for more clovers that day with Quil, if she hadn't eaten one… But if she hadn't eaten it, she might not have defeated Belen. *At least then, Perin would have been alive.*

Twenty-Five

Tavarra

Tavarra refused to leave Perin's body behind. She planned to take him to the Stone of Desire, like she had wanted to with her sister. Nezarra had been dead and shredded. A measly wound was all that had punctured Perin, and she knew it would work. Rhona wasn't quick enough with finding a clover, and the prisms weren't meant for saving a life.

"We can try taking him to the Stone of Desire," Tavarra said, not removing her hand from Perin's stomach.

Rhona clasped Tavarra's wrists. "It's too late. The journey's too far—we wouldn't make it with him. With Luca, all that time ago, it only worked because they made it there almost immediately."

Her hopes melted away in her chest. Like Rhona's mother and Perin, no one in the village woke up.

Rhona took Tavarra to the clover-filled meadow where Perin used to go, the one he had wanted to take Tavarra to. The one he never would, except for this final time where he was dead and she had carried his body there. It had been another person for her to lay to rest, and Rhona helped her dig the hole, then they sprinkled as many clovers as they could with his body in hopes that, wherever he was, he'd have plenty of wishes. She had buried her sister, couldn't bury Eza because there had been nothing of her left, and now Perin. It was… There were not deep enough words to describe how she felt.

Before they left, Tavarra placed Perin's ring on a leather string—a piece of him would be with her on this journey. Beside Perin's gift, she strung a shell she had kept in her pack from Eza and tied the leather around her neck. She only wished she had something from Nezarra.

As she stayed on Rhona's heels, who frequently doublechecked her directions to make sure they were right, Tavarra ignored the battle inside her chest that raged to come out for all those who had died around her. Her parents, her sister, Eza, and Perin.

She was angry at first with Rhona for doing what she did by knocking her out. A part of her always would be, because she could have helped them, could have kept Perin from dying.

"You can go back and find Quil—I can do this on my own," Tavarra said weakly as they trudged through a thorn-covered trail. She had lied—she didn't think she could last more than a few moments by herself.

"We're going together." And that was it, Rhona was determined and done with talking. There was a bit of Perin inside her with that stubbornness.

Tavarra didn't want to get close to anyone ever again. She didn't know if she should just give up and not bother continuing on the track to a stone that may not even be there.

Together, they walked down narrow paths and passed through a shallow swamp. When they stumbled upon a steep muddy slope, Tavarra clung onto her middle.

"I just can't…" She collapsed in front of a large mahogany boulder, wrapping her arms tighter around herself. Dried mud continued to cling from her waist down after crossing through the swamp. She hated thinking it, but she wished she had drowned in that shallow pit—she wanted the suffering to come to an end.

Rhona plopped down beside her and lifted Tavarra's chin in her hands. "It shouldn't be long now. If we have to walk to the ends of Laith to find it, we'll do it. I'm not going to let my brother's last wish be in vain."

Taking a deep breath and shutting her eyes for a moment, letting Rhona's words sink in, Tavarra rose to her feet to continue. "Every time he defended you and tried to prevent his father from hurting you, he got hurt, you know that? His chest and back are covered in scars because of what his father did to him. When he came upon the Stone of Desire, he even begged it to help you. He probably wanted me to keep that a secret, but I wanted you to know in case you are ever angry with him."

Rhona's eyes widened. "What do you mean?"

"He wouldn't have wanted you to have seen how affected he was, too, but he loved you."

Tears started to well up against Rhona's lashes. "Let's keep going."

The leaves of the bright trees started to change in colors to pink, orange, and black. At that point, her energy had drained, yet somehow she pushed herself to run as fast as she could in the eastern direction. She searched for an alabaster stone with a rose-shaped top. Nothing. With all her heart, she wished Eza was there to guide her.

While she and Rhona ran, the world became a dizzying storm. After running for what felt like seasons, she slowed down, searching in all directions.

Perhaps this place never existed, after all. Perhaps the humans had really always been in Laith. She pushed those thoughts away because Perin hadn't hallucinated about seeing the Stone.

They continued wandering in the route that Perin's letter read, where he had once gone to get the Stone to help Rhona, but had never gotten an answer from it. While she wished for a small glimmer of hope buried in her chest to rise, she started to not believe in it. What if it didn't answer her, either? But then the light of the twin suns released their rays on a large, pale stone. Her breath caught in her throat.

"Do you see it?" Rhona's jaw fell.

Tavarra blinked, praying that it was true as wet streaks streamed down her cheeks. "I see it." Almost not believing her eyes, she slowly approached the Stone, as if it would run away from her before she could press her hand atop it.

Even then, when her hand touched the grainy surface, she still felt like it might disappear. Her hand trembled, and she tried to calm herself by inhaling deeply.

"May I ask you a question?" Tavarra's voice came out in a hoarse whisper. For once in her life, she wanted something good to happen—not only for herself, but also for Eza because they had searched together for the Stone for so long. Her shoulders slumped when no reply came. What did she think anyway? That a stone could really speak to her?

She held her hand firmly against the rock and demanded this time, "Will you talk to me? I've come so far, and waited so long to see if you could help me."

Moments later, when Tavarra had given up hope, given up on everything, a quake beneath her hand shook the ground. She took three steps back and then another one for good measure as she stared at the pebbles of dirt vibrating.

From behind her, Rhona gasped, watching on in wonder.

Under Tavarra's stunned gaze, the Stone protruded from the ground, growing to a massive size. The rose on the top became its back as the Stone unfolded, letting arms and legs spring forward, followed by a bald head sliding out of an imaginary shell.

Lids creaked open to eyes of onyx meeting hers. The creature had no mouth, but somehow it spoke to her, the voice echoing inside her head. "What is it you desire?" The sound was rough, booming.

What she wanted was to reverse time, what she yearned for was to bring people back from the dead, but what she'd desired, what she always had … was to dwell in the land of Laith. But not as the creature she was.

"Is there a way you can remove the curse of the beast? Whether I stay on land as a human, or have to return to the sea as a dweller … it doesn't matter anymore. I can't live like this another day or night." She heard the hopelessness in her voice, but was too far gone to try and act brave.

Crawling forward, the Stone extended its neck to where its face was almost touching hers. It cocked its head. "We both know it does matter."

The Stone retreated, and she thought it was leaving her, until it extended its hand. She stared at it a moment longer before realizing it wanted her to step into the open palm.

Tavarra gave Rhona a look of desperation, her heart slamming against her rib cage, not knowing if she should do this—after Eza, after Perin. It seemed selfish.

"Go on." Rhona motioned her forward.

"After seven years, Perin was the one human I would have trusted. I would have trusted for him."

"You can trust me, and I'll be here for you." Rhona took a few steps back for Tavarra to complete the journey on her own. However, she was close enough in case Tavarra needed her.

Dropping her pack on the ground, Tavarra moved forward until her feet were in the center of the open hand. Large fingers came around her, beginning with the pinky. Darkness enveloped her, but she wasn't scared of it or the thought of the Stone's hand crushing her. Tavarra closed her eyes to let the world become even darker. She didn't let her thoughts seep in, only let herself be.

Finger by finger, the Stone's hand reopened. Finally, she peeled her eyelids apart to the world above. It all looked the same. *She* looked the same as she stared down at the tangerine fur on her arms and legs, felt the sharpness of her teeth, took in her claws.

But then unimaginable pain pulsed through her, her knees

buckled, and Tavarra fell to the ground. She knew with all her blackened heart that she was going to become the beast. Permanently. She screamed for mercy, she howled for death, and she begged to not wake up again—it felt like it would never end. When her skin, muscles, and bones stopped aching, she rolled onto her back, breathing heavily through her nostrils.

"Am I dead?" she asked in a hushed tone.

"No, that wasn't what you desired," the Stone boomed in her head.

She lifted an arm, terrified at what she'd find, but it was smooth skin. With a jerk forward, she ran her tongue across her teeth—they were no longer sharp like thorns.

Peering down, she expected a tail of plates, but that wasn't there, either. However, the scars from her chains still rested at her wrists.

"The curse is gone, and you will remain here in human form. If you ever decide to return to the sea again, it's impossible."

Tears rained down her cheeks again as she fell to her knees in front of the Stone, covering her face with her hands.

"You have experienced a lot of death, and there will be more of it to come, but you will find happiness, too."

Before Tavarra could ask anything else, the Stone dragged itself backward and curled into the rose-shaped rock, sinking back down into the dirt.

She looked up at the tops of the trees brushing the sky and still couldn't bring herself to smile. Staring up at the dark clouds, she thought once again of her sister who was dead because of her, a best friend who was killed because she had wanted to help a monster, and a man who died—one she could have loved if given time.

Tavarra glanced down at her clawless hands, then gripped the ring and shell around her throat. "I won't be happy, if ever, but for now, I feel relief, and that's what will have to satisfy me in the end.”

Rhona rushed forward and wrapped an arm around Tavarra. “You’ll be happy one day, maybe not now, but one day. Let’s go home.”

Tavarra didn’t have a home anymore.

Epilogue

Rhona

Rhona had taken one of the tents from her village and left everything and everyone else behind. She couldn't bury the whole village. Her mother was gone, and there were questions that she would never have answers to.

On the way back from the Stone of Desire, Tavarra had been afraid at night. She still thought that the beast inside her would come out, but it never did. Rhona didn't know how long it would take Tavarra to overcome her fear and trust she was safe now.

As Rhona pushed herself ahead, huge chunks of her felt broken. She would never see Perin's frowning face again, never get the chance to truly beat him with a sword, and never see what could have been between him and Tavarra.

He had been a skilled liar and a fierce protector her entire life. She wanted to be angry that he'd never told her about the scars. Instead, it hurt her worse, as if his scars were now hers to bear.

Tavarra chose to go away for a while—she wanted to visit the ocean and give it a proper goodbye. Rhona hoped she would come back to Quil's village, and she would always have her home open for her. Even if it was only her tent.

When Rhona bounded down the grassy incline, her insides twisted with nervous fury, her heart pumping harder than it ever had. It was morning, around the same time they had always met before she'd been taken away the first time. Rhona wasn't sure if he'd even be there.

Taking a deep inhale, she parted the branches. There, in front of the river, sat Quil, his dark hair brushing his shoulders. It had only been a little over a week, but it felt like an eternity since she'd seen him. Her heart pounded even quicker when he turned around, his golden-brown gaze meeting hers.

He wasn't smiling.

Tears poured from her eyes. She dropped the folded tent from her back. Not caring if he was angry with her, she ran and wrapped her arms around his back, because she needed him. Quil didn't wait to hug her back this time, his arms automatically went around her, his fingers entangling in her curls.

"I'm mad at you," he whispered in her ear.

She knew he would be. "But you're here."

"I'll always be here."

"My brother… Eza… Mother…" The sobs prevented her from saying any more, but he knew, and pulled her closer.

Releasing her arms from around him, she took a step backward, her eyes fixed on his. He leaned down and brushed his lips against hers. The way he felt about her, the way she felt about him, it was all in that single kiss.

When she pulled away, Rhona took the pouch from around her neck. She took out the two prisms—one of the whitest of ivories, and the other the blackest of obsidians. Inside, the eyes were both still there, their power quiet. She had one more promise to fulfill.

"Do you want to go on this adventure with me?" Before he could answer, she held up her hand, needing a distraction. "But first, can I have one dance? I still have the pan flute you once gave to me if you need it."

In response, he pulled out a flute from his pocket, lifted it to his lips, and played the richest of melodies. As the night started to fall, she released her emotions through her movements for everyone who had ever suffered, especially her brother, Perin. Under the starry sky, Rhona danced and danced, with the sound of Quil's love flowing straight into her veins, giving her hope that new stories would be told.

Did you enjoy Veiled By Desire?

Authors always appreciate reviews, whether long or short.

Want more Cruel Curses? Check out Shadowed By Despair, Book Three, in the Cruel Curses series!

Sometimes the land chooses for you…

Perin expected eternal darkness after his death, yet the land of Laith has other plans for him. Snapped awake with a desperate hunger for flesh, he fights the urge to feed, knowing that once he gives in to temptation, there is no turning back.

Tavarra's deepest desire was always to be human. By the time she was granted her one true wish, the journey had already claimed those she cared about, including Perin. Alone and on the brink of forgetting how to truly live, she searches for new purpose.

When Perin finds Tavarra, it gives them both the strength they need. Despite the unpredictability of him being the monster this time, Tavarra chooses to help break Perin's curse by journeying with him to retrieve an enchanted liquid for the Stone of Desire. Tied by fate, a sizzling attraction to one another, and loneliness, they must cross the sea into a deadly part of Laith, and find the liquid, before Perin's increasing hunger overtakes him.

Also From Candace Robinson

Wicked Souls Duology
Vault of Glass
Bride of Glass

Marked by Magic Duology
The Bone Valley
Merciless Stars

Cruel Curses Trilogy
Clouded By Envy
Veiled By Desire
Shadowed By Despair

Faeries of Oz Series
Lion (Short Story Prequel)
Tin
Crow
Ozma
Tik-Tok

Cursed Hearts Duology
Lyrics & Curses
Music & Mirrors

Immortal Letters Duology
Dearest Clementine: Dark and Romantic Monstrous Tales
Dearest Dorin: A Romantic Ghostly Tale

Campfire Fantasy Tales Series
Lullaby of Flames
A Layer Hidden
The Celebration Game
Mirror, Mirror

**These Vicious Thorns: Tales of the Lovely Grim
Between the Quiet
Hearts Are Like Balloons
Bacon Pie
Avocado Bliss**

Vampires in Wonderland Series
Rav (Short Story Prequel)
Maddie
Chess
Knave

Acknowledgements

Writing a book, even though it's a companion, is such a tough thing. This idea has been in my head since 2003 and it took me a bit, but I finally got the story I wanted—many suns, moons, and manuscripts later.

Nate and Arwen, you two are my favorite people in the whole world, and we are still like the Three Musketeers.

My editors! Live, you are my favorite content editor in the universe and your comments mean everything to me! Jackie, you helped me so much with your suggestions and wonderful adjustments to tighten up the story and make it better. Hannah, you created the perfect sequel cover!

Alexa, Gerardo, and Amber R., your early reads helped so much with the structure of this story, and you three have the best judgment. Patricia, Victoria, and Kattie, you guys have been here from the beginning and continue to be what keeps me wanting to make more stories. Donna and Amber H., you two are my true book sisters and have gotten me through the ups and downs of everything.

Lastly, to the people who take the time to read this book, thank you so much for giving me that extra bit of strength like Tavarra has.

About the Author

Candace Robinson spends her days consumed by words and hoping to one day find her own DeLorean time machine. Her life consists of avoiding migraines, admiring Bonsai trees, watching classic movies, and living with her husband and daughter in Texas—where it can be forty degrees one day and eighty the next.

Connect with Candace:

Website: https://authorcandacerobinson.wordpress.com/
Facebook: https://www.facebook.com/literarydust
Twitter: https://twitter.com/literarydust
Instagram:
https://www.instagram.com/candacerobinsonbooks/
Goodreads:
https://www.goodreads.com/author/show/16541001.Candace
_Robinson or ignore that and just try searching for Candace
Robinson!

www.ingramcontent.com/pod-product-compliance
Lightning Source LLC
Chambersburg PA
CBHW030819210726

48290CB00002B/663